Watch for More Novels by Delray K. Dvoracek

from Indigo Sea Press

indigoseapress.com

The Prague Double

By

Delray K. Dvoracek

Saber Books
Published by Indigo Sea Press
Winston-Salem

Saber Books
Indigo Sea Press
302 Ricks Drive
Winston-Salem, NC 27103

First Saber Books edition published
December, 2015
Saber Books, Moon Sailor and all production design are trademarks of Indigo Sea Press, used under license.

For information regarding bulk purchases of this book, digital purchase and special discounts, please contact the publisher at indigoseapress.com

Manufactured in the United States of America
ISBN 978-1-63066-242-4

To my wife, Verlene,
and my two sons, Kamron and Kent.

—Delray K. Dvoracek

CHAPTER ONE
Frankfurt, Germany, June, 1974

She quietly entered the bedroom, clad only in her robe, and when she switched on the small lamp, he stirred and rolled over.

"Ten o'clock," she said as she stroked the side of his face. He was quiet for a moment, and when he opened his eyes to glance at his watch, she kissed him on the forehead. "Do you want some coffee before you leave?"

"That would be good." As she left the room, he crawled out of the bed and reached for his clothes. Within a few minutes, he was dressed, strapped the shoulder holster in place and slipped on a sport coat.

His coffee was waiting for him when he walked into the kitchen. He sat and wrapped both hands around the cup and slowly sipped at it. She was attractive no matter what she wore, no matter how she was dressed, but his mind was elsewhere, focusing on tonight's rendezvous.

"How long will you be gone?" she asked.

"I don't know for sure. Don't wait up. If it gets late, I'll go to my apartment and call you tomorrow."

"You look tired," she said.

"I am tired." He drank the rest of his coffee, and when he got to his feet, she followed him to the door.

"I love you, Frank," she said, as he wrapped her in his arms.

"Don't I know it." He gave her a firm kiss, smiled and left.

Surprisingly, the night air outside was calm and refreshing, giving him renewed vigor from the short rest. It was no more than a fifteen-minute drive back to his apartment, where he parked his car in the garage and locked it.

He headed for the street, where he saw the Mercedes parked, and

1

when he opened the driver's door, she slid over to the passenger side.

"Hi," he said, as he got in. He checked the rearview mirror, pulled out onto the street and drove off.

* * *

Arthur Farrington increased the speed of the Volvo, his eyes glued to the Bundesstrasse. A long stretch of pavement lay before him, its surface shimmering from the reflection of the moon. To his left, he could now see the lights of Darmstadt, so he knew he was getting close.

Arthur Farrington did not normally travel so fast at night, in fact, he was not accustomed to hurrying through anything. He was patient in his work, methodical and careful, but prone to outbursts of anger whenever things weren't going his way. If Arthur was at all daring, it was usually with his mind.

However, tonight he was daring with the speed he was maintaining. Even Clarence, sitting next to him, dutiful as he was, voiced his concern.

"Arthur, for crissake, slow down!"

At six-one and nearly three hundred pounds, Arthur filled the seat behind the wheel. His hands were huge, his face fat with a double chin, but in spite of his obesity, he was very capable, and he had been a CIA agent for twenty-two years.

Clarence, his partner, was a shade shorter and physically fit for his fifty-plus years. His silver hair and bushy silver mustache were two characteristics that allowed one to pick him out of a crowd instantly. He, too, was very capable in his own way.

Arthur's eyes were still fixed on the road. It was not every night he was called out of bed by Inspector Heinrich Gastmann, the chief of the *Frankfurter Polizei*. Arthur Farrington wouldn't disturb a night's rest for just anybody, but Gastmann was a good ally in Frankfurt circles.

"For God's sake, Arthur, slow down," Clarence charged again.

Arthur grunted and eased his foot off the gas pedal, his eyes never once leaving the road.

When the Volvo sped over a rise, flashing blue lights lit up the countryside at the bottom of the hill where two German police cars had pulled off to the side of the highway. Other vehicles had slowed, but were being flagged on by a policeman. As Arthur neared, he could make out the tracks of a vehicle that had left the road.

Arthur puffed out a huge breath. He pulled up and shut off the engine, and as he and Clarence Tripson emerged from the vehicle, two policemen approached them.

Arthur introduced himself.

"*Ah, Herr Farrington*," said one of the officers. "*Da drueben*," he said as he pointed off in the direction where the tracks led.

"*Danke*," responded Arthur as he tugged at his collar to fight off a chill. Arthur and Clarence crossed the few yards of open field until they came to an embankment.

Down below in a narrow gully, two men with flashlights were standing near the wreckage of an automobile.

"Inspector Gastmann?" Arthur Farrington hollered.

A flashlight blinded Arthur for a moment. "*Herr Farrington*," came Inspector Gastmann's voice. "*Komm herunter.*"

The inspector shined the light for the two men as they carefully made their way down the slope. A car had come to a rest at the bottom of the twenty-foot trench, its front wheels and grill jammed into the wall of the shallow creek.

"*Schau mal an*," said the Inspector as he shined a light on the man behind the wheel. Arthur Farrington jerked back in horror bringing on a knotted stomach and the feeling of nausea creeping up his throat. The sight of blood was repulsive to Arthur and would force him on occasion to vomit. He gulped in huge mouthfuls of air as he stared at the bloodied and unrecognizable face of the dead man.

Arthur shoved a handkerchief up to his mouth and turned away.

Clarence Tripson knew Arthur's weakness. He reached inside the window of the vehicle and pulled the dead man's head back, then began searching for a wallet.

"I have his identification card," said Inspector Gastmann in

3

broken English. The short, squatty German produced the ID and shined the flashlight on it. "That's why I called you."

"Good Lord!" exclaimed Clarence. He stared at the identification card hardly able to control his voice. "A-Arthur..."

Arthur was standing some distance from the vehicle throwing up what little of his digested food he could.

Clarence turned to the Inspector and motioned to Arthur with his hand. "He can't take this stuff."

"*Das ist selbstverstaendlich*," said the Inspector.

"I'll be all right in a moment," said Arthur. He wiped his mouth and had a sickly, embarrassed look on his face. He tried to regain some composure. "Who is he?"

Clarence held out the identification card, and when Arthur took it from him, his hands were trembling. The color of the ID alone told him the man was from the CIA. "Oh, Jesus," said Arthur. "Frank Vulcek."

"*Ya, sicher*," said the Inspector. "I thought you would want to know this before I make a report." He waited patiently expecting Arthur to respond.

"Y-yes, *danke schoen*," answered Arthur. He held up the ID again. "Frank Vulcek," he repeated weakly. He refused to face the consequences of the agent's death. He could only see the man's pummeled face in his mind. The unforgettable mass of broken flesh would plague him for days, and he knew he would dream about it.

"Is it him for sure?" His voice was still weak, fearful.

Clarence reached back inside the vehicle once again as the Inspector shone the flashlight for him. Arthur turned away while the two men made their inspection.

"It's him," answered Clarence. "Who's the woman?" he asked the Inspector.

"Helga Schleier. Do you know her?"

Clarence shook his head. "No."

"Her face is also badly... marked," said the Inspector searching for an English word to described the girl. "She's dead, too. It's not surprising. No one could survive this...*Unfall*," he finished, substituting the German word for *accident*.

A few seconds passed, and then Inspector Gastmann hollered to an officer above. *"Rufen Sie den Krankenwagen!"*

Arthur turned slightly and looked at the wrecked vehicle again. "Inspector, I would appreciate it if you would not report Frank Vulcek's death."

The Inspector seemed stunned with the request. "Oh? *Warum denn nicht?"*

"It is... a matter of security," said Arthur. "I ask this as a personal favor of you. *Eine Bitte,"* he added quickly in German. His mind was functioning clearly now, and he knew well what the consequences of Vulcek's death would lead to. For the moment, it was necessary to keep Vulcek alive—at least in the newspapers. He needed time to report the death to his superiors at CIA headquarters, time to devise an alternate plan if one could be devised.

"Eine Bitte," repeated Arthur.

"It is unusual, but..."

"I don't care if you report the girl's death, but Vulcek... *Bitte,"* Arthur asked again. He was not one to ask such favors, but he desperately needed this one. The German Chief of Police was a man who worked strictly by the book, and he rarely bucked the authorities. But he had informed Arthur first about Frank Vulcek's death, and that was going through Arthur's mind now.

"Tja, tja, eine Bitte," mumbled the Inspector as he bent his head downward. Arthur could imagine the Inspector's mind whirling with the request. Somehow though, Arthur felt the man was just biding some time to display his authority.

"Okay. Das tue ich fuer Sie."

Arthur understood the reply perfectly. *"Danke, Herr Inspector."*

Gastmann probed. "A matter of security?"

"Yes," answered Arthur. He hesitated. "I regret that I cannot tell you about it. But rest assured, it is a matter of high importance."

A wry smile formed on the man's face, and he nodded. "Your people have helped us... *manchmal,"* he finished in German. "I do not forget such favors."

The grin was still on his face when Arthur extended a hand. "Thank you again, Herr Inspector." The Inspector gave the customarily one shake with his hand and cocked his head at the same time. The gesture reminded Arthur of the Gestapo.

Arthur and Clarence made their way back up the embankment and returned to their car. Before Arthur stepped in, he made an inspection of the ground where the tire tracks of Vulcek's vehicle broke the grass. He glanced back up the highway in the direction from where the vehicle had come, and then again studied the area where the vehicle had left the road. The highway made a wide bend where he was now standing. It was an unusually clear night, one of the few that had not been invaded by the typical fog that seemed to engulf the German landscape.

His eyes studied the highway again. "It's not a very sharp turn," he said out loud.

"What?" asked Clarence.

"Nothing," responded Arthur. He climbed into the Volvo and started up the machine, made a U-turn and headed back toward Frankfurt.

The vehicle had barely made a kilometer when Clarence spoke. "Now what?"

Arthur shook his head. "I don't know. We were so close. Only a few months away."

"Seven weeks," corrected Clarence.

"Damn," said Arthur as he slammed a hand against the wheel. "Why did this have to happen? I suppose he was drinking. The turn wasn't that sharp."

"Or speeding."

"Yeah." Arthur grunted. "I've never known him not to speed." A moment passed. "The plan was insane anyway," he said as if the statement would ease his disappointment.

"I told you that from the beginning."

Arthur pulled a face. "Don't remind me." His eyes were back on the road again. "Did you get the girl's name?"

"Helga Schleier."

Neither of the two knew who she was.

"Check her out," said Arthur. "Who she was, where she lived, what her connection with Vulcek was."

"Probably just a girlfriend," mused Clarence.

Arthur shrugged. "Maybe, but check her out anyway as a matter of security."

Arthur Farrington's mind drifted away from the girl and once again visualized the bloodied face of Frank Vulcek. He wished he weren't so squeamish. He wished he could be more like Clarence, at least when it came to viewing dead bodies. That was an aspect of his job that he never thought he'd get used to, and luckily, dead bodies in his profession were a rarity.

Another several kilometers passed, neither of the men speaking, each involved in his own thoughts.

"It's hopeless," said Clarence. "We'll have to call off the Prague deal."

Arthur unconsciously heard his words, his mind still on the scarred face of Frank Vulcek. He was picturing the bloody image of the dead man's face differently now. He had been barely recognizable, the Inspector had said. Even Clarence took a second look to verify it was Vulcek.

If Vulcek had survived the accident, what would he look like? Face scarred—nose broken...?

"No!" Arthur exclaimed. He blurted out the word so loud that Clarence jumped.

"No! We're not calling off the Prague deal yet!"

The reflection of the dash lights gleamed off of Arthur's glasses. A plan was beginning to evolve in his mind. A wide grin covered his face, creating more folds in his chin, and Clarence knew exactly what he was thinking.

"We're not done yet," Arthur said, almost inaudibly.

"What about the car?" asked Clarence.

"What?"

"That wasn't Frank's car."

"Check it out," said Arthur. His eyes were glued to the highway, and he was barely doing fifty kilometers.

"I think we can do more than fifty," said Clarence.

"What? Oh, right."

Arthur stepped down on the accelerator.

CHAPTER TWO

The massive six-wing structure was known as the I.G. Farben building. It had once housed the SS elite troops of the German Army, and after the war, General Eisenhower had used the complex as his European headquarters. On the sixth floor in one of the wings were several offices that Arthur Farrington controlled as head of CIA operations in West Germany.

Most of the building was used by the U.S. 7th Army and other government agencies, however, within the cream-colored complex, a number of German businesses conducted their daily routines. The building even boasted several small coffeehouses and a nice restaurant on the seventh floor.

The I.G. Farben building lay in the heart of Frankfurt in Gruneburgpark, a highly visual structure from the heavy traffic of the surrounding streets. During his longevity with the CIA, Arthur had worked out of buildings much more open than this one—buildings that seemed so obvious that they were not obvious.

Arthur liked the secretive nature of his operation, yet the openness of it. He came and went to work daily as if he were just another *Arbeiter* in the community, as did all the staff members who worked for him. It was not at all unusual to stop and chat with a German businessman in the same building. He had done it on several occasions, and he knew enough German to get by.

His wife had become accustomed to his routine. The children, now in college, had always been told their father worked for the government. In Washington D.C. where Arthur had spent many of his early years, it seemed almost everyone worked for the government. In fact, if one lived in the Capitol City, it seemed unusual if he wasn't connected with the government in some capacity.

Delray K. Dvoracek

As a case officer, Arthur Farrington was well respected. His job was to collect information from his field men and forward reports to CIA headquarters in Langley. But for the past 48 hours since Vulcek's death, Arthur's job was plaguing him. He had just lost his top operative in West Germany, the best he had ever known. Never in his career had Arthur ever lost an operation, and now he was being tested.

Arthur was one of the few who knew what Frank Vulcek's mission was, but he did not know all aspects of Vulcek's activities. The man was a loner, secretive, unorthodox in his methods, which Arthur often disliked. However, the one thing he liked about Vulcek was that he always achieved results, which made Arthur look good.

Arthur cursed himself as he sat at his desk. He should have pushed Frank Vulcek further, forced him to divulge *everything* he knew about the Prague assignment. He had tried often in his diplomatic and subtle manner, but the operative always managed to elude his probing questions.

Arthur finally made up his mind what he wanted to do, but Clarence Tripson thought he was insane. He even said it to his face, which gave cause for Arthur to throw him out of his office, but such physical abuse was not in his nature.

Of course, Arthur would make all final decisions, but he liked to have the support of his colleagues, especially Clarence. Support meant power when he would eventually call Mr. Kendrid in Langley.

Arthur turned to the preliminary report on Frank Vulcek's death, which had already been sent to Kendrid via the scrambler. Arthur could imagine what the big guns in the Capitol were thinking. They must be trying to salvage the Prague case much like he was right now.

Arthur thought he had a solution, and although he passed on the saving idea to some of his fellow workers, no one as of yet had jumped up and down with enthusiasm. He hoped he could count on Clarence, but even he was hedging.

Arthur grunted, picked up the Frankfurter Zeitung and read the headlines. Chancellor Helmut Schmidt was in a never-ending battle

10

of inflation and unemployment. It appeared the Nixon Watergate Scandal was coming to a head after nearly three years of investigation, and the two East Germans, who a month ago had tried to float their way to freedom in makeshift rafts across the Baltic Sea north of Lubeck, were coming up for trial.

His intercom buzzed.

"Yes?"

"Miss Feldman has arrived," his secretary reported from the outer office.

"One moment, please. I'm finishing up some paperwork."

Arthur Farrington stuffed the newspaper in a drawer, leaned back in his chair and locked his chubby fingers together across his stomach. With the arrival of Miss Feldman, the pressure was on.

He reviewed mentally what he wanted to discuss with her. He had to make it appear natural, which was hard for him to do, and that's why he had never become an operative like Frank Vulcek. He could not act very well, he wasn't very good at lying, and he didn't carry a weapon.

He raised his big frame up from the chair, snugged up his tie and crossed to the door in huge steps. Miss Feldman was the first line of defense that might help salvage the Prague assignment.

"Come in, Trudi," he said as he opened the door. He would not normally use her first name, but it seemed appropriate now.

She was a striking woman with smooth features and beautiful unblemished skin. Her hair was sandy, cut shorter now than what Arthur last remembered. Arthur had met her on a couple other occasions, however, most of his contact with her had been through other operatives, messages and notes. That's the way the operation had been carried out so far. By seeing her today, Arthur had broken one of his own rules, but he firmly believed he would be seeing more and more of her.

Trudi Feldman entered the room with a faint, but welcome smile on her face. "Mr. Farrington," she said, as Arthur motioned for her to sit down.

He watched her, observed how she discreetly crossed a leg when she sat. "I know this must seem unusual, my, ah, summoning you here today. But I..." Arthur stopped. He had memorized what he wanted to say, but nothing was falling into place. He silently swore to himself as he picked up a newspaper clipping and handed it to her.

She read the article, which had a picture attached. Arthur carefully watched her eyes, studied the expression on her face, looking for some hint of recognition in the person's photo or name mentioned in the clipping.

Trudi looked up, amused. "Helga Schleier. Should I know her?"

Arthur scowled, hoping for a different response. "She was a secretary for a law firm here in Frankfurt."

The information passed unnoticed as Trudi read a line from the German article. *"Einsiger Auto Unfall in der Naehe von Darmstadt,"* She said and looked up. "An auto accident. What does this have to do with me?"

Arthur did not want to make the next statement. "The woman was not alone in the vehicle." He hesitated, his gaze on her eyes expecting a reaction. "She was with Frank Vulcek, and he's dead."

Her eyes hardened like stones, and after a few moments, she focused on the article again. Arthur saw her lips quiver and expected to see some tears, but there were none.

"The Prague case," she said, her face emotionless.

Arthur puffed up his cheeks and eased himself into his chair. He knew his course of questions, but they weren't coming easy. "You knew Frank quite well, didn't you?"

"Mr. Farrington, you assigned me to work with him."

Arthur clasped his fingers together. Mr. Kendrid from the CIA headquarters had assigned her, but yet she was working directly for him.

"I know," said Arthur. "What I meant was, you perhaps knew him a little better than just as an operative on the Prague case." The sentence came out crudely, and he wished he had phrased it better.

"I slept with him, if that's what you mean," she said bluntly.

"I didn't mean to insinuate that, ah..."

"That is exactly what you meant, isn't it?"

12

Arthur cringed. "Yes," he said finally. "That's what I meant."

"Yes. I slept with him. Several times. We dined together, we spent some weekends together, we..."

"Miss Feldman," Arthur interrupted. "I did not wish to pry into your personal affairs. I'm more concerned about the situation in Prague."

She lowered her eyes, and then, almost inaudibly, she said. "I knew something was wrong when he left last night."

"He was with you last night?"

"Yes. I woke him at ten, he left shortly after."

"Did he say where he was going, or who he was going to meet?"

"No. You know how he was."

Arthur knew only too well. "I'm sorry about all this. I knew that you and Frank had a, ah…"

She didn't appear to be listening. "It appears to me the Prague assignment is over."

"No! Not yet!" His sudden outburst startled her. Arthur heaved himself out of his chair and paced. "Not yet. There's a way we can salvage it."

Arthur came back to his chair, desperately searching for the right words. "Suppose we were able to find another Frank Vulcek?"

Trudi Feldman was struck with the suggestion. "I would say that was highly impossible."

"Why?" He knew why, but he wanted to hear her reasons.

"There isn't another person around like Frank." She was staring for a moment. "Mr. Farrington, I don't quite understand your questions."

The excitement danced within Arthur. "Just suppose we could find another person like Frank? Someone who resembled him, someone who talked like him, walked like him..."

"Someone who spoke perfect German and Russian?" she asked.

Arthur sank his head.

"Someone who thought like Frank?" she went on. "Someone who made love like Frank, someone who..."

"Yes! Yes! Just suppose we did find someone like him?"

13

"You won't."

Arthur slumped back in his chair, and then, like a mummy coming to life, he blurted out again, "Just suppose!"

The door opened and his secretary peeked in. "Is everything all right here, Mr. Farrington?"

Arthur's face was red from embarrassment.

"Everything's fine," said Trudi. His secretary quietly closed the door.

Trudi was silent for several seconds. "Mr. Farrington, do you know what you're asking?"

He nodded. His words were weaker, calmer now. "I know I'm asking the impossible. But just suppose..."

"Do you mind if I smoke?" she inquired suddenly.

The question struck Arthur odd. "No, no. Go right ahead." He watched her pull a cigarette from a case and light it up, all the time thinking that perhaps she might have some second thoughts about his insane idea.

"I thought the idea of the Prague case was risky to begin with," she said candidly. "And now you're trying to suggest someone else can take his place. I would say it's near impossible."

Arthur felt the world collapse around him. He stuck his elbows on the desk and held the sides of his head with his hands. He slowly shook his head admitting defeat.

"But then," she went on, "I've done other things that were near impossible."

Arthur sparked with the words.

"The biggest problem would be someone with Frank's likeness," she said.

"Yes, yes. I know. I think we can solve that."

"He would have to speak German fluently and have a good command of Russian."

"Yes."

She put the cigarette to her mouth and inhaled a mouthful. "He was crazy, you know. He never had any fears. He took everything one day at a time." Her face saddened as if she were on the verge of

14

tears, and then she looked up again, her composure coming miraculously back to her. "I knew someday I would lose him."

As sad as she looked, she was still a beautiful woman, thought Arthur. "That's why I need you," he said. "You knew much more about Frank than I ever did, and I knew him for several years. I only knew him professionally, but you knew him personally. How he talked in crowds, how he thought, how he reacted around people, how he..." It was no longer necessary for Arthur to go on. "Will you help me if I find another Frank?" he asked almost pleading.

Trudi stared at Arthur. She had unconsciously been listening to his words, not understanding all of them but comprehending his line of questions. She thought about Prague and what would take place in less than seven weeks. It all seemed impossible, but if Arthur thought he could find another Frank...

"Yes," she said selfishly. "Yes. If you can find another Frank."

Arthur felt a burden drop from his shoulders. He had brought her over to his line of thinking, but now he needed more support.

"That's two of us," he said as he reached for the phone.

"I beg your pardon?"

"Oh, nothing," muttered Arthur, unaware he had spoken out loud. He triggered his intercom. "Clarence? Will you come down to my office for a moment?"

Arthur sat silently, observing Trudi Feldman. His mind was working again, forming a new set of questions.

The door opened and Clarence stepped in. When he saw Trudi Feldman, he knew immediately why Arthur had summoned him. He also knew that once again, he would probably be giving in to another one of Arthur Farrington's insane ideas.

CHAPTER THREE
CIA Headquarters, Langley, Virginia

Arthur Farrington stared at the calendar on his desk and marked off another day. Three precious weeks had passed since he and Trudi Feldman arrived in Washington D.C.

He leaned back in the leather-backed swivel chair, dejected with the 21 marks on his calendar. He had been using this office supplied by his superior, Mr. Kendrid, and for all practical purposes, he hadn't accomplished anything since his arrival.

He had been working sixteen-hour days, seven days a week, rarely taking time to even leave the fourth floor of the building, except to eat. This morning he had even come to work unshaven. He couldn't remember when that had happened the last time, or whether it had ever happened. He was happy someone had an electric razor in one of the offices.

He now felt his face, rubbed his chin just to confirm he had a clean face. His suit needed pressing, and he wished he had brought four instead of two, but he had packed in a hurry not realizing he would be here this long. Two suits, four shirts, several changes of underclothes and a couple ties. He had forgotten to pack socks and had to buy some on arrival.

He pushed his attire and grooming habits aside and turned to the computer cards on his desk. The computer of the fourth floor complex was rapidly exhausting the possibilities. He needed a man around thirty-five years of age preferably with dark hair. His height should be around six feet, give or take an inch, and he should have a heavy build. German fluency was absolutely essential along with a decent knowledge of Russian. It certainly wouldn't hurt if he were daring and adventurous, something for which the computer seemed to have no category.

It would be beneficial if the man had lived in Germany, but Arthur wasn't counting on that.

Knowledge of firearms would be helpful.

It would be advantageous if he were single.

European travel overseas was recommended, but that rapidly became another category deficiency.

These were the qualities Arthur had asked the computer the first time. He was optimistic that he would easily come up with hundreds of candidates from the military services or active agents, but the computer had produced only six decent possibilities!

Six out of thousands of entries! The scant results stunned everyone in the complex.

Arthur revised the questions for a second try. He erased the single category, expanded the age category and removed the firearms.

The same six came up plus eight more.

The dossiers of the fresh candidates lay on his desk in front of him. Disgruntled, Arthur began reading through them to see if he had overlooked anything, and after perusing the first half dozen, and, totally dejected, he flung the entire stack in the air and watched the papers flutter to the floor.

When he looked up, Mr. Kendrid, his frame silhouetted in the doorway, was looking at Arthur over his bifocals. "New way of filing things?" he asked. He quietly closed the door and took a seat across from Arthur's desk.

"I just thought I'd check on your progress," he said, as he scanned the dossiers on the floor. "I'm guessing things aren't progressing as you would like them."

The sarcasm in his voice bit deeply. Arthur simply nodded, his face flat and bland. "We have fourteen possibilities, and already, eleven of the candidates have been rejected."

"I thought you had over a hundred possibilities."

"Yes, but only fourteen remotely resembled Vulcek. One man looked very promising, but when Trudi went to Alabama for an interview, she discovered his photo resembled Vulcek better than he

17

did in person. That's what we're up against."

Kendrid sifted through the photos he was holding in his hands. "I see. What about this fellow in Connecticut?" he asked as he held up the photo.

Arthur studied the photo "He looked good on paper and had an excellent command of German and Russian, but when Miss Feldman interviewed him, he said if he considered any assignment, he would have to take his boyfriend along."

Mr. Kendrid shrugged. "So where does that put us now?"

"We've narrowed the categories again. Ten year spread in age, three inches on the height, German and Russian moderate."

"I thought the man had to be fluent in both languages."

"He does," said Arthur as he shook his head. "But it's hard to find a person with all the necessary qualities who is fluent in one language let alone two. And there's yet the matter of a security clearance."

"We'll deal with that when you find a candidate. *If* you find a candidate," Mr. Kendrid corrected himself.

Arthur blew out a huge breath. "And motive. The guy needs a motive."

"You find the man, we'll give him the motive. Compen-sation can be mustered up from a number of funds."

Mr. Kendrid stood up. "Time's running out, Arthur. Have you considered any other options?"

Arthur's face remained blank.

"I see." Mr. Kendrid headed for the door. "Keep me posted," he said as he exited the room.

Arthur Farrington was sick of computer cards, sick of faces and sick of all the dead ends he had come up against. Time was running out, like Kendrid said. He had been reminding him of that every day for the past week. In Kendrid's view, what had initially started out as finding a needle in a haystack had become a needle in a hayfield.

Arthur blew out a puff of air and looked at the mess of dossiers scattered on the carpet. He had just finished gathering them up and had them on his desk when Trudi Feldman knocked lightly on the door and entered. She was wearing a blue suit and carrying some papers.

"More candidates?" he asked.

She sat across from him. "Yes. We ran another set of categories through the computer this morning."

"What qualifications have we restricted ourselves to this time? Male and living?"

Trudi smiled at the sarcastic remark.

For the first time in twenty-one days, Arthur Farrington smiled at his own little joke. He raised his hand up as if pleading. "I'm sorry. My remarks were uncalled for."

"I understand." She placed the new dossiers on an uncluttered corner of his desk. "We reversed a couple categories this time."

"And?"

"We put Russian first, German second, tapped some civilian resources as well as men discharged from the services, and we got a couple look-alikes."

Arthur nodded as he glanced at the pile of papers. "I'll try to go over them before the day is over."

"Why don't you start with them now?"

The question drew Arthur's full attention. He reached for the dossiers and hadn't even touched them when his eyes remained fixed on the top photo.

Arthur stared unbelieving at the likeness before him. As accustomed as he was to imagining Vulcek's face with cuts and scars or a broken nose, he didn't have to use much imagination on this man.

"His eyes," said Arthur.

When Trudi placed a thumb over the eyes and forehead of the man, Arthur jumped with excitement. The man's nose and jaw were remarkably similar to the features of Frank Vulcek.

"Just his eyes," said Arthur excitedly as he mentally placed a set of dark glasses on the man. "Did Frank ever wear dark glasses?"

Trudi flipped a page to a composite photo of the man's face wearing sunglasses.

"I had the people in the lab make this up."

Arthur was unable to take his eyes off the likeness. The overall facial appearance was very good, and his hair was about the same color.

"Jesus!" said Arthur. "I'll take him even if he's a midget!" He read over the remaining physical attributes of the man and then commented. "Five foot ten, one inch shorter than the real Frank Vulcek and a few pounds lighter. Eight years in the military, Russian descent." Arthur looked up. "Russian descent? With a name like Garner?"

"His given name was Granovik. His parents were Russian. When he came to the States, he changed his name. He's fluent in both Russian and German."

Arthur was delighted with the information.

"We ran down his military records. He also happens to be a pilot."

"Uh-huh."

"But evidently not a very good one. He crashed two military aircraft before he was grounded."

"That's very good."

Arthur quickly thumbed through the following pages. He stopped on one particular page and began reading, his eyes whipping from left to right with the lines. "Two court-martials."

"Yes, but he beat the rap on both of them. "He's looking better all the time."

"Isn't he?" The look on Trudi's face bore all the excitement of her voice.

Arthur folded the records and neatly placed them on his desk. "What's he doing now, this..." He read the man's name off the records again. "This Phillip Garner."

"We don't know."

"Where's he live?"

"We don't know. He moved since his last address."

Arthur reached for the phone.

"We're already checking on it." The smile never seemed to leave her face now.

20

Arthur sat back in his chair very pleased with her efficiency. It was nice to have someone working on a project without having to be commanded into everything like Clarence required.

"Miss Feldman," said Arthur, as he rose from his chair. "I'm tired of ham sandwiches at my desk. Suddenly I have a real appetite. Would you care to join me for dinner tonight?"

Trudi offered a smile.

"I'll buy, of course," he said.

"I expected you to."

Arthur returned the smile and took her by the arm. "What else can you tell me about this fellow?" he asked as they left the room.

CHAPTER FOUR
Two days later, South Bend, Indiana

The cabby dropped her off in front of the aviation facilities. This small airport lay on the outskirts of the city, the home to small one and two-motor aircraft. The big airliners utilized the South Bend Regional Airport.

When she entered the building, no one was present, but a sign hung on the door. On it, a note was scribbled in pencil.

In the hangar

She pushed the door open and saw a fellow dressed in coveralls and a ball cap working on the engine of an aircraft. On the tarmac in front of the open hangar, a small aircraft was taxiing by, it's engine drowning out her steps as she walked up to him. She stood for a few seconds behind him, realizing that he did not hear her approach.

"Excuse me," she said elevating her voice. "I'm looking for Phillip Garner."

When he turned around, she could not help but gape at him. There was no doubt he was the person she was seeking.

"You that journalist that called?" he asked as he wiped his hand on a rag.

"Yes." She knew she was staring.

He thought she was looking at the aircraft. "She's big up close, isn't she?" he said as he motioned to the ancient two-motored Beechcraft. "Writing an article on independent operators, are you?"

She was still staring at him, mesmerized with his extreme likeness of Frank Vulcek.

"Ah, yes, yes I am," she answered as she held up a clipboard. Goosebumps were running across her skin.

"Well, you can ask all you want, but I have to give this baby a test flight. Got anything against flying?" He waited for a response, and when none came, he asked again. "Ma'am?"

"Fine, fine," she answered. "I'd love a ride. Yes, why not? That would be…good."

She realized how stupid she must have sounded, but he didn't seem at all perturbed, since he dropped the cowling on the motor, locked it in place and motioned for her to come with him.

Before she knew it, she was sitting in the co-pilot's seat as still as a manikin, watching his hands move as he flipped switches, as he pumped fuel into the carburetor, as he set radio frequencies. She could not keep her eyes off of him, still unbelieving how uncanny his resemblance was to Frank Vulcek.

"Need to buckle up," he said as one of the propellers began spinning. In no time, a puff of smoke spewed out of the engine, and now the second propeller was whirling to a start.

"Bit loud, isn't it?" he hollered over the noisy engines. "Model 18, built in 1937.

As he maneuvered the aircraft out of the hangar, he was speaking into the microphone, and sometimes he was talking to her, filling her in on the aircraft's capabilities, but she had a difficult time hearing what he was saying. He halted the aircraft just short of the runway, ran up one engine and thumped a finger against a glass until the needle jumped into normal range. He pulled the throttle off of that engine and ran up the power on the second engine, made a few instrument checks, then cocked an ear listening to the engine. The aircraft rattled and vibrated so violently that she was sure it would fall apart.

"Lookin' good," he said. Again, he spoke into the microphone, and then glanced toward the south end of the runway. She looked, too, and spotted the small craft on final approach for a landing.

He turned to her. "You look a little flushed. You aren't going to get sick on me, are you?"

"No," she answered.

"Got about a minute before we're cleared for takeoff. So, what's your name again?"

Delray K. Dvoracek

* * *

Arthur Farrington had never been to Indiana before, and he appreciated this hot, early July day. The brilliant sunshine outside was unlike anything Arthur had experienced recently in Germany.

He sat at the desk in the room of the Holiday Inn rereading Phillip Garner's dossier. The man was a natural for getting into trouble and was equally good at getting out of it. He seemed to be as smooth as a good quality wine slipping down one's throat. Everything Arthur read about the man pleased him very much. Phillip Garner's qualities by far exceeded all the other candidates.

Arthur rose from behind the small desk and moved slowly to the window overlooking the city. He stretched for the longest time, not realizing he had been sitting for more than two hours. Carrying out the mission in Prague had become an obsession for him, yet if the mission failed, it would not be his fault, of course. No one could have foreseen the premature death of Frank Vulcek, and so far, the dead man was still alive, at least on paper.

This mission was of utmost importance, a danger to national security if it wasn't pulled off. Arthur assumed that's why Kendrid had let him go this far. He was mildly surprised his boss had not already put the entire Prague case aside, but there was too much at stake, too much to lose, everything to gain if the deception could be pulled off.

He glanced at his watch. Trudi was simply supposed to meet Garner posing as a journalist, make some inquiries, and if he seemed a good possibility, bring him back to the hotel. Certainly, by now she must have gained some insight about the man's character.

What patience Arthur possessed was slowing eroding away. He paced across the carpet of the room and back to the window, then sat at the desk and again began reviewing the dossier before him.

Another hour passed before he got up from the desk and went to the window. "What in hell is holding her up?"

*

Phillip Garner banked the aircraft and turned onto the final at the airstrip. He gently throttled the engines back and lowered the flaps as he edged the nose up on the craft. In seconds, the plane drifted downward above the runway and finally settled with nary a bounce. At the second exit, he turned off and followed the taxi strip back to the flight station.

Outside the hangar, he cut the engines, and as soon as the propellers spun to a stop, he exited and offered a hand to Trudi.

"Miss Feldman," he said as he helped her to solid ground. "Feeling all right?"

"Wonderful."

"You hardly said a thing during our ride."

He had no idea how taken she was with his actions. "Too excited to talk or even take a note," she answered. "Thanks for the tour."

If she was any judge of character, he seemed to like her from the moment she introduced herself. He was cordial enough on board the aircraft, yet, she believed it was because he was on his best behavior. She was new to him, but little did he know that he was not new to her. She could not drive from her mind how much he resembled Frank Vulcek, especially now while he had a pair of sunglasses in place. It was so strange sitting next to him in the aircraft, as if he really were Frank.

"If you want to wait inside the station, I'll button this baby up and be right with you."

"Fine," she said and headed across the tarmac.

* * *

Arthur's impatience was rising like the tide when the phone finally rang. He grabbed the receiver and answered, "Yes?"

"Arthur?"

He recognized her voice. "Where are you?"

"At the airport. He offered to take me for a plane ride and I couldn't refuse. We just landed."

Arthur's mouth hung open.

"He's got a lot of Frank's qualities."

The excitement jumped in Arthur. "Will he do?"

"You'll have to make that decision. He wants to take me out to dinner, so I'll bring him right over."

Arthur wanted to know more about the man. "Trudi, how does he..."

"He's coming," Trudi interrupted. "I have to run."

"Trudi!"

No one had ever hung up on Arthur Farrington before, but this time he didn't mind. He sat at the small desk again, smiled defiantly, slipped the dossier into the desk drawer and closed it.

Arthur knew Phillip Garner was an independent operator out of the small airfield. He held a commercial license but evidently was suspected of flying more than just passengers and simple cargo. Arthur had had to turn a few screws, but there was no doubt in his mind that he now had enough information on Garner to make him the Prague double—*if he qualified*, that is. And if he didn't qualify, the FBI could have him back.

While Arthur waited for them to arrive, he had practically worn a path in the carpet. It was nearly an hour later when he heard voices in the hall. They were laughing when they entered, but the laughter abruptly quit when Phillip Garner saw Arthur sitting in a chair.

Arthur rose slowly, silently, unable to take his eyes off the man. "Incredible!" he blurted out. Phillip Garner, only an inch shorter than Frank Vulcek, had practically the same build, but now, his face was cold, emotionless, like Frank appeared most of the time.

Garner gave Trudi a curious look. "What's this all about?"

His voice wasn't the same as Vulcek's, Arthur noticed, but he liked the tone of it.

Garner's eyes were back at Arthur. "What's going on here?"

Trudi's jovial manner was also gone. "This is Arthur Farrington, the man I work for."

Garner realized he was not talking to the editor of a newspaper. He snapped at Arthur. "And who do you work for?"

"The CIA," said Arthur calmly, as he produced his credentials.

Garner's face turned to surprise. He studied the big man's

appearance, guessed he was wearing a two hundred dollar suit and guessed his middle-aged look of success was probably genuine. But he was still on the defensive. "What does the CIA want with me?"

"Please, have a chair," Arthur offered.

"I prefer to stand."

Arthur liked the curt and snide response, liked everything he had observed so far. "We have a bit of a predicament," he said as he produced two glossy photos from the desktop. He handed them to Garner and waited for his reaction. One was of Frank Vulcek, a rare picture with a pair of dark glasses in place, and the other was of Phillip Garner, both depicted in quarter profile.

"A remarkable resemblance, don't you think?" Arthur said.

"So, somebody looks like me. You've got the wrong man."

"That remains to be seen," said Arthur, pleased with the man's response. "Before I go on, I must ask that our conversation remain in strict confidence."

Garner grunted. "What makes you think I have to keep anything in confidence?"

Trudi saw the disgruntled look on Arthur's face and answered. "Phillip. At least listen to what Mr. Farrington has to say. That's all I ask."

Garner hesitated and then gave a slight nod. Arthur began his memorized speech. "The photo of the individual you have in your hand is that of Frank Vulcek. He was working on an assignment for us, but unfortunately met with an untimely death. It is of utmost importance that we carry out his assignment, if we can, and very soon. If we didn't have such a time factor, we might have been able to devise other ways."

"Other ways to what?"

Farrington hesitated, searching for words. "Other ways... to carry out the assignment."

"How did this Frank character die?"

"In a car mishap."

Garner turned to Trudi seeking confirmation.

"That's right," she confirmed. "Frank died in a car accident."

27

"So what do you want from me?"

"Well," Arthur continued, "you bear a remarkable resemblance to Frank Vulcek."

"So?"

"So, we could use you."

"For what?"

"To carry out the assignment. Besides the resemblance, you have several of the qualities we're looking for."

"Like what?" he snapped.

Arthur drew in a deep breath, now a bit perturbed with the short, sarcastic remarks. It was becoming more difficult for him to cast the man's impolite mannerisms aside. "You speak German and Russian fluently."

"How do you know that?"

"We've done a little research on you. Born in the Ukraine of Russian parentage, immigrated to Germany. Lived in Hamburg up until the age of twelve, then immigrated to Canada. When your father died, you and your mother came to the States."

Arthur liked the stunned look on Garner's face. "Your mother has been dead for six years. Up until the day she died, she spoke very little English." Arthur clasped his hands behind his back and rocked forward on his toes. "That's how we know you speak German and Russian."

"What else do you know?" Garner asked, as if the information had not impressed him.

"We know you were a pilot in the military, and we know you cracked up a few planes. Evidently that was the reason for your discharge."

"I volunteered to leave the service. I have an honorable discharge."

Arthur pulled the dossier from the desk and flopped it on the top. "According to this, I would say you were more like encouraged to leave the service." When Garner did not respond to the statement, Arthur went on. "And we know you're the outdoors type."

"What does that mean?"

28

"It means you're a hunter and fisherman."

Garner knew Farrington wasn't interested in the fisherman part.

"You possess a handgun collection," said Arthur as he turned a page. "Rather good shot, too. That's a favorable factor."

The comment slipped out of Arthur's mouth involuntarily, but Garner, more curious now, took a chair, which made Arthur feel like he was finally making some progress.

"It seems to me," Garner observed, "you're looking for a spy to replace a spy."

Arthur was surprised to hear the use of the word, *spy*. There was a nonchalance about the way Garner used it, but Arthur was blunt. "As a matter of fact, we are. However, we prefer to use the term agent."

Garner laughed out loud. "You think I'm stupid enough to become a goddamn spy?"

"No," said Farrington trying to remain calm. "But you might be smart enough."

Garner looked at Trudi, his eyes narrowed in disgust. He was suddenly out of his seat and headed for the door. "You can go to hell."

Farrington despised the response, a phrase that Frank Vulcek had used on him a couple times. "Would you rather go to prison?"

Garner abruptly stopped. When he turned around, the look on his face indicated that Arthur had stirred his mind. Arthur's confidence was soaring. "We know, of course, that you have a few financial problems running your airstrip. Your business does require money to run it, doesn't it?" Arthur didn't wait for a response. "And of course, when one desperately needs money, one turns to desperate measures."

It appeared that Arthur now had Garner's full attention. "In your case, it appears you made a few flights to South America with, shall we say, a rather unusual cargo?"

Garner once again sat down, and when he crossed a leg, Arthur knew he was ready to listen. Arthur thumped a finger on the dossier again. "However, things in here could be handled differently

29

assuming an arrangement could be worked out." Arthur waited patiently for Garner's response.

"What sort of arrangement?" The snappy and snide remarks that normally accompanied his responses were gone.

"Some sort of compensation could be arranged," said Arthur. He could tell Garner's mind was calculating.

"How long will you need me?"

"Three weeks, perhaps four."

"What do I have to do?"

Arthur smiled inwardly. "Sort of the same kind of work you were doing before. Deliver some merchandise to Prague, Czechoslovakia, except this time the merchandise is legitimate and the pay could be rather substantial."

"What sort of merchandise?"

"You'll find out later."

"I don't speak Czech."

Trudi was quick to respond. "Neither did Frank Vulcek."

Garner's mind was clicking, his eyes back on Farrington. "What else?"

"That's it." Arthur lied.

"That's it?"

"That's it."

Garner glanced at Trudi. "That doesn't sound very exciting."

"That's usually the way it is," she said. In most cases, that was the truth, but she knew this assignment would be different. She had been instructed to handle a question like that in a simple manner.

"You said there would be compensation," said Garner suddenly. Excitement was riding his face. "A thousand a day."

Arthur was unprepared for the amount, in fact, he was somewhat astounded that the figure wasn't larger. But then, Phillip Garner did not know exactly what he was bargaining for. "I believe that can be arranged."

Garner glanced at the two photos on the desk. There was no doubt he resembled the dead man, Frank Vulcek, and there was no doubt they wanted him badly. They had gone to a lot of trouble to

30

reach him, and yet, the assignment seemed too simple. Why would the CIA pay him a thousand a day just to deliver some merchandise to Prague?

He reflected on what Trudi had said only a few moments earlier. *Usually the assignments of agents weren't very exciting,* or words to that effect. He had read enough about CIA activities to know that was probably the case. He had once met a retired CIA agent who maintained that his work had amounted to nothing more than a drab desk job. Perhaps it was that simple.

The money was good. Twenty-one thousand dollars in three weeks, maybe more. That would more than take care of the expenses he was running up at the airfield.

He also suspected he was being watched by the FBI, and now Arthur Farrington had confirmed it. The big man had explained it all too clearly when he said one would go to desperate measures if he needed money.

He had no choice, but he reminded himself that Farrington had agreed to a thousand a day—and not reluctantly.

"The money is good," said Garner, his words directed at the big man. "But there's something else."

"I'm listening."

Garner stood up and paced. "Since you people are so good at digging up records, maybe you're just as good at burying them."

Arthur knew precisely what Garner was driving at. "Go on."

"A thousand a day and a clean slate on my pilot record."

"That," said Arthur, "is a little more difficult to arrange than it appears." Arthur was lying again, and he was amazed at how easily he had done it. It was an option he had already considered and discussed with Kendrid, an option Kendrid had already agreed to only because he was sure Farrington couldn't come up with a Prague double.

"I'll see what I can do," said Arthur, not wanting to give in so easily.

"I want a clean slate," demanded Garner. He glanced at Trudi, as if asking whether such an arrangement could be made.

Trudi was straightforward. "If anything can be done about your record, Arthur's the one who can do it."

Garner sat again, his face full of thought. "I'll need some time to think about it."

Arthur pushed the issue, feeling confident he had the man. "You have just thought about it. Yes or no?"

Garner glanced at the photos again and was reasonably sure what kind of information the dossier held. "This is blackmail."

Arthur said nothing and was ever so pleased with himself and Garner's choice of words. When Garner first entered the room, Farrington had seen the tough side of the man. He was defiant and belligerent and carried an air of arrogance like that of Frank Vulcek. He was impulsive, but decisive, and now he appeared sure of himself. He had bargained well and made reasonable demands.

"I'd have to get my affairs in order at the airport."

"That's a reasonable request."

"I would like...at least a day to think this over."

Arthur knew he had him. "All right."

"Okay," Garner finally said.

Arthur nodded, jubilant inside himself, but hoping he didn't show it. He liked the character of Phillip Garner, but he wasn't sure he liked the man. But then, he had not gotten along that well with Frank Vulcek either. His only regrets were that he could not divulge the full nature of the assignment, and that he might well be signing Phillip Garner's death warrant right now. If Garner knew the complete circumstances and had his choice, he probably would have opted for prison.

"What happens now?" asked Garner.

Arthur rose quickly from his chair. Just because he thought he had the man for the job, there were still some obstacles. "I have to get back to Washington, so I'll leave you in Miss Feldman's hands."

Garner was mildly surprised. "What's your role in all this?" he asked her.

"I was working with Frank when he died."

Arthur saw a glint of a smile on Garner's face.

"We'll be working together?" Garner asked.

"To a degree," she answered with a slight smile.

Arthur directed a few final comments at Trudi. "I want you to start briefing Mr. Garner on Frank's background. Anything and everything you can think of. The more time you can spend with him, the better."

"When does all this start?" asked Garner.

"By tomorrow at this time, you will already have earned a thousand dollars," Arthur said as he extended a hand. "Thank you, Mr. Garner."

Arthur turned and exited the room.

Phillip Garner stood quietly, pensively. He felt a little more at ease now that he knew she would be working with him, and he liked her in spite of the masquerade she had put on.

"I knew you weren't a journalist," he told her.

"No you didn't," she countered.

No, he didn't, but he didn't want to admit it. He still had his apprehensions about the assignment, but if a woman was involved, it couldn't be that dangerous. After all, on occasion, he had balanced his life against danger. In Viet Nam, one wheel gave way when he landed his jet, but he had escaped from the craft before it went up in a ball of fire. In the states, he had dumped a jet in the Arizona desert, having extended his fuel consumption. That was basically his fault, but he had luckily gotten out of the court martial. Arthur Farrington was correct when he said earlier that he had been forced out of the military. Garner could have fought that issue also, but he decided to move on with his life.

Starting up his own private business at a flight station seemed like a good idea, but he was out of money now. It didn't pull in the capital he thought it would.

There were other issues—flying a false flight plan to Argentina. He thought his cargo was legitimate, but it turned out that he was delivering guns and other military hardware. He had flown as a co-pilot with a fellow named Bucky Pearson. Garner didn't know about the cargo, but Bucky did. Garner had had suspicions up to this point that he may have been under surveillance, and today, Arthur verified it. It appeared that they had caught Bucky.

He did not know what legal channels he had in case he was indicted, and ironically, he never did receive any money for the flight. Arthur was right when he said running this commercial flying business required money. Garner possessed an ancient twin motored Beechcraft in his hangar that needed a few more thousand dollars to make it legally air worthy, and until it passed the five hundred hour inspection, he was broke.

His gaze came back to Trudi who had been quietly sitting, watching him. "Is this assignment going to be as easy as I think it is?"

"No," said Trudi. "For the next several days, you're going to have a lot of homework."

"I'm good at math."

Trudi remained all business. "You'll be reviewing dozens of photos, people that Frank knew. You'll memorize their names and faces, you'll know their habits, their jobs.

"I'm going to tell you everything I know about Frank. How he thinks, how he works, what he drinks, his moods and his favorite swear words. How he walks, how he drives, how he is so good at getting under the skin of everybody around him.

"You'll be wearing his clothes, his ring, you'll carry his wallet and you'll know everything there is to know about his background.

"You'll be given a cover story. You'll live in his apartment, you'll drive his car, you'll eat what he eats, drink what he drinks..."

"Whoa!" said Garner. This was not at all the same person he had just taken for an airplane ride. Somehow this innocent, good-looking woman had caught him completely off guard. Her initial meeting fooled him into thinking she was a journalist on assignment, but she was rambling on like a teletype machine. He liked her charm originally, but now he was having second thoughts.

"Is there any easy part to this job?" he asked innocently.

"Yes. You'll get to sit in a chair and relax while the plastic surgeons remake your face."

He stared at her. "What?"

"You already look so much like him, so it won't require much. Frank Vulcek went through a windshield. You'll need a few scars here and there."

She felt her emotions getting away from her. She could not become involved with this man, even though the temptation lingered heavily within her. It suddenly frightened her. She had known Garner for only a few hours, but he was so much like Frank Vulcek. She had lost Frank once and she did not want to go through it again.

"You were in love with him, weren't you?" he asked.

Her silence was the answer.

"I'm sorry I asked."

She seemed in a trance, and then her composure came back, but her voice was cold. "We have a lot of things to discuss. Shall we start with dinner?"

He smiled. "I said I'd take you out."

"I'm hungry, so I hope you have enough money to cover it."

"I will by tomorrow."

As they left the room, he was adamant. "I'll memorize what I have to and do whatever this Vulcek fellow did, but there's no way in hell they're going to do plastic surgery on me."

"It will only be temporary. Just a couple scars here and there."

"I don't care. Nobody touches this face!"

CHAPTER FIVE

Two days later, a limousine picked up the two at Dulles International, and within the hour, the limo veered off the turnpike and entered the CIA complex. Garner had seen photos of the complex, but now that he was on the grounds, he seemed antlike in size.

The vehicle passed through two checkpoints with ease, since Trudi had all paperwork in order. From the underground parking lot, and with badges attached to their clothing, they made their way by elevator to the fourth floor where Arthur Farrington's office was located.

"Ah, Mr. Garner," Arthur greeted as he stuck out a fat hand. "Good to see you. Nice trip, I assume?"

"It was all right."

Arthur almost considered the answer an insult, since Garner's tone matched the staunch look on his face.

"Miss Feldman, good to see you." Arthur clasped his hands together as if he were about to deliver a lecture. He addressed Garner again. "Miss Feldman will show you to your temporary quarters, which are in this very building. Once you've settled in, we'll begin."

"Begin what?" Garner asked.

Arthur seemed puzzled. "Well, there are those who would like to ask you a few questions in order to see if you fulfill our needs."

"I thought I was already on the payroll."

"Indeed you are, but of course, there are others here who must, ah, judge whether, ah, you're the right man for the job." Arthur was hedging with his statement, and now Garner realized that just because he was here didn't necessarily mean he qualified for the assignment, whatever it was. In the back of his mind, he kept thinking about his past activity flying to Argentina. For the last twenty-four hours, he thought his record would be cleared, but evidently that was not yet definite. And of course, he was still thinking about the compensation.

Trudi escorted Garner to a floor below, where a room was assigned to him. It was comfortable enough, furnished much like a hotel room, except it had no windows, but the room service was good; his one bag was already lying on the bed.

"If you'd like to freshen up a bit, please do so," Trudi suggested. "In another half hour, I'll be back to take you to the cafeteria."

"Are your quarters nearby?" he asked.

"Next door. See you in thirty minutes."

When she was gone, a smile crept into his face. He was happy to have her as an escort but wondered how long that would last.

He undressed and showered and threw on a different set of clothes. In exactly thirty minutes, she rapped lightly on the door, and when he said come in, she entered.

"Ready?" she asked. She was dressed in a rich, cream-colored sweater and a gray skirt, and he could smell a light and fresh perfume.

"You certainly changed in a hurry," he commented as she headed him toward the elevator. "I'm impressed."

"Showered, too."

He raised an eyebrow and grinned. "Now, I'm really impressed."

Somehow, he believed he might be in for a night of entertainment, or at least would spend most of the evening with Trudi, but after they ate, she escorted him back to his room where he remained for the night. Disgruntled, he turned in early.

* * *

In the morning, Garner was up and dressed by seven when his phone rang.

"Sleep well?" she inquired.

"Fairly well."

"Breakfast?" she asked.

"What time?"

"One minute." She hung up, and almost immediately, he again heard the light rap on his door. She was wearing a light blue blouse and a black skirt this time, but the perfume was the same.

"I'm beginning to like this job," he mused as they headed for the elevator.

"Don't get too used to it," she said. "Your day starts at eight o'clock and I won't see you until eight tonight."

She couldn't have been more correct. After breakfast and back on the fourth floor, Trudi introduced him to Dr.Vladislav Kuranik, an older gentleman, mild and meek in appearance. In a rather small room, the man sat across from Garner, studying some paperwork before he initiated a conversation in Russian.

"Perhaps we could begin by discussing your background," he offered in a soft voice.

"It's all written in my dossier, I'm sure," Garner answered speaking Russian.

Dr. Kuranik offered a wry smile. "Of course it is, but I am here to check your proficiency in Russian."

For the next thirty minutes, they covered his background, how he eventually reached the United States, his stint with the military, and in particular his capabilities as a pilot, which he found amusing.

Since he was a pilot, Kuranik went on to discuss varied topics. They talked about military terminology such as tanks, flanking maneuvers, naval sea craft, bombsites, various fighter aircraft, and finally, they spent several minutes discussing missiles, something Garner was unfamiliar with. The Russian seemed to be just as interested in Garner's knowledge of the topics discussed as well as his command of vocabulary. Near the end of the session, Kuranik handed Garner a sheet of paper and a pen. He was asked to listen to several sentences, and afterward, all he had to do was write down verbatim in Russian what the man said. That was easy.

Nothing about the interview seemed to spark anything specific in Garner's mind, except, just before they concluded, Kuranik asked, "Are you familiar with the Russian military's file and rank?"

"No. Why do you ask?"

"Just curious."

"I think you're more than curious."

"Mr. Garner, I just ask the questions, you answer them."

"Which means you don't know why you've been instructed to ask that question."

Dr. Kuranik was silent for a few seconds. "Our interview is over now."

"And so I can leave?"

"No. Werner Baumgartner will be here momentarily."

Seconds later, the door opened as if on cue. Garner looked across at the rectangular mirror on the wall and figured earlier it may have been a two-way mirror. Now, he was sure he had guessed correctly.

When Baumgartner stepped in, Kuranik stepped out. The German was a tall, middle-aged man with thick blond hair and shining blue eyes, definitely Arian in Garner's mind.

"*So, sollen wir anfangen?*" he asked in German.

"*Warum nicht?*" Why not, Garner answered, "*Aber pass auf. Es ist moeglich, dass jemand uns beobachtet.*"

On the other side of the wall behind the two-way mirror, two other Germans, who were observing the interview, both laughed out loud. Arthur, whose German proficiency was limited, looked at the two, curious with their reaction.

One of the Germans clarified. "He told Werner to be careful, that it was possible they were being watched."

Arthur beamed, happy with the translation. A half hour earlier, Arthur had been in this very room with two Russian speaking gentlemen observing Garner, and now, the same microphone easily picked up the conversation going on between Garner and Baumgartner.

After fifteen minutes of being questioned on similar topics that the Russian had asked, one of the German observers commented, "He's good. I'd easily take him for a German."

"Is his German as good as Vulcek's?"

"Definitely."

When the interview was over, Arthur went next door, where he beckoned Garner to come with him.

As the two walked down a corridor, Garner asked, "How am I doing?"

Arthur grunted. "So far so good."

"Does that mean I passed?"

"So far."

Arthur entered another room where three other men were waiting.

"This is Mr. Kendrid, the man I work for," Arthur said as he introduced a man bigger than himself. "Meet Howard Walser and Oscar Halverson," Arthur said introducing the other two. "These two gentlemen have a few questions if you don't mind, Mr. Garner."

"Do I have a choice?"

None of the three found the comment remotely funny.

Walser, a mousy fellow with just a wisp of hair riding above each temple began the questioning. "Have you ever been married, Mr. Garner?"

"Once."

"And?" Walser inquired

"Once was enough."

The little man jotted something down.

"No children?"

"I'm sure you know that answer already."

Walser grunted. "Have you ever been accused of a felony?"

"Yes."

The man looked up. "Could you elaborate?"

"Accused and acquitted."

The others chuckled at the answer, but Walser's face remained unchanged. "Mr. Garner, I don't believe you should take these questions so lightly."

"Mr. Walser," Garner said as he leaned forward. "You're asking me to become a spy, so who gives a goddamn if I've been married or ran a red light. Why don't you ask me some spy questions?"

The men in the room all looked at Walser waiting for his

response. "Like what?" he asked.

"Like whether I could betray a friend or kill somebody. Stuff like that."

"Well," Walser answered, "then let's cut to the quick. "Could you betray a friend?"

"If he requires betraying, he isn't a friend."

Walser didn't bother to write anything down. "Could you kill somebody?"

"I did my share in Viet Nam. Best to get him first, if he's out to get me." Walser looked over at big Mr. Kendrid and nodded. It must have been a signal of some sort, since Arthur and Mr. Kendrid left the room and closed the door behind them.

Outside in the corridor, Kendrid began walking Arthur back to his office. "This fellow could be a walking bombshell. How did you run across him?"

"Miss Feldman found him. He's arrogant as hell, isn't he."

"He certainly is. Howard got a couple of the heavy questions out of the way early. Didn't even have to work up to it."

Mr. Kendrid stopped at Arthur's office. "I want Howard's report when he's finished. Find out if this man of yours can shoot, and then send him over to see Kurt."

"Yes, sir."

"And tell the boys in the lab to prepare for him. We might as well get a jump on things." Mr. Kendrid headed for his office.

"I've alerted them already, but Garner's not too keen on having his face worked on," Arthur said.

Without turning around, Kendrid answered, "That's your problem, Arthur."

When Arthur walked into his office, Kendrid's words were still on his mind. He dialed his secretary, and when she answered, he asked, "Where's Miss Feldman?" He paused, and then, "Find her and send her to my office."

* * *

41

The rest of the questions Walser asked seemed insignificant compared to the first few. The other man, Oscar Halverson, didn't even ask one question. It made Garner wonder if this second fellow was in the room simply as an observer. Evidently they had enough information, since Walser escorted Garner down to the indoor firing range, where a husky man named Russ took over.

Outfitted with a set of ear covers, a .357 Remington and a box of shells, Garner loaded the pistol and fired six rounds at a twenty-five foot target.

The pattern was six inches across. He reloaded and fired another six rounds from fifty feet. The pattern spread was nine inches.

"Not bad," said Russ as he handed over a .38 Beretta. Garner shoved in the clip, pulled the action back and emptied the clip into a fresh target at the fifty feet range. Even from this distance, Russ could see the uniform pattern.

"Want me to fire another clip?" Garner asked.

"That won't be necessary," the husky man said. He gathered the weapons and ear covers from Garner and made a quick phone call, and when he hung up, he pointed Garner to the lounge. "Have a seat. Someone will be down to get you."

Garner spent the rest of the morning with a younger fellow named Kurt Johnson, probably in his late twenties, he guessed. Kurt supplied Garner with three maps; one of St. Louis, one of Frankfurt, Germany and the surrounding area, and one of Prague. On each of the maps, strategic locations were marked by numbers, and separate photos were numbered corresponding to the locations.

"Memorize the numbers and the places they represent," Kurt told him. You have one hour and twenty minutes at which time I'll be back to quiz you."

"Jesus Christ!" Garner remarked when he saw how many places were listed.

"Is he on there?" young Kurt said as he left the room.

* * *

It was a strange test, Garner thought, and he had no idea how well he did on the quiz. Over one hundred locations were listed, and the young fellow covered every one of them. He guessed if he remembered half, he was doing good, and after he was quizzed, the young fellow simply said, "Thank you, Mr. Garner." Then he handed over a pile of photos on which parks, streets, bars, buildings, rivers and a host of other locations were depicted, all from the Frankfurt area.

"More items to tax your memory," was all Kurt said.

Under each of the photos, a word was written to describe the subject. A half dozen photos depicted Frank Vulcek's apartment building on Taunusstrasse, some from the outside, some from the inside.

Street signs were labeled, the street in both directions from Vulcek's apartment were depicted as well as a photo of Frau Kutcher, Vulcek's landlady. Several photos of additional men and women, whom Garner presumed that Vulcek knew, added to the memorization process.

Vulcek owned a Peugeot, and a series of photos appeared that depicted it from every angle. What Garner presumed was important was the license plate number, which he for certain memorized.

At the end of the afternoon, he was exhausted, his mind so full of trivia that he could hardly believe he could store much more knowledge without his head breaking apart.

Two hours into his studying, young Kurt Johnson returned. "Mr. Garner. Ready for a break?"

"Yes, I could use one."

"Good. Follow me."

The young man escorted him once again to the basement near the firing range where he had been earlier in the day, and where he was introduced to a muscular and very tanned looking lady named Freya. "Freya, meet Mr. Phillip Garner. You've got him for the next two hours."

Young Kurt turned to Garner. "You'll be spending a few hours a day here for the duration of your stay. Have at it."

Delray K. Dvoracek

Freya, with cropped, short sandy hair and built like a stocky bull, was crammed into a top and shorts that were far too small for her. From the back, all he could see was muscles rippling in her legs and tight cheeks under her shorts as she led him into an exercise room where several other men were working out.

"*Your close,*" Freya said with a strange accent, as she handed over gym shorts, a sweat shirt, tennis shoes and socks." She pointed him to the men's locker room. "*Venn you reddy, vee verk.*"

When he came out of the locker room, she was waiting for him, and for the next two hours, she definitely worked him. She placed him on a dozen different exercise machines. For some reason, he thought sure she was working him hard just to judge his stamina and endurance, but he was not about to let her win him over, so he fought the leg presses, lifted the weights, did chess presses and anything else she demanded. When he thought he was finished, she had him make six rounds around the track. After two hours, he was whipped, and when he finally was released for a shower, he soaked under cold water for a quarter hour.

After he dressed, Freya handed over a schedule for the next six days. Almost every day was labeled at a different time, and although he could not remotely understand the demand for the physical training, he did feel refreshed once he left the gym. And on a positive note, he had been told to find his way back to his room without an escort this time.

It was near seven o'clock when he lay down on his bed fully dressed. He checked his watch, remembering that Trudi said she would see him at eight. He barely had his eyes closed when he was fast asleep only to be awakened by a light knock, yet he remained still, his eyes still shut. When he finally opened his eyes, Trudi was sitting on the edge of his bed.

"Hungry?" she asked.

He smiled. "Famished. Why is it I only get to see you when it's time to eat?"

"Because I have a busy schedule. I can't be at your side every minute of the day."

44

"Why don't you try?" he asked as he touched her hand.

She pulled her hand away and stood up. "Let's go, Mr. Garner."

It wasn't as if Phillip was headed out on a date. She took him to the same cafeteria downstairs, where a host of other CIA workers could dine twenty-four hours around the clock. The ambiance of the eating room was similar to that of a Burger King.

Garner was mildly surprised to discover the cafeteria half full, even at this hour. After passing through the line, they took a corner table.

"Frank ate a lot of meat," she suddenly said. "He was a steak and potatoes man, not much for pomes frits or dessert, and he liked salads on occasion."

"What did he drink?" Garner asked.

"Usually water."

"I meant the hard stuff."

"Brandy or beer."

"At least he had some good qualities." Garner thought he would throw some humor into the conversation, but she wasn't responding.

"He tipped well, too, even though the gratuity comes with the price of a meal in Europe."

"What'd he do in his free time?"

"He worked late hours, never stopped."

Garner picked at his food. "I assume he spent some time with you."

She looked down, a saddened look on her face.

He felt sheepish. "I'm sorry. I hit a sore spot, and I apologize."

"No need to. It's something I'll have to get used to."

They ate in silence for a while. "How was your day?" she finally asked.

"Grueling." He smiled. "Well, not exactly grueling, but they've got me reading a lot of stuff, looking at photos, memorizing names, dates and places. They even wanted to know if I could kill somebody."

"What did you tell them?"

He shrugged. "If the incentive is right, I suppose anybody

could." She was still looking down. "Did Frank Vulcek ever kill anybody?" he asked.

She hesitated a moment. "I don't know."

The hesitation was long enough to make Garner think she wasn't telling the truth. Arthur and Trudi had, after all, picked him to replace a spy. If Vulcek was anything like the spies he had read about in novels, perhaps he did kill somebody. Garner had spent part of the morning firing a pistol, and now that he thought back, perhaps having proficiency with a handgun held more significance than what he earlier imagined. Guns were second nature to him, but for sport, and certainly not for killing somebody.

"How many others did you interview before you picked me?"

"A few."

"Nobody else qualified?"

"Some did, but none resembled Frank like you do."

"What am I getting into?" he asked.

"Delivering some merchandise to Prague."

"I'm firing pistols and memorizing a hundred names, faces and places, and I've been mapped to death. And why am I scheduled to work out in a gym every day?"

"Physical exercise relieves your mental activities. It's good therapy."

"All this just to be a delivery boy?"

"It's simply precautionary. Chances are you won't use hardly any of the information you're learning. But one little piece of information that you remember could be your..."

"Salvation?" he finished.

"I didn't phrase it right," she said.

"No, you phrased it right. I should have asked for more money."

The statement took her by surprise. She thought he was contemplating the danger that the assignment might entail and was having second thoughts about going through with it, but *money* was his driving force. Money never motivated Frank Vulcek, she knew. Frank worked for the thrill of it.

"I need to retire," she suddenly said. "Tomorrow's a big day for me, and another big one for you, I'm sure."

"I'm sure," he agreed.

They dumped their trays and returned to their rooms.

CHAPTER SIX

The next day started out with a quiz on the information he was to memorize the first day, and when that ended, the young fellow, Kurt Johnson, presented an hour-long slide show. More photos of Frankfurt, especially the *Zeil*, the main thoroughfare running through the city. Other landmarks showed up on the screen, such as the Opera House, which had been gutted with a bomb during World War II, as well as the bombed out church in the center of the city.

It seemed every bar within the proximity of the main train station area was on display—the Dolly, the Star, the Swing, the Neu Yorker. Why he had to be able to recognize *Bologna's*, an Italian restaurant, he did not know, but evidently it was important to Vulcek, as was the *Troika*, a Russian restaurant and bar.

On and on the photos came as the young man rattled off the importance of each slide, so fast and so furious that Garner could hardly keep up, and when the fellow finished, he started all over again.

By late morning, Garner was ready for the gym and some mental release the physical exercise would grant him. Afterward, he had another quick bite in the same cafeteria, eating alone.

That afternoon, his first meeting was with a dentist. His teeth were fine.

A nurse at a station took his blood pressure and a blood sample and then sent him on to see a doctor. The physician was an older gentleman with a gray mustache and beard, and when Garner entered his office, the man was looking over some papers and didn't seem in the least bit in a hurry to accommodate him.

"I'm Doctor Borgen. So you're the fellow from Indiana," he finally remarked.

"Yeah. What's that mean to you?"

"Nothing. Don't believe I ever met anyone from Indiana before."
He asked Garner to strip off his shirt, and as he ran a stethoscope
across his back and chest, he asked, "Are you on any medication?"

"No."

"Ever have any trouble breathing or heart palpitation?

"No."

"Ever been treated for drugs of any sort?"

"No."

"Did you get laid last night?"

Garner stiffened. He was sure he had heard the man correctly.

The doc chuckled. "I just threw that in to see if you were paying
attention. Chest seems okay, but then, this is just a quick check.
When was the last time you ran a mile without stopping?"

The question seemed to be a bit strange, Garner thought, but he
let his mind wander back a few years. "Probably with the Air Force,
some five or six years ago."

The doc felt along the sides of his neck. "Be a good idea to get in
a mile each day downstairs in the gym. Tell Freya I sent you."

"I'm already working with her."

"Ah. The boys are way ahead of me. Good. She's something,
ain't she?"

Garner didn't know what he meant.

The doc studied some paperwork again and made a few
notations. "How old are you?"

"Thirty nine."

"Got a lot of muscles."

"Who, me?" Garner asked.

"No, Freya." He looked up. "Well, you too. If you take care of
yourself, you might get another couple good years in before you
expire."

"What?"

"Just a little joke," he chuckled. "Everybody around here is
always so damn serious. Kind of breaks up the monotony for me.
You're good to go."

* * *

When he left the office, he was somewhat surprised to find Trudi waiting for him, and then, he was not surprised, since he hadn't been given instructions where to go from here.

"Hi," she said.

"What? Is it time to eat again?"

She smiled. "No. Something more important than that."

As they walked to the elevator, she asked, "How did your day go?"

"You asked me that yesterday."

"Today's a different day."

He laughed. "Well, if somebody dropped me off at the main train station in Frankfurt, I could find my way to Frank Vulcek's apartment with my eyes closed. I know every bar that he frequented. I can eat blinis and borscht soup at the Troika and pizza at Bologna's. I know the Opera House hasn't been used since World War Two, and I even know where to purchase a ticket for an excursion on the Rhein River."

"Anything else?"

"I may need a cap on a tooth, but it's not pressing, and this doc I just saw is the only person I've met here with a sense of humor."

"Did he ask if you slept with somebody last night?"

"As a matter of fact, he did."

She laughed. "Doc Borgen asks everybody that. I understand Freja has you up to eight laps."

"She and the doc are shooting for a mile."

They got off the elevator and headed for a door that simply said *Lab*.

They entered what appeared to be a reception office, but Trudi walked him through into separate room.

Inside, a tall, distinguished man with slick black hair and wearing a white lab coat was waiting for him. He looked more like a used car salesman than a surgeon. He was standing in front of a wall on which three rows of photographs were strung out on wires from left to right. The first row was that of Frank Vulcek, some full-face shots, some at a three-quarter view, some in profile.

The second row beneath them were photos of himself in similar positions, and the third row depicted another set of photos of himself exactly like the row above, but all of the photos on this third row were depicted with scarred tissue about the eyes, a definite scar across his forehead and a deep gash on the left side of his throat.

"Good God!" Garner exclaimed.

"I can assure you it's basically painless," the man in the white smock said.

"I don't give a damn about the pain. I'm not interested in messing up my face." He turned to Trudi. "I told you that."

"That's not a problem," the man said. "We'll utilize dyes and plastic skin for the scar tissue. Inside of six weeks, it will all wear off. That which doesn't, we can surgically remove. A couple months from now, you'll be back to normal."

Garner stepped closer and examined the retouched photos of himself with the scars in place. "You won't fool anybody." He pointed at the row of himself with the drawings of the scars in place and grunted. "These made up photos of me don't even resemble Vulcek."

"Oh?" the man replied. He pulled two of the photos off the wall with the composite scars in place, one a headshot, one a profile. "You don't think these resemble Frank Vulcek?"

"No."

The man smiled. "These two photos are Vulcek. The rest up there are you."

Garner gaped at the two photos, looked up at the remaining photos on the wall and then turned to Trudi. She simply nodded.

"You people are insane," he said.

Trudi narrowed her eyes. "I told you plastic surgery would be required."

Garner again studied the composite photos. "Yeah, but Christ, I had no idea it would be this extensive."

"We've done bigger makeovers than this," the lab man confided.

"This is an easy fix, four days at the most."

"Four days?"

"Couple hours each day," the man said.

Arthur entered the room from behind them, carrying a manila envelope in his hand. "How's everybody today?" he asked. "Getting ready for surgery, Mr. Garner?"

Garner glared back, insulted with the smart remark and the smile on Arthur's face as well. Arthur pulled a photo from inside the envelope and held it up. "I believe you know this man."

He was the pilot Garner had flown with to Argentina. "Bucky Pearson."

"Right," Arthur said. "The FBI has Mr. Pearson in custody as we speak, and he's been very cooperative. It seems your name has come up a few times. However, I've talked to Mr. Kendrid and we believe we can persuade the FBI to drop all charges."

Arthur placed the photo back in the envelope, turned and left the room.

"Evidently I've passed all tests," Garner said to Trudi.

"Yes, everyone is pleased with your responses and qualifications."

"So, all that's left is this surgery?"

"Oh, no." Trudi said. "You'll be working on names, faces and places every hour you're not in surgery."

"Doesn't sound like much fun."

"There's Freya in the gym," she reminded him.

He did not find the remark remotely funny. Freya was cordial enough, but physically, she was nothing more than a walking piece of sinew and muscle.

"Mr. Garner," the surgeon said. "We'll expect you here at eight in the morning for the next four days. No food or drink after eight tonight. Is that clear?"

"Yes."

Trudi took Garner by the arm and walked him out of the office. "Hungry?" she asked.

* * *

At eight the next morning, a young lady dressed in white met Garner in the same office and ushered him into the adjacent operating room, where everything appeared as sterile as he could imagine.

"My name's Marci," she said. "Would you remove your shirt, please?"

She proceeded to take his blood pressure, and as she did so, she was reviewing a chart. "You don't smoke?"

"No."

"Nothing to eat or drink since last night?"

"No."

"Are you allergic to anything?"

"No."

"Your blood work looks good."

"Aren't you going to ask me if I got laid last night?"

Marci turned a shade of red. "I see you've already met Doc Borden."

The surgeon came in and began stringing up the same photographs Garner had seen of himself the day before. "Mr. Garner," he greeted. "I'm Harold. Obviously you've met Marci. Glad to have you with us this morning."

Garner thought it strange that the surgeon introduced himself as simply *Harold*, and now the man was whistling as he examined the photos. Garner looked around. He was sitting in something like a barber's chair, but he did not see anything that remotely appeared to be surgeon's tools. "Where did you acquire your medical degree?" he asked the surgeon.

"I don't have one, but Marci is a registered nurse and anesthetist."

Garner was mystified. "What are your credentials?"

"Seventeen years with Universal Pictures."

"You're not a surgeon?"

"No, I'm a makeup artist." He turned to his assistant. "We'll do

53

just the dyes today."

The chair buzzed as Garner felt himself dropping into a reclined position. He watched patiently as Marci and Harold slipped on elastic gloves, and then Harold pulled a drawer open in which several syringes were located. Another drawer exposed several small vials with various colors in them.

Before he knew it, the young lady shoved a needle into his arm, and a few seconds later, he remembered her saying *You should begin to feel sleepy.*

* * *

He awoke from the drowsiness, and in short order, his eyes focused to see Arthur's face staring back. He glanced about to see Trudi next to him.

"Amazing," Arthur remarked. "Very good, very good."

"Feeling all right?" Trudi asked.

Garner offered a faint smile. "Time to eat again?"

She chuckled. "Feel like getting up?"

He reached a hand up toward his eyes feeling a stinging sensation. "Give me a mirror."

Harold shoved one in place.

"Jesus!" Garner said as he stared at the red and dark colored sockets about his eyes. He stretched up and saw the same coloring extending from his right ear lobe down to his collarbone. They had punctured his skin with needles like a tattoo-artist. Disfiguring the eyes was most important, they had said, and they were doing a good job of it so far.

"It's a good start," said Harold. "You might feel a bit queasy for the next hour or so, but it will wear off. See you tomorrow same time."

When Garner got out of the chair, he did feel a bit light headed. After putting his shirt back on, he walked out with Trudi and Arthur. "What's on the agenda for the rest of the day," he asked.

Arthur answered. "Kurt Johnson this afternoon, Walser and

54

Halverson tomorrow. Tell Freya in the gym you're taking today off. How's the face?"

"Still stings."

Arthur just nodded. When the three passed his office, he entered, leaving Garner and Trudi alone. She noticed that he was slightly unsteady as he walked. "Feel like just talking for a while?" she asked.

"That would be a welcome change."

At the end of the corridor, a door opened to a balcony where they sat in two comfortable chairs shaded by an overhang. To the south, the sunshine lit up the landscape with a deep brilliance as the noise of autos on the freeway sent a rushing sound across the way.

From somewhere, Garner could hear birds singing. "What is that, a songbird of some sort?"

She listened. "I don't know."

"Would Frank have known?"

"No. Frank and nature weren't one and the same. I don't think he ever took time to notice the beauty that surrounded him. He was too involved in his work."

"That's too bad."

"He wasn't much of a people person either. He and Arthur never got along very well. Frank was very perceptive and productive, however, Arthur played off of him and always took the credit."

"And that bothered Frank?"

"No," she said. "Whatever Frank accomplished, he did for himself. Work drove him. He was always a part of the action. That's what he liked best."

"And you loved him, didn't you?"

Trudi looked off pensively before she answered. "He had his tender moments, but I never knew for sure what was going on inside his head. We could be having dinner somewhere, and suddenly he would be staring off, as if I wasn't even there, thinking about something. He never seemed to relax.

"That last night, before he...died. I knew something was wrong."

Garner let a few seconds pass, seeing that her gaze and thoughts were elsewhere. "Why are you telling me these things?" he finally asked.

"Because you need to know how he acted, how he reacted, how he thought. My best advice to you is to remain aloof if you ever run across anybody who mistakes you for Frank, and I know someone will. It may not be any of the faces Arthur is so intent on showing you with his slide shows and photos, because Frank dealt with a lot of people that Arthur never knew about."

Garner's mind was working furiously to digest what she was saying. It appeared to him that Vulcek was not only a loner, but somewhat of an outsider.

That afternoon, Garner spent most of his hours with Kurt Johnson running through the same names, faces and places, and he was quizzed to death on everything.

Toward evening, he expected Trudi to come knocking on his door, but Arthur informed him that she had left the CIA complex and was headed back to Germany. The mere thought of her being gone disturbed him. She knew more about Frank Vulcek than all the men put together here at Langley, and somehow, he felt what information she had to impart would be much more valuable than all these locations and buildings he was forced to memorize.

Arthur treated him to dinner that evening in the same cafeteria. For someone who was heading up the Prague assignment, whatever it was, Arthur said very little. "Everything going all right for you?"

How could he respond other than to say it was, since everything here was planned for him. He had absolutely no say-so in what he was doing, and if he could have been granted a wish, he would have wished to have Trudi back.

In the morning, he was back at the lab where Harold and Marci, his nurse, froze his face with Novocain. His face was numb as they formed the first layer of plastic skin and fashioned it to his face. He listened to their medical jargon, having no idea what *caudal support of the temporal* meant, or *multiple scars on the medial canthus*. All the while the two worked on his face, he occasionally caught a glimpse of himself in a mirror beyond them. He watched them glue the synthetic skin in place that marked his eyes and forehead. They also fashioned a *slight nick*, as they labeled it, on the bridge of his nose.

With most of the work done about his eyes, Harold held an electric blower to his face that shot out warm air to dry the so-called scars. As the plastic dried, his own skin tightened as if squeezed together with a pair of pliers.

"You'll get used to the sensation," Harold consoled him.

"How will I ever get this crap off?"

"This is not crap, my good friend," he answered. "Surgeons make you look pretty. We makeup artists make you look unpretty. That's a real challenge." He chuckled. "You know, if I could get your face on a movie screen, I'd win an Oscar for best makeup artist of the year."

"You're that good?" Garner inquired.

"When I get done with you, you'll think you're Mr. Vulcek."

"Did you ever meet Frank?"

"No," he said. "I never had the misfortune."

That answer triggered Garner's mind. He made up a lie. "I understand he killed a couple men."

"I have heard that rumor, but of course everything here at Langley is a rumor until somebody discovers it isn't." He stood back and shut off the electric blower. "Beautiful. Beautiful work, don't you think, Marci?"

The following two mornings they worked on his throat, and two days later, after another brief inspection by Harold to make sure every piece of his disfiguration was solidly in place, he ended up in Arthur's office.

Mr. Kendrid was there when Garner arrived, wearing dark glasses.

"My god!" Kendrid exclaimed. "They did a hell of a job."

Garner sat across from the two men and removed his glasses. Even without them, Harold said he could easily pass for Vulcek. Harold had considered fitting him with colored contact lenses, but eventually the decision was made that the color of his eyes was close enough, and his hair was virtually the same, except now he combed it back like Vulcek used to wear it.

"It's a remarkable resemblance," Arthur stated. "Your voice isn't the same, but it's guttural, like Frank's. If anybody confronts you..."

"I know," Frank finished as he pulled away his collar. "Just show them the scar." His throat appeared as if it had been sliced open.

Arthur opened a drawer and produced a wallet. "It's Frank's. It contains your new face on the ID, your driver's license and three hundred Marks." He placed a ring alongside it. "Frank's ring."

Garner slipped the ring on his finger. It was a perfect fit.

The last item Arthur produced was his passport. The photo was different than his ID, and the date of issue was a few years earlier. It already had stamps in it from Germany, Italy and Czechoslovakia. They had thought of everything.

"At 6:15 tomorrow morning," said Arthur, "a limo will be waiting downstairs to take you to the airport. Once you arrive in Frankfurt, you're on your own. Make the rounds like you've been instructed, and if you run across something, we'll be in contact."

"How do I contact you?"

"You'll find out."

"What about Miss Feldman?"

"What about her?"

Garner threw his arms open. "She spends the better part of a week with me and then simply disappears?"

"She has a job, too," he said, as if the answer was sufficient. "Good luck to you." Arthur rose and extended his hand across, and although Garner shook it, he still had his mind on Trudi.

Mr. Kendrid was cordial enough as he offered his hand. "Thank you, Mr. Garner, for being so cooperative."

For being blackmailed, Garner was thinking, as he left the office. Back in his room, a small suitcase with appropriate clothes was on his bed, and alongside was his plane ticket.

He did not eat that night, nor did he sleep well.

CHAPTER SEVEN

The intercom inside the 747 clicked on. "We are now starting our descent into Rhein Main. Please fasten your seat belts and observe the no smoking signs. Thank you."

Phillip Garner sat in a seat near the rear of the aircraft. The dark glasses he was wearing reflected in the window as he glanced down at the hazy night-lights of Frankfurt.

Though he had not slept well the night before, not once during the flight had he felt tired. It all happened so fast. In a short ten days, he had had so much knowledge pressed into his head that it was impossible to relax. The full implication of what he was doing and where he was going suddenly struck him like a baseball in the face.

His mind raced, untiring, not for a moment able to erase any of the newly acquired data that occupied his thoughts.

He could understand why he needed proficiency in German, but when he asked why he needed to speak Russian, they had told him simply because Vulcek could speak it.

During some of his last sessions with Walser and Halverson, he had seen a few film clips of the real Frank Vulcek, saw how he walked, how he swung his hands. It wasn't much to go on, but it was better than nothing. Strangely enough, they did not have any tapes with Vulcek's voice on it, thus the need for the scar on the throat, a good excuse for the change in his voice box.

He removed his glasses and felt the scars about his eyes and throat. At first, the implanted scar tissue had left him with a stinging sensation and a tightness of the skin, but that had disappeared already, like Harold said it would.

"From the war?" the man asked, who was sitting next to him.

Garner realized that without glasses, the man was concerned about his looks. The man pulled up his pant leg to show a brace

59

wrapped around a skinny leg. "D-Day. I took a bullet before I even got off the landing craft."

Garner simply nodded. "Vietnam. A mine blew up in my face."

The man offered a hand. "By God, put her there, friend."

The aircraft thumped on the runway, and when he glanced out the window, lights of the terminal flitted by. More lights glared in the night, then red and green flashing signs advertising the small businesses in and around the terminal.

He had once visited Frankfurt when he was a boy, but he did not recollect anything of the city. What he knew now about the city was what Langley had pounded into him.

A half hour after the aircraft came to a stop, he picked up his bag and was quickly herded into a line headed for the *Passkontrolle*.

Within a short time, he handed over his passport to the German in the black customs uniform. The official glanced at the passport, looked up and then examined the passport photo again.

"Die Brille wegnehmen, bitte."

Garner removed the tinted glasses and watched as the customs man again examined the passport photo.

"Danke sehr," he said and let Garner pass. The *Zollkontrolle* did not even examine his suitcase.

Once outside, the cool, heavy fog penetrated his skin. He slipped into his raincoat as a taxi pulled up, and a few minutes later, he was on the Autobahn. Off to his right, he could see Rhein Main Air Force Base, which occupied the north side of the Frankfurt-Main Flughafen.

A few kilometers later, the taxi driver swung on to Morfelder Landstrasse, and it wasn't long until they crossed the Fridens Bridge, a name he recognized from Langley.

The Hauptbahnhof loomed out of the fog, and though it was near midnight, the streets were as crowded as if it were midday.

The driver sped past a few street islands and zipped around a trolley car. The lights of the Dolly Bar, one of Vulcek's hangouts, flashed to his right. The Pan Am neon sign blinked on and off, blue, huge, on the top of the building across from him.

Oom-pah music poured out of a bar as the driver moved on. The city and its sounds had an enticing ring, which reminded him of Winnipeg, where he had lived many years. It was not the same, of course, but Winnipeg and its downtown district were not totally unlike the city center of Frankfurt that he was now observing.

The taxi skirted down Taunusstrasse and flew past the bombed out Opera House, another familiar picture from Langley, and soon after, they were driving down Reuter Weg. The names of the streets were registered in his mind, and after a few more blocks, the driver turned off, and magically, there it was.

He had seen enough photos of the brown, brick corner building, and though it was night, a lamp pole illuminated enough of the structure. An iron gate at the entrance broke the low cement wall surrounding it, and a gateway beyond led to a courtyard where the garages stood. It was all as he had imagined, as if he had been here before.

Garner paid the driver and watched him drive off. A chill invaded him momentarily as he tugged at his raincoat collar and pushed through the iron gate. He entered a breezeway and opened the main door with a key. The staircase led to a wide hallway on the second floor. The door to Frank Vulcek's apartment was to the left. He crossed quietly on the runner, set his bag to the floor and had just got another key when a door opened behind him.

"*Oh, Herr Vulcek! Sie sind wieder zu Hause!*"

It was Frau Kutcher, Vulcek's landlady. Garner recognized her immediately. She was wearing a tattered gown and a head covering that was sloppily wrapped around her hair.

"*Ja. Ich bin wieder zurueck gekommen,*" he answered.

She stared at him. "? *Oh, was is'n da los mit'm Hals? Und die Augen?*" She gasped and threw her hands up to her face.

He touched the scar at his throat and answered her in German. "I... had a car accident, you know. I had to have an operation."

She grimaced. "Oh, my God! I'm so sorry. He didn't tell me you were hurt so badly!"

Garner was alert. "Who didn't tell you?"

"The man who was here. Your friend. He didn't tell me. I'm so sorry!"

"Did he leave a name?"

"Oh, no. He never did."

He never did. That meant the visitor had been here more than once. "Can you describe him?"

Her eyes dipped as she tried to recall. "Well, I only saw him twice. And it was dark a little bit, you know. He was a tall man, and thin. And a beard." She swiped at her chin. "Yes, a beard like... like that artist fellow, you know."

He guessed she meant Van Gogh.

"Do you know him?" she asked.

"Yes," said Garner. "I think I know who it was." He didn't have the faintest idea.

"*Ein moment! Ein moment!*" She was gone for a second, and then returned with a handful of mail. "Your friend asked if you had any mail. He said he would forward it to you, but I remembered what you told me about your mail. I kept it for you."

Garner nodded. "Thank you, Frau Kutcher." She stood waiting as if expecting something more. Garner reached into his pocket, produced a couple Marks and tucked them into her hand.

"Oh, thank you, Herr Vulcek. It's so nice to have you back again. I knew you were coming. Your suits arrived a few days ago.

"*Schlaf gut!*" she said and disappeared behind her door. Garner's mind couldn't keep up with his thoughts. He had just passed the first test with a person who knew Frank Vulcek fairly well.

As he entered the room, he was surprised how calm he had been, especially since she had sprung so suddenly upon him.

He closed the door and switched on the light. The room was exactly as Trudi had described it. A huge, double bed practically covered the length of one wall. A wardrobe stood against another wall, and inside were the suits that Trudi said would be there.

Several shirts lined the wall alongside them, and below were three pairs of Vulcek's shoes and a pair of slippers.

A small end table sat next to the head of the bed, and next to that was a roll top desk. To his left, an ell-shaped opening five feet wide led to another door where the toilet was located. He turned on the light in the small bathroom, then switched it out again. Back in the bedroom, he slipped off his coat and sat on the bed for a few minutes, still keyed up from the flight.

Ten minutes later he finished a shower. It felt good, hot, relaxing. More tension had built up in him than he realized, and with the warmth came a welcome comfort.

He sat on the bed once again wearing a robe that belonged to Frank Vulcek. Vulcek wore fancy suits and evidently spent money freely, but Garner never would have guessed it by the simplicity of this apartment.

The tall, thin visitor with the beard was a mystery. From all the photos Garner recollected at Langley, none remotely came close to Frau Kutcher's description of the man.

He turned his attention to the letters Frau Kutcher had given him. The first two were bills, which he put aside. The third was a short note.

Call me as soon as you arrive. It was signed, *Irmtrod,* and there was a phone number underneath. The stamp on the envelope indicated it had been mailed two days ago. His mind was back on the photographs again and the names he had memorized. Irmtrod was a name he would never forget, but it brought no recollection. And who would know he was arriving now?

Perhaps this note was from one of Vulcek's contacts. It was near one in the morning, but he picked up the phone and dialed, his curiosity growing. The phone rang twice, three times.

"Allo?" It was a girl

He answered in German. "Ah, hello. This is Frank." He was curious but calm as he waited for her response.

"I thought you would be arriving earlier," she answered in English.

Garner smiled. "Trudi?" He looked at the scribbled message. "Irmtrod? Is that your real name?"

He heard a faint laugh. "Yes. How was your trip?"

"Good."

"Are you tired?"

"I should be, but I can't sleep."

There was a short silence. "Why don't you come over. I'll make you a drink."

Garner didn't hesitate. He quickly wrote down her address on Marianplatz and asked how to get there. She was about to hang up when he quickly said, "Wait a minute!" Garner was looking about the room wondering where Vulcek's car keys were.

"The keys are in the upper right hand drawer in the desk," she said, as if she had read his mind.

He found them. "Got 'em. I'll be right over."

It didn't take Garner long to find the Peugeot Frank Vulcek owned, since the numbers on the garage doors matched the apartment numbers. He slid into the bucket seat behind the wheel, and after grinding for a few seconds, the engine caught. He raced the motor a few times, and in a cloud of blue smoke, he pulled out of the garage.

Reuter Weg led him back to the Opera House where he turned on to Hoch Strasse, and at the park, Marianstrasse took him to Marianplatz.

He wheeled the car around the circle and pulled over. He had just started up the few steps to the building when another vehicle entered the circle behind him. The car normally wouldn't have drawn his attention, except when it turned in his direction, the lights switched to bright and then back to dim again.

Garner curiously watched as the Mercedes, dark in color, passed by on the street. It kept going and turned the corner at the end of the block.

For a moment, he wondered if the car had been tailing him, but then another car entered the circle, and it, too, passed by on the street and turned the corner. Garner shrugged off the suspicion and entered the foyer of the apartment complex.

He located her number and rang, and when the door buzzed, he pushed his way in. He climbed the stairs two steps at a time and made his way down the hallway. He stopped for a moment when he reached the door. It was slightly ajar, and it was dark from within. He tensed as he eased it open.

"Trudi?"

She was sitting on a couch behind a low table on which a couple candles burned.

"Hi," she greeted.

He stepped in and closed the door behind him.

"I hope I'm not interrupting your séance."

She smiled. "Not at all. She rose from the couch clad in a floor length white robe.

Garner liked what he saw. "It's not every day I land in Europe and am greeted by such a beautiful lady."

"Where are your dark glasses?"

He patted his breast pocket. "I don't usually drive at night with dark glasses."

She came closer and studied his face. "They did a good job on you. Would you like a drink?"

"Yeah. Frank preferred brandy, but I prefer scotch."

"I only have brandy."

He shrugged as he removed his raincoat. She mixed a drink at a cabinet and handed it to him, then sat on the couch again and lit a cigarette from the flame of the candle.

"Would you like a cigarette?"

"Frank didn't smoke," he said. "I don't either."

She smiled again. "I was just testing you."

He sat in the other corner of the couch. "I've already had a visitor," he said, not knowing what else to say.

That caught her by surprise. "Tonight?"

"No. Some time ago. A friend, evidently. He wanted to forward my mail, but Frau Kutcher wouldn't let him."

"Did you get a description?"

"Tall, thin and with a beard."

Trudi raised a shoulder. "I don't know who it was."

"Could he have been one of Frank's contacts?"

"Possibly."

Delray K. Dvoracek

She seemed to be staring at him as he nurtured his drink. Figuring her out was not easy. At moments she seemed cold, and then abruptly she looked warm and beautiful behind her saddened gray eyes. Like now.

The saddened eyes changed. "Tomorrow evening you should start making your presence known."

Garner nodded. "I intend to." Those were orders from Arthur Farrington. He was to start dropping in on all the nightspots Vulcek frequented and make it known that Frank Vulcek was back in circulation.

Garner twirled his drink around in his hands. "What do I do if I find someone who knew Frank?"

"Just tell them you're back in business. Tell them about the accident."

"Is that all?"

"Frank wasn't much of a talker. If a person has a tip or something, accept it and pay him off."

"What kind of information might I expect?" he asked.

"A name. A meeting place. Most anything. Just accept the information and..."

"And pay him off," finished Garner. Her eyes were cold again, staring like a zombie. She had asked him to come over, but now he wondered why. Her smile was inviting, yet, she was stoic as if her thoughts were in another world. He wondered if a good slap would bring her around.

She put out her cigarette, pulled her knees up and folded her arms around them.

Garner felt frustrated. "Did Vulcek have any enemies?"

"He may have, but there's nothing to worry about. You'll be out of here in a few days."

"Do you know when?"

"No."

"But you just said a few days." She didn't respond. "For someone who's supposed to be helping me through this wild... whatever it is, you aren't making things easy." He put his drink on the table and stood up, and with his raincoat in hand, he headed for the door.

"Wait," she said. The coldness drained from her face, and her eyes brought on a saddened look. She was close now. "It's just that..."

"That what?"

"It's just that you look so much like him. You are so much like him."

Any anger Garner felt before was suddenly gone. She was so beautiful, and now he realized the reasons for her cold responses.

Her sad eyes were on him, but he knew she was seeing Frank Vulcek. He couldn't find any words to console her as he slipped his arms around her. There were no tears in her eyes as he drew her to him, held her firmly against her. She hugged him tightly as if weeks of concealed emotions were draining from her body.

Then she whispered in his ear. "Will you make love to me?"

He kissed her with a tenderness that he did not even know he possessed. Her lips were soft and warm, and he did not care if she wanted to make love to Phillip Garner or Frank Vulcek. Tonight he would play either role.

CHAPTER EIGHT

At three in the afternoon the next day after a ten-hour sleep, Phillip Garner woke with a big smile on his face. He hadn't expected to spend the night at Trudi's, but it was all in a night's work, he told himself. This was the longest he had slept in weeks, perhaps months.

Trudi was gone, but she left a couple of hard rolls on the dining room table for his breakfast and a short note, which he quickly read.

"I enjoyed it, too," he mused.

He dressed, ate quickly and then drove through a drizzling rain back to his apartment where he showered. With a different set of clothes on, he sat at the roll top desk looking out over the courtyard. The room was chilly for a July morning. And although two radiators were in the apartment, there was no thermostat in the room. He knew the Germans habitually kept their apartments cold and combated the chill with heavy sweaters.

He opened the wardrobe, rummaged through a lower drawer and found a sweater. What was underneath caught his attention. In a shoulder holster was an automatic pistol. He recognized it immediately as a Beretta, the same weapon he had fired back in Virginia. He retrieved the gun from the holster and extracted the clip. It was full. He pulled back the action on the automatic just enough to see a bullet was in the chamber. This weapon was fully loaded and ready to fire.

He wondered if Arthur Farrington carried a weapon. Or Trudi? He shoved the clip back into the handle, put the automatic back in the drawer and pulled some articles of clothing over it, hiding it as it had been before. Wearing the sweater, he sat again, where several paperbacks lined the top of the desk. Garner found it amusing that most of them were espionage type novels.

He started searching through the desk drawers, for exactly what, he didn't know. In one drawer he discovered a half-empty box of cartridges, which indicated that perhaps Vulcek had fired a few from the Beretta.

Stuffed into pigeonholes under the roll top, he found four opened letters. He scanned the contents of the first three but found nothing interesting.

The last letter was from a glassware company in Frankfurt, a bill for six Rosenthal crystal glasses. Garner remembered his drink last night was in a Rosenthal glass. He guessed Garner had given them to her as a gift at one time or another.

He put the letters back and continued his search but found nothing unusual.

His eyes were drawn once again to the paperbacks on the top of the desk. They all seemed to be of uniform height and width except for one, which was slightly taller. He pulled the book from its place and began flipping the pages.

At the end of the novel, an onionskin envelope fell out. Inside was a short typed note:

Dear Sir,

Our firm should like very much to consider in detail the matter, which we discussed at an earlier meeting. Please feel free to call for an appointment.
M.T.

It was typed in German, which wasn't unusual, but he kept coming back to the words *our firm.* This was simple white paper with no return address at the top and none on the envelope. What firm would send such a note?

The postmark was dated May 5. If he remembered correctly, Arthur Farrington said they had been searching for a substitute for Frank Vulcek for about three weeks. That meant Vulcek must have been killed about a week after he received this letter.

He reflected back. Farrington said Vulcek had driven off of an embankment somewhere in the vicinity of Darmstadt. Garner had just seen a map of Frankfurt and the surrounding area in Vulcek's desk. He found it, spread it out and located Darmstadt about 25 kilometers to the south.

Something was not adding up. Farrington said Vulcek had fallen asleep at the wheel, but since his automobile was in the garage, whose car was he driving?

Garner jumped when the phone rang.

"Ja," he answered simply.

The voice came in German. "Frank, you were much more fortunate than Helga."

Garner was careful with his response. "She wasn't as tough as I am."

He heard a faint chuckle. "Are you back in business?"

"Of course."

"You sound like you have a cold."

"You'd sound the same if your face went through a windshield."

There was a long silence. "I'll meet you tonight."

"Where?" Garner inquired.

"Same place, same time."

Garner cursed. He wanted to suggest a place he knew of, but the man had hung up. Obviously, the man on the other end of the conversation wasn't working for the CIA. Garner wanted to call Farrington, but he had been given no telephone number or address. A safety precaution, Farrington had said somewhere along the way.

Trudi was gone, too, and he had no names of any CIA people in Frankfurt other than her and Arthur. He had agreed to that in Langley, but he wasn't accepting it now.

He retrieved the map again. On the backside was a city map of Frankfurt. He started looking for any pencil marks that Vulcek might have made. He himself had often circled addresses or streets on maps for quick reference.

His patience paid off. South of the suburb of Sachsenhausen was the Frankfurter Stadtwald. Vulcek had circled one end of the Jacobiweiher, a small lake within the forest area. The only other mark Garner discovered was a circle around Marianplatz, where

The Prague Double

Trudi had her apartment.

He had nothing better to do until evening, so he folded up the map and headed for his car.

* * *

He made a few wrong turns, but eventually, he located the area marked on the map. The only building in this vicinity was a huge mansion on a large, beautifully landscaped ground. A closed set of iron gates fronted a long driveway, which formed a circle in front of the home. The entire ground was surrounded by a high, wrought iron fence. Garner had no idea what significance, if any, this may have meant to Vulcek.

He spent a good part of the day simply driving around the city, familiarizing himself with the streets, and in the early evening, he dined at the Troika in downtown Frankfurt, evidently one of Vulcek's favorite spots.

He ordered a meal, and while waiting for it, a gentleman dressed in a fine black suit approached him.

"Frank. It is you, is it not?" he inquired.

Garner had removed his dark glasses, and when he looked up at the man, he recognized him from one of the photos in Langley.

"Izaak," Garner said as he offered a hand.

The man, a Jewish proprietor of the Troika, remained with his eyes fixed on Garner's face. "I heard about the accident, but I had no idea how severe it was."

"I'm alive," Garner responded."

"We have all suffered. Eat and drink well. Tonight you are my guest."

As the man walked off, Garner knew what he meant by *We have all suffered.* Izaak Goldman was a survivor of Ausschwitz, one of Hitler's death camps.

Garner had now met two people who knew Vulcek, and evidently he was passing for the man. Izaak did not even inquire about his voice, which Garner found unusual, but then, he had been advised to throw in a raspy sound whenever he spoke. It was a good cover, and it appeared his voice had also been accepted by the man who had telephoned him earlier in the day.

His meal came, and while he ate, a violin player accompanied a big baritone singer as he sang his way through several Russian numbers. Garner looked about the room while he dined, but he did not recognize any other faces. Apparently, the only one in the restaurant who knew him was Izaak.

Afterward, he drove to the Star Bar, ordered a beer and walked about the lounge carefully scrutinizing the crowd. He did not recognize anyone, and no one approached him.

His next stop was the Europa Bar. Again, after hanging around for over an hour, he thought someone might recognize him as Frank Vulcek, but the result was the same.

To a degree, he was angered that someone hadn't recognized him during the night, yet, at the same time, he was relieved. It was always possible, of course, that someone knew him but had not approached him. Without the dark glasses, he certainly drew enough stares. The bars were so dimly lit, he could barely see with them on. He was at least doing what Farrington had instructed him to do, but since no one had remotely recognized him, it occurred to Garner that perhaps Vulcek wasn't as well known in these circles as Farrington thought.

The phone call that afternoon was still plaguing him. He didn't know when or where to meet the mystery man, and on an off chance, he thought perhaps it might be in one of these nightspots.

He easily located the Dolly Bar, a dive across from the Bahnhof, and other than a few girls who tried to push off some drinks on him, nothing exciting was happening.

It was almost midnight when Garner pulled up to the Neu Yorker Bar. He had given up wearing the dark glasses completely. Who in his right mind would wear dark glasses at night anyway? He decided that if anybody knew Vulcek, they would have to get used to him the way he looked without them.

He barely was inside the door when a man came up behind him. "Hi, Frank. Good to have you back." The man studied Garner's face.

"Damn. Did a number on you, didn't it? Are you holding up okay?"

"I'm getting used to it." In his mind, Garner was quickly reviewing the photos he had memorized back at Langley. This man had an ugly scar across his forehead, something Garner would never forget, but he had no idea who this man was.

"Got you a table in the corner," he said. "First one's on me."

It made sense now. Evidently he was the owner, since he signaled for a waitress to come over. A straight brandy came with a beer chaser, so obviously the owner knew what Vulcek's drinking habits were. The young waitress, whose bosom was practically falling out of her halter, took the Mark tip and scooted away.

Garner innocently looked about the smoke-filled room. Two strippers were showing their wares and writhing to a band that was thumping out *Night Train*. It took several minutes for them to work themselves down to their pasties, and when the music ended, they gathered up their scanty clothing and hurried off stage just as a solo-sax player started blaring away.

He had called Trudi earlier a couple times with no response, but he headed for the phone anyway to give her another try.

He pushed himself through the crowd to the phone, dialed Trudi's number and had some German Pfennigs ready in hand in case she answered. He let it ring several times, then jammed the phone back on the hook.

When Garner turned to head back to his table, he rubbed elbows with a man who stared at him, his interest more than just curiosity.

"*V-Vulcek! Du!?*" the man stammered.

Garner knew he had found someone who was more than just an acquaintance of Vulcek's. Garner spit out an insulting response. "Yeah. Me. Surprised?"

The man turned and quickly fought his way through the crowd toward the doorway. Garner watched him for a moment, then ran after him, but by time he made his way outside, the man had crossed the street and was running along the sidewalk.

"Wait!" Garner hollered. The man kept running and disappeared around a corner. When Garner reached the corner he saw the man step into a Strassenbahn.

Garner cursed as he ran back to his car. Within moments, he made a U-turn on the street and raced after the streetcar.

He easily caught up to the Strassenbahn, and through a window, he could see the man he had met in the bar. The tattered captain's cap he was wearing was an easy mark. The man had his face pressed up against the glass, but he obviously did not know Garner was in the Peugeot.

When the streetcar reached the Hauptbahnhof, it glided smoothly through the islands and veered off to the right to the front of the train station.

Garner swore. He had to follow the traffic to the left around the islands.

When the streetcar stopped, Garner saw the man get off. He raced the vehicle to the end of the circle and pulled up at the curb, and then he ran across the square where he saw the white hat disappear into the train station.

Once inside, he ran the length of the train tracks, glancing down each platform, but it was useless. He was searching for the white hat, but if the man was smart, he more than likely had removed it.

By the time he returned to his car, he was cursing the fact that he lost him.

It was almost one in the morning when he arrived at Trudi's. He didn't expect her to be home, but he rang anyway and was mildly surprised that she answered.

The door was open slightly like it had been the night before, and when he entered, he heard her call from the kitchen.

"Hi, Phil. Hungry?"

He smiled, recollecting that they seemed to have met in Langley usually when it was time to eat. "No, I'm not. Hi," he greeted. She came out of the kitchen, crossed to him and put her arms around him.

"I tried calling you a few times today."

She gave him a light kiss. "I'm a working girl, you know. One still has to have a cover."

"You keep late hours," he said.

"Just like you."

"What's your cover?" he asked.

"I work for a chemical firm."

"Where?"

"The main office is in Fulda."

"Where's that?"

"Near the East German border."

She mixed him a drink, and as he retired to the sofa, he was hashing over her answer. "What was Frank's cover?"

"I missed you today."

"I missed you, too. What was Frank's cover?" he asked again.

"He was a salesman."

"What did he sell?"

"Anything and everything. Whatever he made up."

"How come he lives in such a small apartment? It doesn't seem like his style"

"That was his style," she said. "He's got one in Hamburg and one in northern Italy."

He remembered seeing photos of them in Langley. "All paid for by Farrington?"

"Of course."

"Frank must have been something special."

"He was the best, and Arthur knew it." She changed the subject. "How was your day?"

"Busy. Does Frank have an unlisted telephone number?"

"Yes."

He nodded. "Well, someone else besides the CIA has it." That drew a curious look on her face. "I think Vulcek's friend must have called."

"What did he want?"

"To meet me. He just said the same place, same time." If she knew where the same place was, she didn't indicate it. "I also met the proprietor of the Troika Restaurant."

"Izaak," she said.

"Yes. And tonight I just met somebody who knew Vulcek in the Neu Yorker Bar."

"Who?"

Garner shrugged. "I don't know. Somebody with a white captain's hat, like a fisherman."

"That was Willie."

"Willie who?"

"I don't know his last name. He was one of Frank's snitches. His information was usually useless, though."

"If he was a snitch, why did he run off?"

"I don't know."

"And how come I never came across his photo in Langley?"

"I told you Frank probably knew a lot of people that Langley was not aware of."

The answer seemed sincere enough. He wished he didn't have so many questions, but his curiosity was prodding him on.

"Do you know where Frank died?"

When her eyes saddened, he knew the question was painful for her. "It was near Darmstadt. He drove off the road."

The questions wouldn't quit. "If he drove off the road, how does it happen I'm driving his car?"

"He was with someone else. A girl." The painful expression had not diminished any. "Her name was Helga Schleier. I don't know who she was."

Garner's mind was working. Helga was the name the man on the phone had mentioned this afternoon. He wasn't sure what sort of information he now possessed, but there was no doubt Trudi was bothered by the fact that Vulcek was with a woman that night.

He rose from the sofa and put his glass on the table.

"Do you want to stay tonight?" she asked.

He had expected that, but Willie was on his mind. "I would like to, but there are a few things I want to check out."

He gently pulled her to him and looked into her saddened eyes. "I'm sorry about all the questions, but I like to be in control of things. I seem to be poking around and don't know exactly why."

He pulled the map from his pocket. "Do me a favor? See if you can find out who owns this place." He showed her the circled area.

"It's a big mansion with a fence around it. Whoever lives there has got a few bucks."

"I'll see what I can do."

He kissed her and headed for the door.

"I'm not working tomorrow," she said.

"I'll call you."

The door had barely closed when Trudi was at the phone and dialed. She waited several seconds while the phone rang on the other end, then, "You told me to call if Phillip was on to something." She paused. "He ran across Willie."

She was silent again as she listened to the voice on the other end. "Yes," she finally said. "And there's something else. He wants to know who owns the estate in the Stadtwald north of the Isenburger Road."

She listened to the instructions from the other end. "Okay. Goodnight, Arthur."

* * *

Phillip Garner returned to the Neu Yorker Bar again where the smoke was thick and the music was still blaring away to three bouncing beauties. He made his way to the bar and waited until the bartender approached him.

"Do you know a guy named Willie?" he asked. "He wears a white fisherman's hat."

The bartender grunted. "*Ja.*"

It didn't appear the man was going to give any more information. "What's his last name?" inquired Garner.

"*Schlepper. Willie Schlepper.*"

"Do you know where he lives?"

"Yeah," he offered. "But if you want to know, it'll cost you 37 Marks."

Garner didn't mind paying the money, but the amount struck him odd. The man produced a slip from underneath the bar. It was Willie's bill in the amount of 37 Marks.

Garner placed two twenties on the bar.

"Third basement door along the river on Speicher Strasse." He snapped up the two twenties and moved away.

Garner went outside into the cool night and checked his watch. He didn't know where Speicher Strasse was and it was late anyway. He decided he would look him up tomorrow.

As Garner crossed the street to his car, he noticed a black Mercedes parked several yards behind his Peugeot. He would not have considered anything abnormal, except someone opened the door briefly and the light went on. Then the person quickly slammed the door shut and remained inside.

Garner calmly climbed into his car and checked his rear view mirror. No one had stepped from the Mercedes yet.

He ground the motor into action, made a quick U-turn on the street and headed in the opposite direction of his apartment. He had barely traveled a block when he saw the Mercedes swing a U-turn like he had. He had no doubts the auto was following him.

He thought perhaps it was a contact, but Farrington had said he would know when a legitimate contact was made.

Whoever was following him was someone other than the CIA, he was sure. He headed into the center of the city and turned onto Berliner Strasse. At the Kaiser Dom he turned right, but before he reached the Alte Bruecke, the Mercedes once again appeared in his rearview.

He turned onto the Main River road, and when the Mercedes was out of sight, he increased his speed. The cobblestone clattered underneath the wheels as he dipped down an incline. As soon as he drove over another rise, he tromped down on the accelerator. In his rearview, he saw the Mercedes fly over a knoll two blocks behind.

At the next circle, he raced around three-quarters and headed across the Untermain Bruecke. Once on the other side, he swung onto the riverfront road and paralleled the Main River in the opposite direction.

When he glanced in the rearview, he was surprised that the Mercedes was no longer trailing him. He couldn't believe he lost the car that quickly, or perhaps the vehicle wasn't chasing him.

He drove around for another ten minutes, and when he was convinced the car was no longer following, he headed for his apartment.

He circled the block twice searching for the Mercedes, and when he was certain it was not around, he wheeled the Peugeot into the courtyard and parked in the garage.

Just as he was about to ascend the steps to the door, a figure stepped out of the shadows.

"*Vulcek. Sie leben noch.*" The tall, thin man had his hands in the pockets of his raincoat, and for some reason, Garner suspected one of them was wrapped warmly around the handle of a gun. He could suddenly feel his heart beat through his raincoat.

"So, you really are alive," the man repeated in German. He grunted. "You're pretty lucky."

"A good man's hard to kill," retorted Garner, throwing the raspy sound into his voice. It was a ridiculous answer he thought as soon as he said it, but it was the only thing that came to mind.

The tall man made a few steps closer, his hands still in his pockets. He was now no more than a few feet away, and he had his head cocked as if he were studying Garner.

"Take a good look," said Garner. "Everybody else does." Garner made sure the light from the lamp pole was hitting him, then pulled his collar back. He wanted the man to see the scars on his face and neck.

The shadowed figure spoke in a softer voice now. "Is the deal still on?"

Garner had no idea what deal the man was talking about, but he guessed it had something to do with the merchandise he was to deliver to Prague. "Maybe."

"Have you got the information?"

Garner didn't know what to answer. When he turned to face the man more directly, a hand in one of the tall man's pockets raised slightly. He was carrying a gun all right, thought Garner, and he needed a fast answer.

Delray K. Dvoracek

"I haven't got the information yet. I'm supposed to make contact here in Frankfurt." He couldn't have given the man more accurate information.

"When?"

"Tomorrow or the next day."

It seemed to satisfy him. "Okay. I'll talk to the man. When you get the information, get hold of me. Agreed?"

"Agreed," Garner said, even though he didn't know how to get hold of him. Vulcek would have known that information.

The man made a motion to leave and then directed another comment. "I see you haven't changed your habits. You still don't make your appointments." With that, he walked out the gate onto the sidewalk strutting like a peacock.

There was no doubt he was the man who had phoned the day before—the man who had told Garner to meet him at the *same place,* wherever that was. Garner watched the man disappear into the night shadows of the tree-lined street, and when he was gone, he headed up the steps feeling a relief drop from his shoulders. He decided before he reached his door that the next time he left his apartment, he wasn't leaving without the Beretta.

CHAPTER NINE

He phoned Trudi when he rose from his sleepless night and told her about the man who had met him at his doorstep the night before. She agreed to meet with him, so he dressed casually with a loose jacket that easily hid the shoulder holster and pistol underneath.

When he pulled up in front of her apartment, she flitted down the steps toward him. "Good morning," he greeted as he shoved the door open.

"Hi." She sat down and gave him a long and heartfelt kiss. "We shouldn't be seeing each other, you know. Especially in the day time."

"I know," he said as he squeezed her hand. He wheeled the car around. "I won't tell Arthur if you don't." She just smiled. "Anyway, those were Farrington's orders, and God knows where he is. He could be in China for all we know."

"He's here in Frankfurt."

Garner nodded. "I figured he was."

"Where are we going?"

"To Darmstadt. Do you know where Vulcek went off the road?"

Her face paled. "Yes. Why do you want to go there?"

"Got nothing better to do."

She was quiet for some time. "You look tired," she finally said.

"I didn't sleep well last night. I'm not used to a stranger prowling around my apartment with a gun in his pocket."

She gaped at him. "Was he the same man who called you the day before?"

"I'm sure of it."

"Would you recognize him if you saw him again?"

"Only if I saw him walk. He was tall, had a pointed beard and strutted like he owned the street."

81

"Turn here," she said.

Garner wheeled the vehicle onto the Bundesstrasse and increased his speed to ninety kilometers.

"How did you manage to free yourself up today? I thought you were a working girl?"

"I called in sick."

"Can you do that?"

"I can do whatever I want."

Garner found that amusing and was happy to see the smile on her face.

* * *

They had driven for close to twenty minutes when Trudi pointed to the spot off to the right. "Over there."

Garner slowed the vehicle to a crawl and crept along for several yards until she told him to pull over. The tracks where the vehicle had gone off the road were barely visible, but it was easy enough to see where they led.

The two crossed the field until they came to an embankment. Down below the imprint in the opposite bank where the bumper and grill had impacted was still visible. Bits of chrome and glass glistened in the shallow stream below.

"What do you expect to find here?" asked Trudi.

"I don't know." Garner looked up and down the creek. "What was the weather like that night?"

"It was clear."

"No fog?"

"No."

Arthur Farrington told Garner that Vulcek had fallen asleep at the wheel, but Garner simply refused to believe that. He looked back from where the vehicle left the road. "They must have both been asleep."

"What's that?" Trudi asked curiously.

"Frank and the woman. They both must have been asleep. Come

on," he said as he took Trudi by the arm and walked her back to the car. He started the engine and swung back on the road headed toward Frankfurt.

"I didn't think you'd find anything here. It's like Arthur said, they must have fallen asleep and driven off the road."

Garner drove half way up the hill, swung a U-turn and headed back down the highway. He was doing eighty kilometers when he sped around the turn. He slowed the vehicle, turned around, went back up the hill and headed back down again, this time doing a hundred. He gripped the wheel harder fighting the auto as it edged its way to the shoulder.

"Watch out!" screamed Trudi.

Garner fought the wheel as the car slid off the road and spun around in the grass. He jammed on the brakes as the car fishtailed around, and in seconds, the car came to a stop just feet from the riverbank.

When Garner looked at Trudi, her face was struck with horror, and as they got out of the car, she was shaking. The rear bumper was hanging over the edge of the bank.

"My God!" she said. "You could have killed us both!"

His eyes were back on the highway again. "I think we both know Frank didn't fall asleep at the wheel."

"Of course not," she scolded. "He was speeding. He always drove like a maniac, just like you were."

"But he wasn't speeding," said Garner. He pointed where Vulcek's vehicle had left the curve at the high speed. "Frank left the highway over there. If he was speeding, he would have ended up where we are now." The distance between where Garner was standing and where the Mercedes disappeared over the embankment was at least thirty yards.

The realization stunned Trudi. "If he didn't fall asleep and he wasn't speeding, then..."

He saw the horror in her face, but he said it anyway. "They were murdered. Someone tried to make it look like an accident."

Her hand was up against her mouth cutting off her own speech.

Delray K. Dvoracek

"Murdered," she said softly.

"Was there an autopsy report?"

Her words were still soft, frail. "Arthur said so."

"Did you see the report?"

"No."

Garner took her by the arm and helped her into the car. "I think we've had enough for one day." Enough for her is what he meant. Farrington had a lot of explaining to do, if he could ever find him.

The mission once again plagued Garner. Why he was supposed to hang around Frankfurt didn't seem to be making any sense. If he was to deliver some merchandise to Prague, why spend time in Frankfurt where the possibility existed of his identity being compromised? And if Vulcek was murdered, his own appearance was sure to eventually startle somebody, especially the person who killed him.

He started the car and headed back to Frankfurt. By the troubled look on Trudi's face, it was obvious she did not know that Vulcek and Helga were murdered.

His thoughts came back to the man he had met last night. He wondered what sort of deal the man was talking about, and he wondered why Farrington hadn't cautioned him. Maybe Farrington didn't know about the *so-called deal.*

The more questions Garner asked himself, the more confused he became. It was one thing to be forced into becoming a spy, but it was another thing to not have the faintest idea who he was supposed to spy on.

He needed more information, and if he couldn't get answers from Farrington, he'd start with Willie Schlepper. It might well turn out Willie possessed useless information like Trudi said, but Garner wanted to determine that for himself.

* * *

They were nearing the outskirts of Frankfurt when Garner suddenly turned the Peugeot off the highway heading toward several long buildings.

"Where are you going?" Trudi asked. It was the first time she had spoken for several kilometers.

Garner's eyes were in the rearview. They had been ever since he saw the black Mercedes pull onto the highway a kilometer from where he and Trudi had spun off the highway. He was sure it was the same Mercedes that had tailed him the night before.

Garner passed three long warehouses, pulled the vehicle over and stopped. The Mercedes slowed a hundred yards behind him and then disappeared from view behind the first warehouse.

"Stay here," Garner said as he stepped from the car.

"Phil, be careful. He may have a gun." The words were backed up by the worried look on her face.

"I'm ready this time," he said as he brushed his hand against his jacket. He quickly ran along the rear of the building, and at the end, he carefully peered around. He ran along the back of the three buildings, and at the end, he again carefully looked around the corner. The Mercedes was a few feet away, facing the other direction, as if waiting for his car to pass by.

Garner drew the Beretta from its place and quickly crossed to the back door. He threw it open, jumped in and jammed the gun against the driver's neck.

The man was caught totally by surprise. "What? Wait a minute! I can..."

"Keep your mouth shut or I'll blow your goddamn head off!" Garner didn't know if he had the nerve, but he wanted the man to believe he did.

"Wait! I can explain!"

"You're damn right you can explain!" Garner slipped a hand over the man's shoulder and pulled a revolver from under his coat. He searched inside his coat and found the man's wallet. When he eased the gun barrel off his neck, the man careened to see who was behind him.

He had a silver mustache on his lip, the same color as his hair. "My God!" said the man. "Y-you look just like him!"

Garner sat back perplexed when he saw the identity card.

"I can't believe it!" said the man again, astounded with what he was seeing.

Garner's eyes were on the card, identical to his own in shape and form.

"Clarence Tripson?" Garner questioned. "Bullshit!" He shoved the muzzle of the Beretta against Clarence's mustached lip.

"Jesus Christ!" Clarence pleaded. "I'm on your side!"

"Yeah? And whose side am I on?"

"Farrington's!" Clarence gulped, the fear never leaving his face. "Trudi Feldman! She's in the car with you! Frank Vulcek! Phillip Garner! You're his double! You just came back from Langley after ten days of indoctrination!"

Garner pulled the barrel away from his lip. "What the hell's going on here? Why were you tailing me?"

Tripson gained some composure. "Farrington told me to keep an eye on you. I was supposed to help you if you needed it."

"Was that you chasing me last night?"

"Yes."

Garner's voice seethed with sarcasm. "Well, you can't tail anybody for shit! I lost you right away. How are you supposed to help me if you can't keep up with me?

"And where the hell were you last night when the tall guy with the gun showed up?"

"What guy?"

"What deal was Vulcek making with this guy?"

"I don't know what you're talking about."

Garner leaned his face right into Clarence's. "Some guy is waiting for me when I return to Vulcek's apartment. He's carrying a gun and he wants to know whether I've got the information yet."

"What information?"

"You tell me. The information is some deal he made with Vulcek. So what's the deal he was talking about?"

"I don't know!"

Garner could imagine the man was not accustomed to being interrogated in the manner he had attacked him. Judging from his answers, Clarence didn't know anything more than he did.

"How do I get in contact with Arthur?"

"You don't."

"All right," snapped Garner. "Then you tell Arthur to get in contact with me. If he doesn't, I might just hop a plane and get the hell out of here."

"You wouldn't do that."

"I've got money and credentials to get me anywhere I want. You tell Farrington to get hold of me or he can take his little game of spies and stick it up his ass!"

Garner got out of the car and handed Clarence's revolver back to him. "Don't shoot yourself."

* * *

"He what?!" Arthur practically screamed at Clarence as he came around his desk. Clarence had never seen him so furious.

"He got the drop on me," said Clarence. In his fourteen years' experience as an agent, no one had ever taken his weapon away from him. "He also said if you didn't get hold of him, you could stick this spy game up your ass."

Arthur Farrington was practically frothing at the mouth, his fists like two rocks, his shoulders hunched up like a killer football player. He jumped up from his chair. "All I asked you to do was tail him! Now, is that so damn difficult?"

"Then you tail the son-of-a-bitch!" Clarence shot back. "My God, Arthur. He was like a damn animal. You never told me he was like that. I thought he was going to blow my head off before I could even tell him who I was."

Arthur shook his head and settled down. "All right, all right." He sat again, angered with Clarence, but he was pleased to hear how Garner was playing his role. It looked like the new Frank Vulcek was taking good care of himself.

"All right," said Arthur again. "Tell me what happened, and all of it."

A sense of relief fell in place as Clarence pulled up a chair. He knew Arthur would get over the heated emotional state he once in a while managed to work himself into.

"He wanted to know who the tall, thin man was." Clarence began.

"I wish I knew. What else did he ask?"

"This guy wanted to know if the deal was still on."

Arthur's elbow dropped off the end of the desk. "What deal?"

"I don't know. Garner said he talked as if he and Vulcek had some kind of deal they were working on."

Arthur slowly rose to his feet and began pacing again. It was beginning to surface now. He knew Frank Vulcek was involved in something more than just the Prague case, and now it looked like Garner was stumbling onto something similar. "What else?"

"He wants you to contact him."

"I can't," said Arthur. "Somebody else is watching him. We can't let anyone know Garner is working for us. You know that."

"He said you better contact him or he's going to hightail it out of here."

Arthur stared at Clarence. "That was just a mild threat. Where would he go?"

Clarence sat back in his chair. "You know, I think the guy likes being a spy."

"What makes you say that?"

"He's got the flair for Vulcek's character. We've got him running all over Frankfurt looking for people we don't even know about. He's making the night scenes, he's been approached by a guy with a gun, he found Willie, he's investigating Vulcek's death on his own, and he's starting to piss you off just like Vulcek did. It's scary."

Clarence's short assessment pleased Arthur to no end. Clarence was the one who said a double for Vulcek couldn't be found, but here he was admitting Garner was a perfect double.

"We'll let him go a little longer by himself," said Arthur. "He seems to be turning up something new every day."

When the phone blared, Arthur answered it. "Hello?" There was a pause. "Yes, Trudi. Clarence is here now." Arthur sat back in his seat and listened carefully. "I know, I know, but we don't know who the tall man is." Arthur made a face. "Trudi, Garner can take care of himself. He'll be all right." Arthur listened while Trudi delivered a long monologue.

Arthur nodded. "Okay, okay. We'll watch him. Keep in touch." He hung up.

"Garner's going to pay Willie Schlepper a visit tonight," said Arthur. He stood, his hands shoved down into his pockets as he crossed to the window overlooking the square below. "Clarence, I want you to change cars, change clothes, lose fifty pounds, cut off your mustache, dye your hair. Do whatever you have to do, but tail Garner, and this time don't get caught with your pants down." He turned around. "Is that clear?"

Clarence nodded, and seeing that he was no longer needed, he left the room.

Arthur turned to a wall map of the city and focused on the area in the Frankfurter Stadtwald. This was the area that Trudi had passed on to him. Garner wanted to know who lived there.

Arthur Farrington already knew. It was owned by Manfried Toller, a prominent, well-respected lawyer in Frankfurt, known widely in many other circles. A preliminary check on the lawyer had turned up one other interesting piece of information. Helga Schleier, the woman who had died along with Vulcek, was the lawyer's private secretary. That might explain why Vulcek had circled the lawyer's home on his map. It looked like Phillip Garner was stumbling onto something that only Frank Vulcek knew about.

The connection among the three at this point seemed to be the best thread Arthur had to hold onto, and he did not want that thread to break.

He sat behind his desk, his eyes still on the circled section of the Stadtwald. He was suddenly on the phone. "Clarence, I want a thorough rundown on Helga Schleier and anyone else who works at Toller's law firm." There was a pause. "That's right, everyone."

CHAPTER TEN

The fog was much heavier now than earlier in the evening. Garner slowed the Peugeot as he passed the signpost indicating Speicher Strasse. It was the third time he had seen the signpost tonight. Twice he had already knocked on the basement door to Willie Schlepper's apartment, but no one answered.

Garner had gone back to a few bars in hopes of spotting the man, but no one had seen him.

Garner parked the car and got out. It was almost one in the morning as he tugged at his raincoat collar, cursing the cold dampness. Almost every day had been overcast. If it wasn't raining, it was drizzling. If it wasn't drizzling, the fog was so thick it was almost impossible to breathe. He wondered how the Germans could stand it.

As he walked along the shadowed riverfront, a gull shrieked off to his left above the Main River. In the distance, a car zoomed across the bridge, its headlights barely visible.

Willie's entrance was at the bottom of a set of cement steps. When Garner reached the stairs, he looked down at the door. The wrinkled cigarette pack he had placed earlier at the base of it was still there.

"Shit," he said as he moved on to a boarded up doorway several feet away. It was shadowed, a perfect shelter from any passer-by. He decided he would wait an hour or so for the man, hoping he would show up.

His mind drifted as he stood, shoulders hunched up, hands in his pockets, his patience already gone. He was sure Farrington would call him that evening, but he hadn't. Maybe he wasn't in Frankfurt, even though Trudi said he was.

It crossed his mind that perhaps Clarence Tripson was running things here in Frankfurt, but he quickly discarded that notion. Clarence didn't have near the perception or savvy that Arthur possessed. Clarence was just supposed to tail him, or so Clarence had told him. He wondered if he was nearby now.

Another car passed off to his left and disappeared across the bridge. Just as the drone of the engine faded into the night, he heard footsteps coming his way. Garner slipped his hands out of his pockets as Willie walked by just feet away. The white hat was a dead giveaway, but the man looked bigger and taller than what Garner remembered. Willie hurried down his staircase and was fumbling for a key when Garner came down the steps behind him.

"Hi, Willie. Retiring for the night?"

Willie whirled around and stared up at Garner. He quickly turned the key and pushed the door in, but before he could get inside, Garner was at the bottom of the steps and kicked the door in, bowling Willie over to the floor. Garner reached around the doorframe and found the light switch, and when he flipped it on, Willie was on his feet.

Garner tensed. Willie was bent over with a long pointed knife in his hand, and he looked as if he would use it.

Garner kept cool. "Look, Willie, I just want to ask a few..." He didn't have a chance to finish. Willie lunged with the fury of a madman. Garner grabbed for his wrist to force away his arm as he sliced at him, but he caught his arm too far back. He grappled with the man and yanked at his arm, but when he did so, the stiletto sliced across his chest, ripping the cloth raincoat through to his skin.

Garner cried out as he jammed an elbow into the man's ribs. He slammed him so hard against the wall that a picture dropped from its place sending shards all over when the glass broke.

Garner fought to loose the knife from his hand, but the man held fast. He couldn't believe the man's strength. For an older man, he was as strong as a bull.

Willie sliced at him again, and this time, Garner got both of his hands on Willie's wrist and flung the man over his shoulder. Willie went down, but he was up immediately. He struck again but was

91

slightly off balance. Garner grabbed his wrist and swung a furious blow into Willie's stomach. Willie keeled over as the knife flew from his hands, but then he brought up a knee aimed at Garner's groin and missed.

"You son-of-a-bitch!" Garner yelled. He slammed another fist into the man's stomach and heard the breath scream out of him. He hit him again and again. Blood poured out of his nose and mouth when he flopped backward against the wall. As he slowly sank to the floor, Garner gave him two more hard punches to keep him down.

Sweat covered Willie's face. His eyes were shut, and he was wheezing heavily from the blows he had taken. Blood poured from his nose, now swelling, broken, Garner was sure.

Garner dropped to the floor, his strength exhausted. He couldn't believe the almost superhuman strength Willie possessed. A burning sensation tore at Garner's chest, and when he opened his raincoat, his shirt was soaked with blood. A slice from the stiletto left a deep gash in his shoulder holster. If he hadn't been wearing it, right now he would be a dead man.

Garner pressed a handkerchief up against the wound and groaned as he threw his head back, still sweating horribly. When Willie started coming around, Garner jerked him by the collar. "Okay, Willie. Who you working for?"

One eye from Willie opened for a second and then began to slip shut. Garner shook him. "Come on, Willie, talk."

"*Ich... kann nicht,*" came the faint reply from his bloodied and torn mouth.

Garner had been in fights before and had never beaten a man so severely, but he wanted information. He pulled the Beretta from its place and stuck the barrel in Willie's eye, and when he clicked off the safety, Willie opened his eye.

Now," said Garner. "You tell me who you're working for or I'm gonna put a little hole in your eyeball."

"*Nein! Nein! Ich kann nicht! Er wird mich toeten!*"

"Goddammit," Garner screamed back in German. "Tell me or I'll kill you!"

"*Von Hauer!*" shouted Willie. "*Dieter von Hauer!*" He screamed the man's name out as if they were the last words he was ever going to utter.

"Describe him!" demanded Garner.

"Y-you know who he is."

"Refresh my memory!"

"Tall..." Willie stopped. He was unconscious, but the one eye with the Beretta sticking in it was still open. Garner released the pressure and the eyelid slipped shut.

The man was breathing evenly now, but Garner knew he would not be able to bring him around. *Tall*, he had said. The one word was enough for Garner. The tall man who strutted like a peacock was Dieter von Hauer.

* * *

Garner lay on his bed feeling the numbness in his chest. The doctor had probed with needles a few minutes earlier to freeze the wound, and Garner watched as the last stitch was tied in place. Trudi sat across from him, quiet, her eyes unmoving from the surgical operation.

"Chances are you'll live," said the doctor as he packed away his surgical tools. He abruptly left the room without asking any questions, as if he had done the very same operation a dozen times before.

"What, no bill?" Garner asked Trudi.

"He works for us."

"Often?" Garner asked.

She ignored the question. "You fool." They were her first words since she had arrived, and they were biting. "Nobody told you to go looking for trouble."

"Nobody told me not to either." He shifted himself on the bed, propped himself up on a pillow and ran his fingers across the bandage. "Couple days and I'll be good as new."

"If you last a couple days."

She was bitter, and her voice showed it. And she was beautiful, too, he was thinking. She was definitely a challenge. He had met some women more beautiful and some homelier, but none with the changing temperament she seemed to have. Even when she was angry, he couldn't help but like her.

He probed the wound with his fingers again.

"Was it worth it?" she asked.

"I got a name. I know who Willie's working for."

"Who?"

"The tall guy with the beard. Dieter von Hauer."

Trudi jerked back when she heard the name. "Von Hauer?"

"Do you know him?"

"No. But I heard Frank mention the name." Her eyes were staring, her memory searching. "Yes. I remember now. One night Frank and I were downtown. He stopped to visit him."

She hesitated. "Well, not him, but a partner of his."

"What partner?"

She thought back. "Toller," she said. Manfried Toller. They have a law firm here in Frankfurt."

The name stirred Garner as he pointed to the desk and asked her to get a letter.

She opened it and began reading the letter out loud. "Our firm should like very much..." She read silently and then finished, "feel free to call for an appointment. M.T." She looked up. "Manfried Toller? I don't know what this means."

"Did Frank ever visit Toller more than once?"

"Only once while I was with him, but I never met the man."

Garner got a telephone book and confirmed his suspicions when he found Toller's address. "This is the guy who lives in the mansion. Do you suppose Arthur knows?"

"I told him you wanted to know, but he never called me back."

Garner wondered if she was telling him the truth. He pursued a different vein. "Why does this Dieter von Hauer want the information I'm supposed to take to Prague?"

"Do you know for sure that's what he wants?"

"When you put everything together, it kind of looks that way, doesn't it?"

When she didn't respond, he felt sure she was covering up something.

"What am I supposed to deliver to Prague?" he asked. When her eyes dropped away, he knew she had the answer, but obviously, Farrington must have instructed her not to tell him. There was a connection among Toller, von Hauer and Vulcek, and it had something to do with Prague. It was very possible that Farrington himself didn't even know. Maybe that's why he wanted him prowling around Frankfurt.

Garner was suddenly tired, and his mind couldn't keep up with the information he had acquired.

"Are you staying tonight?" he asked her.

"Would you like me to?"

He smiled. "I may need some medical attention."

"That's a funny way of putting it," she said.

Garner watched as her long fingers slipped off her nylons. She reached behind her neck and undid her zipper, then daintily stepped out of the dress and hung it over a chair. She faced him, removed her bra and then scratched under each bud-like breast for a moment. Clad only in her panties, she slipped under the covers.

"You're lovely," he murmured just as his eyes slowly began to close.

"Are you going to sleep on me, Phil?"

He didn't hear her.

She pulled a cover over him, then stroked his hair. She gently ran her fingers across his scarred eyes, along the sides of his nose, around his slightly open lips.

Her eyes saddened. "Oh, Frank," she whispered as she kissed him on the cheek.

She turned off the lamp and warmly slipped under the covers.

CHAPTER ELEVEN

Every chair in the reception room to Manfried Toller's law firm office was leather. The long, oak table in front of the wall of law books was bulky and massive and looked as if it had been placed there one time only and would never be moved again.

Crystal Schmidt, Manfried Toller's new, private secretary, sat behind her desk, dressed in a rich, blue suit and matching blouse.

Toller entered the room and glided silently across the thick carpet. He was a tall man with thick blond hair, light blue eyes, a strong nose and a heavy squared off face—all qualities, which so represented the true German master race. In Frankfurt circles, he was considered a brilliant mind in the field of jurisprudence.

His voice too, was heavy and commanding, yet charming when the moments were right.

"Herr Toller," greeted Crystal. "Welcome back. How was your trip to Berlin?"

Manfried's warm smile met the moment. "Fine, thank you." He produced a small black box from his pocket and handed it to her.

She seemed excited to receive the gift but simply raised her head and said thank you, though she did not open the present.

If Manfried Toller was annoyed by her decision not to open it at the moment, he didn't show it. "Anything while I was away?" he asked as he sat on the edge of the desk.

"Hamburg called about the stocks, and the newspaper would like a statement about the Mueller case. There were three phone calls. I put the names and numbers on your desk."

"Very good," Manfried said as he stroked the side of her face. "Anything else?"

"Dieter would like to see you. He said it was urgent."

"Tell him I'm back and send him in." Manfried stroked her hair, then picked up his briefcase and went into his office.

As soon as he disappeared inside, she turned her attention to the gift Toller had brought and carefully opened it. The set of diamond earrings sparkled with elegance. She looked up at his office door, closed the box and set it in a drawer and then dialed Dieter von Hauer's office.

Manfried Toller removed his Austrian-made Loden suit coat, smoothed down the sleeves and hung it in the closet. In a small mirror, he made a thorough inspection making sure every blond hair on his head was in place. Satisfied, he sat behind his plush desk and was opening his briefcase when he heard the light knock.

Dieter von Hauer entered, he, too, dressed well in his vested suit. Although Dieter wore a beard, something Manfried Toller did not particularly like, he tolerated it only because the man always kept it well groomed.

Dieter sat in a leather-backed oak chair across from Toller and patiently waited. Toller finally placed the briefcase to the side, produced a nail file and began to manicure his nails.

"Anything from Berlin?" Dieter asked when he knew Toller was ready to listen.

"No, nothing." The words were short, almost insulting.

"Nothing at all?" asked Dieter.

"No. Rozmanov told us to sit tight for a while until they can figure some other way to get the information."

Dieter gave a sly smile. "I think I have the solution."

Toller looked up curiously. "Oh? And what's that?"

"Vulcek's still alive."

"What?"

"He's still alive."

"Impossible."

"There was no mention in the newspaper of his death," said Dieter.

Manfried stood up and stiffened. "No, there wasn't. I just figured since he dropped from sight, he must have been killed along with Helga." He looked away. "We both suspected he was with her that night. The paper mentioned her death."

Dieter knew that the chief of police was a friend of Toller's. "You talked to Inspector Gastmann?"

"Yes. He said she was alone." Toller paced around his desk constantly stroking his chin, a nervous habit. "Maybe he's not alive and it's just a rumor. I don't think Inspector Gastmann would lie to me."

"I talked to Vulcek. That's no rumor."

Toller frowned, unbelieving at what he had just heard. "You talked to him? Are you sure it was him? I mean, the car was completely demolished."

"It was him. His face is a mess and he sometimes wears dark glasses to cover up the scars. His voice isn't the same, but he had his throat slit like he had an operation."

"You're sure it was him?" Toller questioned. "Inspector Gastmann said..."

"Manfried," interrupted Dieter. "I was only a few feet from him. There's no mistaking it. He's alive. And if you want a second opinion, go see Willie Schlepper."

"Why Willie?"

"Because Vulcek caught up with him last night. He's lying in the hospital with a broken nose and three busted ribs."

"Vulcek did that?"

"I had Willie snooping around for me. He panicked and flashed a knife. You know Vulcek when he gets mad."

Toller was back at his chair, his mind on Inspector Gastmann. He knew the Inspector had lied when he said Helga Schleier was alone in the vehicle. He had expected that, but what he didn't expect was that Vulcek would show up again.

"He said he's still willing to deal," said Dieter interrupting Toller's thoughts.

Toller swung his chair away and pretended to look out the window. He couldn't believe Vulcek had survived the accident.

"What's the next move?" Toller asked.

"He's supposed to contact me as soon as he has the information."

Toller swung the chair around. "He doesn't have it?"

"He said he would in a day or two."

Toller nodded, which indicated to Dieter that their discussion was over. Dieter reached the door and turned. "Are you going to call Rozmanov in Berlin and inform him Vulcek's still alive?"

"What?" Toller got to his feet. "Oh, yes. I'll call right away. I'm sure Berlin still wants to deal. I'll take care of it myself."

As soon as Dieter was gone, Toller picked up the phone and dialed, but he did not call Berlin. His grip tightened around the phone when someone answered. "This is Toller," he said in a low voice. "Vulcek's still alive." While Toller listened, his face twisted into a rage. "I don't want any of your goddamned excuses! He's got the information, and I don't care how you get it, but get it! And this time I want him dead! Do you hear? Dead!"

CHAPTER TWELVE

Arthur Farrington finally called. The only information Garner was able to salvage from the conversation, was the fact that Arthur was actually in Frankfurt. Arthur knew Garner had been cut up by Willie Schlepper, and his only comment was, "You should be more careful."

That infuriated Garner, and his frustration grew when Farrington said he knew nothing about Dieter von Hauer or Manfried Toller. How could the man not know anything about them especially when he had had a couple days to run a check on them?

To Garner, it appeared von Hauer was the man Vulcek had been interested in most, and when Garner inquired what he should do if he were contacted by Dieter again, Farrington simply said, "Sit tight and keep out of sight for a couple days." And then he abruptly hung up.

Garner decided he wasn't going to keep out of sight. No one was going to hang up on him and leave him in the dark.

He took Trudi out for dinner, dropped her off at home and made the rounds in the bars again. Four hours later and disgruntled that he hadn't dug up anything, he headed for his apartment.

It was almost midnight when he returned and found a note stuffed under his door.

Mitternacht, Das Goldene Pferd.

It was signed, *Dieter.*

Garner quickly located the address of The Golden Horse Gasthaus in the telephone directory. It was probably the meeting place where Dieter had referred to a couple days earlier—the appointment he was unable to keep.

The Gasthaus was on the Morfelden road, at least a twenty-minute drive. He glanced at his watch and cursed. It was a few minutes to twelve. He was already late.

He couldn't call Arthur because he had no number for him, and if he called Trudi, she would try to talk him out of going.

He grabbed a jacket from Vulcek's wardrobe, threw it on and ran down to the garage. If he couldn't get any answers out of Farrington, maybe he could out of Dieter.

* * *

Traffic along the Morfelden road was sparse. Both sides of the lane were lined with trees, black and lonely in appearance under the illumination of the headlights. Wherever the Golden Horse Gasthaus was located, it was certainly remote.

The neon lights suddenly came into view, and as he began to slow the vehicle, he reflected on what Dieter von Hauer looked like. That night in the dark, the only recognizable traits were his height and beard. That and his strange peacock strut should be enough to pick him out of a crowd.

When he emerged from the vehicle, he made a quick inspection of the parking area. There were a dozen cars or so, but no one was visible at the moment.

He could hear laughter and a band playing from inside, and as he approached the entrance, he patted his breast pocket, reassured that the Beretta was in place.

The interior of the Gasthaus did justice to its country location. Every wall was filled with trophies of stuffed animal heads, and a hundred mugs or more were lined up one after another on a high wooden shelf that ringed the room. The spaces in between the stuffed animal heads were jammed with swords and knives of every kind.

The Gasthaus was divided into two rooms. In the first, Garner didn't spot anyone who remotely resembled Dieter von Hauer. The second room was crowded with people, where all the singing was coming from. Another quick inspection told Garner that Dieter von Hauer was not among them. It was possible he had arrived too late and missed him.

He returned to the first room and went to the bar. "Pilsner," he

101

said to the red-vested bartender. The man gave Garner an extra-long look, nodded and drew up the beer for him.

Garner found a corner table and sat down, and when he glanced back at the bar, the bartender was gone. Then he spotted him behind an aluminum-like grillwork near the kitchen. The man returned, and now Garner realized he had been at a phone. Garner was back at his beer wondering whom the man in the red vest had called, but he brushed off the incident. Time slid by as he ordered a second and third beer.

He visited the men's room, and when he returned, music and laughter from the back room seemed to get louder by the minute. A young German couple entered and made their way over to a table near his. They casually glanced at him and then glanced some more, he was sure, at his scarred face. He had given up wearing the dark glasses, which seemed to draw everybody's attention, but he didn't care.

Two more men entered, both tall, but neither of them was Dieter. One of them went to the bar, a big man. The one that was walking in his direction was bigger. Both were wearing long raincoats, and the man that was approaching had a hand in his pocket. Garner was fairly sure it wasn't there to keep warm.

Garner slipped his hand from his beer and was reaching for the opening of his coat.

"*Nay*," commanded the man in German only a few feet away. He sat at the table and glared at Garner. "You just don't stay dead, do you Frank?"

Garner's mind raced, just like his heart. He was mentally going through all the photographs of the men he had memorized back in Virginia, but he did not recognize this man or the man at the bar.

"Finish your beer, Frank." The man edged in closer, and now Garner could feel the metal of the gun jab his side.

"Where's Dieter?" Garner snarled.

"I suspect he's sleeping," came the cynical reply. "He's an early riser, you know." The man was so close to Garner that he could smell cigarette smoke on his breath. He studied Garner's face. "You ain't

102

as pretty as you used to be. I understand they had to build you a new voice box."

He jabbed the gun further into Garner's side. "Let's go, and keep your hands at your side."

When they reached the door, the second man from the bar joined them. Once outside, one of them pulled the Beretta from Garner's holster as if he knew it would be there. They shoved him in the direction of the parking area, and as they began crossing the lot, a car pulled into the driveway.

If Garner were to create a scene, now was the time in full view of another vehicle. He swung a violent punch into the midsection of the man on his left, and when he did so, the man screamed out when his gun went off in his pocket. Garner turned ducking from the second man, but he was too late. He felt the gun barrel thump on his head, and when he went down, stars blasted like fireworks in his brain.

His eyes were closed now, but he could hear the man who had fired the gun in his pocket cursing violently. Then came a heavy kick to his stomach, forcing him to gasp for air. His eyes were open again in time to see a man emerge from the vehicle that had just entered the lot.

A flashlight flicked into his face as the man lifted Garner's hand and tugged at his finger.

"That's his ring," he heard the third man say.

When the first two jerked him to his feet, he caught a glimpse of the third man. All he noticed was his thick, blond hair, and then his mind faded into darkness.

CHAPTER THIRTEEN

Garner woke to a throbbing head and a face burning with pain. He forced his eyes open, but he was only seeing out of one. The surroundings of the room remained out of focus for a minute while he waited for his head to clear, and then, slowly, the realization of what had happened to him began to materialize.

He could taste blood in his mouth. He ran his tongue over his teeth to see if any of them were loose.

They had worked him over, the two thugs that had picked him up at The Golden Horse. Instinctively he tried to reach for a handkerchief, but then came the realization that he was tied in place to a heavy wooden chair. His hands were bound in back of him and lacking any feeling. He rolled his shoulders, forcing some sensation into his system.

His feet were tied to the legs of the chair. To test his toes, he curled them upward, and then he worked his hands some more, hunched his shoulders. A lone bulb dangling from a ceiling cord offered the only light in the room.

Directly ahead of him seemed to be the only exit from this basement prison. The door was wooden with a small window cut out in the upper center.

He struggled again to loosen his hands, but they were bound securely. He sank back in the chair, the throbbing in his head once again pounding. As best as he could, he let himself relax, forced himself to think. He didn't know the two men who had beat him or their connection with von Hauer, and he wondered who the third man was—the man with the blond hair.

He remembered they had made reference to Vulcek's ring, and evidently all three believed he was Frank.

His face was stinging severely, and right now he would give

anything to soak it in cold water. Even a tiny drink would be... He suddenly heard footsteps from outside the room. Someone was coming down a set of stairs. The back of his throat tightened when a key slipped into the door. The lock clicked loudly in the silence, and the door opened with a loud creak. It was the bigger of the two men, and he was limping, and his teeth were clenched as he neared. Garner saw the rag tied above his right knee where a trickle of dried blood had stained his pant leg.

The man stopped a few feet in front of Garner, all the while slapping a huge fist into an open palm. Fear shot through Garner's whole body. This was the same man who had beat him into unconsciousness before. They wanted the information he was supposed to deliver to Prague, but he couldn't have told them if he wanted to. Farrington was smart. That's why he had never divulged what the merchandise was supposed to be.

"Did you have a nice nap, Frank?" the man half grunted, half laughed. He bent down into Garner's face, the heavy smoke on his breath a familiar odor. "Ready to talk yet? If you don't, Herman will be coming down with the needles."

Garner's skin crawled.

He laughed again. "You'll wish to hell you talked, Frank."

"I told you I don't have the information. I won't get it until..."

Garner's head snapped when the man struck a blow, and it snapped again with the next blow. The pain in his face was so heavy that he couldn't feel any more.

"You son-of-a-bitch!" the man hollered as he pointed to his bloodied knee. "You did this!"

Garner barely saw the foot coming, and when the sole of the man's shoe slammed into his chest, the air lunged out of him. His chair reeled over backwards, sending him crashing to the floor. Stars shot out of his mind when his head struck.

At the same time, he heard the big man holler out in pain and saw him go down. His bad leg had buckled from underneath him when he delivered the kick. The big man struggled to his feet and limped out of the room, and when the wooden door closed, Garner heard the distinct sound of a key turning in the lock. The lone bulb above him was out suddenly, and then came the shuffling sound as the man limped his way up the stairs.

Garner stared up into the empty darkness. From somewhere upstairs, he could hear muffled voices. Moments later, he heard a door close, and shortly after, a car started up and drove off. Evidently, one of the men had left. What was the man going after? Needles? Garner shuddered when he thought of it.

He wiggled his feet again and felt them move. He instinctively moved his hands, then moved them again. This was strange. They were no longer numb! He wiggled his fingers just to make sure his body wasn't playing tricks, and now, for certain, some feeling was coming back to him!

He remembered he had heard a cracking sound when the chair crashed to the floor. His right hand was still tied, but it felt looser. When the chair toppled, a slat or two must have broken out of the back. He imagined in his mind how the slats fit into the seat.

He hooked his toes under the legs of the chair and forced his feet upward. When he stretched his hands apart, he gained some free line, but not enough to arch his arms up over the back of the chair.

He had no choice. He would have to topple the chair to one side to expose the back. The man upstairs might hear the chair fall, but if he could free himself now, there was only one man to contend with instead of two.

He forced his body weight to the right, trying to bring the chair over, but it wouldn't go.

Weakened from the effort, he sat still, puffing, letting his strength return. Sweat poured over his face and burned his eyes.

But he took the pain as he forced the weight of his body to one side of the chair, and then rocked all his weight to the other side. The chair teetered for a second and then dropped to the cement.

Garner was alert, deadly quiet, listening for the man upstairs. But, nothing. He arched his arms backward up over the chair, his muscles stretching and burning. His arms dropped to the inside of chair, and within a minute, he worked his hands free. Then he freed his feet and rolled away from the chair, stretching his body, feeling a renewed strength charge inside of him.

Resting on his knees, he flexed his fingers and wrists. A quick swish of his sleeve wiped away some sweat from his forehead.

Once on his feet, the feeling came back and he concentrated on his surroundings. The only light in the room was a thin ray coming from the outside staircase through the small window in the door. He silently made his way to the door and tried the handle, but it was secure like he feared it would be.

What light came through the window beamed on the upturned chair, and beyond the chair he could make out some burlap bags on the floor. A plan began to evolve. He carefully groped his way along the wall of the basement, searching, feeling any and every object his hand touched. And then his fingers found a lovely, long metal pipe. He returned to the upturned chair and set it back to the position it was in when the man kicked him over.

Working as fast as he could, he removed his shoes and pants and then stuffed the burlap bags into the pant legs. He fashioned the pants and shoes in position on the chair and wrapped ropes around them to make it appear like his legs and feet were tied securely.

Very carefully, he reached up and unscrewed the light bulb in the socket and then made his way back to the door with the metal pipe held firmly in his hand. When he looked back at the chair, there was no mistaking it. His pants and shoes in the dim light appeared as if he were still tied in place.

A smile covered his face as he balanced the pipe up and down in his hands. His only concern was that the third man might be upstairs, but it didn't make any difference. Right now, he had nothing to lose.

"Hey!" he hollered. The pipe trembled with excitement in his grip.

"Hey, you!" he shouted again. "Come here!"

He heard someone stir, and within seconds, the man was at the top of the stairs. Garner gripped the bar more tightly when he heard the familiar limp of the man descending the staircase. A shadow crossed the small window, and he knew the man was right outside.

107

He heard the man trigger the light switch a few times, and when the light did not go on, the man curse under his breath.

The loud click when the door unlocked sent a shiver up Garner's spine. When the door opened, the man stepped into the room and looked at the dummy legs on the chair. "So you're ready to talk, huh?"

"You're goddamn right!" hollered Garner as he leveled the iron pipe across the man's temple. The man went down without a sound, and although there was no blood visible on his head, Garner knew the man would never be able to hear what he had to say.

Garner rolled the man over and pulled a Walther automatic from his shoulder holster. Immediately he was at the doorway looking up the stairs, but there was no noise, no movement of any sort. Garner glanced at the dead man on the floor. He had never killed a man, but he felt no remorse in sending this man to Hell. He could only think of the beating he had taken, all for a piece of information he didn't even possess.

Garner returned to the chair where he pulled the burlap bags from their place and quickly donned his pants and shoes.

He silently climbed the stairs and made a quick inspection. He was in a small home somewhere in the country, he guessed. A living room was off to his right, the kitchen to his left. A hallway door opened to a bathroom where he could clearly see a stool and sink. Two more doors led to bedrooms, both empty as he suspected.

In the bathroom, he ran cold water into the sink and soaked his face with wet towels. The cold was so refreshing, but when he looked into the mirror, he cringed. Harold and Marci in the plastic room back in Langley would have marveled at his new look.

The right side of his face was swollen where he had been pistol-whipped, and although his left eye was puffed up, he was seeing out of it now. The only mark on his nose was the one Harold had put there, and a quick inspection indicated it hadn't been broken. He had taken a lot of punches, but all they did was add to the messed up face he already had.

He soaked the towel a final time and draped it over the back of his neck, and now, as some of the pain subsided from his head, he felt the hurt coming on in his chest. He guessed he might have a cracked rib or two.

A glance at his watch told him it was 7:30. Heavy dark clouds hung threateningly outside, and he wasn't sure if it was evening or morning.

He was about to walk out the front door when a set of headlights shown in the distance. A car was coming up a long driveway. Garner moved away from the door and pressed himself flat against the wall. It was the second man returning. Garner made his way back to the bathroom, switched out the light and left the door partially open.

Moments later, the second man entered carrying a package under one arm. In the kitchen, he glanced around seemingly not alarmed with the absence of his partner.

After a few moments, he called out. *"Klaus? Klaus, wo bist du?"*

"He went to see the angels," said Garner as he opened the door. The man turned, his eyes gaping into the gun barrel of the Walther.

He threw his hands into the air. "Wait, Vulcek!" he protested. "Wait! I think we can work something out!"

"You're goddamn right we can," scowled Garner as he approached the man. "You talk, I'll listen." The man was shaking, exactly how Garner wanted him.

"Wh-what do you want to know?"

"Who hired you to rough me up?"

"Toller."

Garner raised his eyebrows when he heard the name. "Why?"

"He wanted to know why you were going to Prague,"

"He knows why I'm going." The man's hands were still shaking as sweat broke across his forehead.

"H-he wanted the information you were taking to Prague."

"How did he know about it?"

"Dieter told him."

So, the man Dieter had referred to was Manfried Toller. The puzzle was taking shape.

"What's your connection with Dieter?"

The man nervously shook his head as if not comprehending the question. "Nothing."

"Come on," scowled Garner. "Dieter works for Toller and you work for Toller. You can do better than that."

"I work privately for Herr Toller. I have never met Dieter before."

Garner couldn't sort out his thoughts. There had to be a connection with the Prague deal. "Did Dieter know you were supposed to beat the information out of me?"

The man swallowed hard. "I was given strict orders never to talk to Dieter under any circumstances. I wasn't even supposed to go near him."

Garner understood the man perfectly, but it didn't make any sense. It appeared that personally, Toller was interested in the information he was supposed to take to Prague, yet at the same time he wanted him dead. Dead? He didn't know that for sure yet.

"What were you supposed to do with me after you got the information?"

The man was really nervous now, fumbling for an answer. Garner raised the Walther a bit.

"Kill you!" the man blurted out.

Dead, thought Garner. The answers were coming, but the picture still wasn't clear. "Who was Helga Schleier?" Garner asked.

"What?" The man was confused with the question.

"Who was Helga Schleier?"

"Well, ah, your girlfriend, wasn't she?"

Garner realized he blew it.

"I mean before me," Garner demanded as if the information the man had supplied was already known.

The man hesitated again. "She was Toller's girlfriend, his secretary. But you knew that. Why do you..." The man stopped mid-sentence and critically studied Garner.

Garner knew what the man was thinking. He made up his mind. "Who killed Vulcek?"

The man's eyes widened into a colder stare when he realized he wasn't talking to Vulcek. "I-I knew Vulcek was dead before the..."

"Before the accident?" finished Garner. "You should know, shouldn't you. Toller ordered the killing, didn't he?"

The man grabbed for his coat pocket in a futile attempt. The bullet from the Walther caught him in the breastbone before his hand made it half way to the concealed weapon. The force of the slug flattened him against the wall. For a moment, he appeared suspended like a picture frame, then slowly, he slid to the floor and crumpled into a fetal position.

Garner froze in place, his arm outstretched, the Walther pointed straight ahead. The realization of killing a second man suddenly struck him. His hand shook uncontrollably now, and without warning, the weapon fired again, sending a bullet through the glass of a window.

A loud thump resounded when the Walther slipped from his hand to the floor. Garner looked at the splotch of blood where the man had backed against the wall. A streak of red followed him down to where he sat.

Nausea crept up the back of Garner's throat. He had just killed two men, but it was little compensation knowing that Vulcek probably would have done the same.

His feeling of sickness slowly turned to anger when he thought about Arthur Farrington. The man had set him up. He decided the next time he saw Arthur, he would personally choke the goddamn truth out of him.

Inside the dead man's pocket, Garner found a set of car keys. When he turned toward the door, he spotted the package the man had brought. The dead man downstairs had said Herman was an expert with needles. Curious, he opened the package, but it contained nothing more than some medical supplies.

Garner spotted his Beretta on the counter, slipped it into his shoulder holster and left the house.

Delray K. Dvoracek

CHAPTER FOURTEEN

Arthur Farrington parked his car along the Boulevard in front of the Frankfurter Polizei building and lumbered up the steps, his nerves beating away. Inspector Gastmann had called demanding to see him immediately.

Arthur was not sweating, but he might as well have been. He already had enough problems. Neither he nor Trudi had seen Phillip Garner for two days.

And he was mad at Clarence. Clarence was supposed to tail Garner, but he lost him. *The guy acts, thinks and drives like a maniac*, Arthur remembered Clarence saying. Garner had run several red lights late at night, and Clarence had tried to run the same lights, however, at one of them, he collided with a truck. He was lucky to get by with a broken finger, but his car didn't fair as well.

Arthur hurried through the reception room and headed for Inspector Gastmann's office. Telephones were ringing, and chattering voices filled the air, but he heard none of it.

He slipped into a hallway and reached Gastmann's domain. "Mr. Farrington to see Herr Inspector Gastmann," he informed the secretary.

"*Ah, Herr Farrington. Der Inspector ist unten. Er wartet auf Sie in Zimmer A-fuenf.*"

Oh, Jesus, thought Arthur as he headed for the basement staircase. He knew what was in room A-5.

He found the door and stared at the German word *Leichenhaus* underneath the number, then turned the handle and stole his way inside. His throat was dry as he approached the man in a white smock sitting at a desk. The distinct aroma of chemicals and other strange smells filled his nostrils.

The man knew who Farrington was and simply motioned with

112

his thumb for Arthur to keep going.

Arthur passed into a second large room, and feeling his stomach churning up his breakfast, he shoved a handkerchief over his nose. The morgue was shiny white and clean, and off to the side next to two moveable stretchers on wheels stood the Inspector with another man. All Arthur could see were the tagged toes sticking out from under two white sheets. The man with Gastmann marked something on a chart and left the room without saying a word.

The Inspector remained standing next to the nearest covered corpse. He nodded and motioned for Arthur. *"Bitte, Herr Farrington, komm hierher."* Arthur nervously stepped closer, the handkerchief over his nose and mouth practically cutting off his breath.

"You had a good sleep last night?" asked the Inspector in his broken English.

"Yes, thank you," answered Arthur.

"Good breakfast, too?"

Arthur nodded and felt his breakfast bubbling in his stomach.

The Inspector reached for the sheet of the first corpse, but he did not lift it immediately. It was as if he were purposely waiting, enjoying every moment of the squeamish look on Arthur's face.

Arthur feared the worst. He knew the corpse would be Phillip Garner, and suddenly he felt the world around him collapsing. The Inspector waited long enough and finally pulled back the sheet. Arthur stared on, eyes wide. For a moment he forgot about his churning stomach and the handkerchief dropped away from his face.

"Do you know him?" inquired the inspector.

Arthur nervously shook his head. "N-no. I don't."

"How about this one?" said the inspector as he exposed the second corpse.

The handkerchief was back at Arthur's face. He felt sick, but he was overjoyed that neither was Phillip Garner. "No. I don't know either of them."

The inspector was back at the first corpse again. "This one was hit with a heavy instrument. Dead instantly." He Looked at the second corpse. "This one was a bit messier," he said as he pulled the sheet back to expose the hole in the man's chest.

Arthur jerked back, uncontrollably sick.

"Of course, there's a bigger hole in his back where the bullet came out." He reached a hand underneath as if he were going to flip the body over. "Perhaps you would like to see it."

"No! No! For God's sake, Herr Inspector!" Arthur choked as he moved away. "W-why have you done this?"

"I thought perhaps you could tell me who they are." The Inspector's cynical voice had not changed any.

"Why should I know?"

"Why indeed?" The Inspector produced a cigar and lit it up, then rocked back and forth on the balls of his feet as he spoke. "Our duty officer this morning was approached by a man wearing dark glasses. He left a note in an envelope."

Arthur was gaining his composure. "A note?"

"Yes. The note told us where to find the bodies."

"Why did you contact me?" asked Arthur. He could hardly wait for the answer.

"Because the note said, tell Arthur." He shoved the note into Arthur Farrington's hands. "And of course, you are the only Arthur I know."

Arthur was sickly overjoyed with the news and still sick to his stomach. "D-do you know who they are?"

"Of course," came the Inspector's snappy reply. "We are not incompetent." The Inspector began reading from a chart. "The first man is Klaus Kastner, the second, Hermann Reigard. Both with prison records, both with an impressive list of criminal acts." He looked up from the sheet expecting Arthur to respond to the information.

Arthur was quick to reply. "Do you know who they were working for?"

"I suspect for themselves. We know they have connections with the syndicate here in Frankfurt. There are rumors that they work for Manfried Toller, but that is perfect nonsense, of course. Herr Toller is a personal friend of mine."

"Yes," retorted Arthur covering his surprise when he heard Manfried Toller's name. "Perfect nonsense."

"*Tja*," said the Inspector. "I thought you would agree. But of course, the question remains, what interest do you have with these two men?"

Arthur was at a loss for an explanation. He didn't know exactly, but there was no doubt Phillip Garner knew. "I frankly don't know."

The Inspector frowned, his voice ringing with snobbery. "You, head of CIA operations in West Germany don't know? And one of your men killed them?"

"I can't tell you. I don't know."

The Inspector shook his head and paced a bit. His cynical smile indicated he didn't believe Arthur. He raised his voice now, spittle spewing out of his mouth. "What do you take us for? Complete idiots?" He threw his hands in the air. "I played your game once and did not report the death of Vulcek. What am I supposed to do with two more dead men?"

"Herr Inspector..."

"What do I tell my superiors? I should be making an investigation on these two men right now!"

Arthur was alert. The Inspector just said he *should be making an investigation* on the two men. That meant he had not conducted one yet. Was the inspector playing a game of his own? Arthur hoped so.

"*Tja, tja*," remarked the Inspector. He had his hands on his hips facing the two corpses. "How much time do you need this time?" he asked.

Arthur could not believe what he heard. "A week."

"Forty eight hours and I make a report."

"Seventy two hours?" asked Arthur. He figured out the Inspector and guessed he had planned to hold the report on the two men all along. It was just a matter of time now, and a display of authority.

All right," snapped the Inspector. "Seventy two hours." He eyed Arthur and smiled. "But of course, there may be favors we might need in the future."

"Of course, of course," agreed Arthur.

115

The Inspector wrapped an arm around Arthur's shoulder and started walking him out of the morgue. "You know, Arthur, we should have lunch together sometime."

* * *

Arthur made his way outside into the fresh air, unaware of the startling sunlight that brought the city of Frankfurt out of its habitual gray into brilliance. There was no doubt Garner had killed the two men, and now he probably took off like he said he was going to do. He feared what Mr. Kendrid in Washington would say, and he cursed himself. He had worked too hard, searched so long.

Arthur was so engrossed in his thoughts that an aircraft could have crashed in front of the police station without his noticing it. He opened his car door and crawled inside before he even noticed the man sitting next to him.

"Hello, Arthur," said Garner. "It's so nice to see you." Garner took off his dark glasses to expose his badly beaten face. "I suspect you're happy to see me, too."

Arthur gasped at the sight.

"Drive," said Garner. Arthur nervously searched his pockets for what seemed like a minute before he finally found his keys.

CHAPTER FIFTEEN

For four days, the two had been enjoying the classy atmosphere of the health spa in the Harz Mountains. "How's my eye look?" asked Garner. He was smiling, enjoying her two-piece swimsuit. Her top was held up by a thin cord tied around her neck, and her bottom barely covered anything.

"Which eye?" she asked.

"My bad one."

"Your bad one looks good."

Garner couldn't take his eyes off her. For four straight days he had been watching her every movement, especially the way she swung her hips. Since they had arrived, an abundance of sunshine was giving her a nice tan, and she looked beautiful in every respect.

He sipped at his beer. *Schoen temperiert*, the waiter had said, yet, it was a little too warm to his liking but probably perfect for Frank Vulcek.

He, too, was enjoying the bright sun. It was amazing how the rays had healed his face to a degree. The swelling had disappeared, and though he had a shiner on one eye, it wasn't far off in color from the scars they had given him in Langley.

Farrington had granted him and Trudi these few days' pleasure and really didn't have any other choice. Garner had threatened to drop the whole masquerade unless he got some answers, and finally Arthur started talking.

Apparently, Arthur did not know Vulcek had connections with Toller and von Hauer. He confessed he had let Garner blunder his way through the streets of Frankfurt.

"I apologize profusely that you had to kill or be killed," he had told Garner.

Every day, Garner was learning something new about Vulcek.

117

Delray K. Dvoracek

The former agent worked the trenches and dug up scum wherever he operated. He loved to spring surprises on Farrington and thrived on deception, but as long as he made Arthur look good, Arthur put up with his insolence.

Arthur couldn't apologize enough for the *discomforts* Garner had gone through, and according to Trudi, Arthur rarely apologized. As of yet, he never admitted that Vulcek and Helga Schleier were murdered, but he at least agreed it was a possibility. All Garner really wanted was the truth from Arthur, and he wanted to believe him.

After all, if he returned to the States, he was probably looking at a stiff prison term. Of course, if he ended up dead, he could avoid prison life, which made him wonder who the real fool was; he or Arthur.

"The water's great!" Trudi hollered from the pool.

"So's the beer," answered Garner. He toasted her and took another drink.

When she hoisted herself out of the water, he caught a glimpse of the cleavage between her breasts.

"What are you looking at?" she said teasingly as she knelt down and ran a towel over her body. She smiled and gave him a quick kiss. "You want to make love to me again, don't you?"

He grinned. "What makes you think so?"

"It's written all over your face. You've had that love-making stare ever since we arrived."

He chuckled. "Is that so bad?"

A waiter was suddenly upon them and had trailed a phone all the way from the lobby. "*Telefon fuer Sie, Herr Vulcek.*" He spun around and walked off.

Garner glanced at Trudi, his playful mood gone as he lifted the receiver. "*Hier spricht Vulcek.*" He glanced at his watch. "Right," was all he answered, and then hung up. His eyes were back on Trudi, and the playfulness in his voice was gone. "Arthur. He said nine o'clock tonight at the department store. What does that mean?"

"He wants to see you at his office."

Garner pulled a face. "It looks like I've graduated. I didn't think

I'd ever get to see where Arthur works." He took a drink from his beer and settled back in his lounge chair. "You were in love with Frank." he said as he eyed her.

She didn't respond.

"You knew him better than anyone."

"Yes." Her eyes saddened with the reply.

"Would Frank ever lie to you?"

She hesitated. "I don't know what you mean."

"Did he always tell you everything?"

"No. I'm sure there were things he kept from me." Her voice was defensive. "Should I have expected him to tell me everything?"

"No, I suppose not. But what about the affair with Helga - Schleier. He didn't tell you about that?"

"No. But if he was having an affair, I don't suppose he would tell me."

"You said, if."

"What do you mean?"

"Maybe he didn't tell you about Helga because he was protecting you."

"From what?"

Garner took in a deep breath. "Do you think Frank could ever sell out?"

"Sell out? You mean..."

Garner nodded.

"Why would he do that? Money didn't motivate him. It was the excitement, the thrill. It was all one-ups-man ship for Frank."

"I don't know if I buy that," said Garner.

"Then why are you still here after all you've gone through?"

That was a very good question, Garner was thinking. He changed the subject. "What do you suppose Frank's connection was with Toller?"

She had a blank look on her face. "What do you think?" She asked the question as if she really didn't want a response.

Garner looked at his watch and offered a warm smile. He leaned over and kissed her, then whispered, "I think we still have time to make love before we return to Frankfurt."

Her gaze stretched beyond Garner for a moment, and then her mood changed. She reached out and squeezed his hand. "I think so, too."

* * *

It surprised Garner, and yet, it didn't surprise him when he parked the Peugeot in front of the I.G. Farben building. It wasn't too far from his own apartment, and it was one of the slides young Kurt Johnson had shown him numerous times. All Garner knew was that it was a government building. Strangely enough, he had passed it a few times in the past week. Little did he know that Farrington was probably sitting in his office when he drove by.

Trudi had a passkey to a rear entrance where a security guard was posted. He recognized Trudi and let them pass.

They took the lift to the sixth floor where they passed through another security guard into a huge reception area. Arthur and Clarence were waiting for them in an office beyond. Arthur was his usual big self, and the only thing different about Clarence was the middle finger on his left hand, which had a splint on it wrapped with tape. Garner assumed he had broken it and wondered how, but he didn't ask.

Arthur Farrington was studying a wall map when he turned to greet them. "You're on time," he said as if he couldn't think of anything else to say. His eyes focused on Garner's face "You look much better, Mr. Garner."

"Yeah, I'm ready to be beat up again."

Arthur frowned, not sure how he should take the sarcasm, but it was a remark Frank Vulcek would have made. He handed two files over to Garner. The first was that of Toller. It contained a photo of the man, numerous newspaper clippings and various other documents.

"He has donated huge sums to various charities," Arthur said. "A personal friend of the Chief of police and mayor and well respected

120

in legal circles. An impeccable record."

"Nothing in here about murder?" Garner asked.

Arthur overlooked the snide comment. "We've checked him out in Berlin, Hamburg, London, Bern. Impeccable credentials."

Garner didn't like what he was hearing.

"He travels a lot. As a matter of fact, he just returned from Berlin today." Arthur was pacing with a nervous gait. "We're checking out his contacts. It may be nothing, it may be something.

"Dieter von Hauer," Arthur went on pointing to the second file. "He also has an impeccable record on paper, but he's far from the spitting image of Toller. He's a law partner, but he's heavily in debt. Gambles a lot, squanders money on women, fancy automobiles, etcetera."

Arthur stopped pacing. "Do you recognize either of them?"

Garner studied the photo. "Could be von Hauer. It was dark when I met him, but I think it's him." He examined the first photo. "This could be the blond-haired guy I glimpsed at the Golden Horse Gasthaus."

Arthur grunted. "These men have good reputations in legal circles. Is it possible you could be mistaken about either one of them?"

"For Christ sake, Arthur," Garner badgered. "Whether I recognized Toller or not, the two men who were beating the hell out of me said they worked for him. What's so hard to believe about that?"

Arthur's lip curled. "Motive," he said. "I'm looking for a motive. And it doesn't appear Manfried Toller has one, but Dieter von Hauer does."

"Motive for what?" snapped Garner.

The question caught Arthur by surprise. He was thinking along lines for murder, but he didn't want to suggest that. He shrugged his shoulders. "Frank Vulcek was working something on the side. I don't know exactly what, but for some reason he was dealing with von Hauer." He hesitated. "It may have something to do with the microfilm Frank Vulcek was supposed to deliver to Prague."

Garner raised an eyebrow. He knew he was to take some

information to Prague, but he had no idea it was a piece of microfilm. His mind was back on Vulcek. It was ironic that Arthur suggested that he may have been working something on the side. That was what he himself had alluded to with Trudi earlier in the afternoon.

Arthur sat uneasily behind his desk and made a face. "Miss Feldman," he began, "I know this must be painful for you, but it's a question of whose hands the microfilm were eventually to fall into."

Trudi stared back. "Frank wouldn't sell out."

Arthur was up again, pacing. He knew he hadn't phrased the accusation with tact, but that was too near the truth, he feared. "It is a possibility we can't afford to overlook."

"That's crazy," she said.

Garner exploded. "What is so goddamned important on the microfilm!?"

"Mr. Garner," Arthur said as politely as he could. "You are not being paid to know what's on the film. You're being paid to deliver it, and that's all."

Garner turned to Trudi. "Do you know what's on the film?"

"I'm the only one that knows," Arthur shot back. "All you have to do is deliver it!"

Garner got into Arthur's face. "Was Willie cutting me up part of the deal? Were the two guys who beat me up part of the deal? They were supposed to kill me once they got the information. Was that part of the deal?" Garner was fuming. "I don't have to deliver shit! All I have to do is walk out of this goddamn insane asylum!"

For the second time within a week, Arthur's anger swelled. "Garner. You can't walk out of here or go anywhere without my say so. A week ago, the FBI asked to have your ass extradited to the States. The only thing standing between you and prison is Mr. Kendrid in Washington and me!"

"We made a deal!" Garner shot back.

"That's right!" Arthur countered. "So live up to it!"

Garner eyed Clarence and came back at Arthur. "You think you've got me by the balls, don't you?"

"You're damn right, and I'm squeezing them."

122

All three men looked at Trudi, who sat with a rather coy look on her face. She had never seen Arthur act like this before.

Arthur took a deep breath and softened his temper. "Mr. Garner. I am your savior or your executioner. You make the choice."

Garner succumbed to the fact that there was no way Arthur Farrington was going to disclose what was on the microfilm. It may well be the way the CIA operated—purely on a need to know basis.

Suddenly it didn't make any difference what the assignment was. There was no way he could go back to the States, at least, not without Arthur's graces, and there was no escape in Europe. Arthur would find him.

Garner looked at Clarence who hadn't said a word since his arrival. Somehow he felt all three in the room knew what was on the microfilm, and he felt betrayed. They couldn't pull off whatever they were supposed to do without him, yet, he was the one in the dark.

"All right, Arthur," he said calmly, as he probed one more time. "You're my savior. If I'm in the middle of this, I should know what's on the microfilm. I might be able to..."

"No!" Arthur interrupted. "There is absolutely no need to know. You could compromise everything if you ever got..." He stopped.

"Caught?" Garner finished.

Everyone in the room was silent.

"Is that all, this time?" Garner asked. "Just deliver the microfilm to Prague and come home?"

"Yes."

"When do I leave?"

"Within 48 hours."

"What happens in the meanwhile?"

Arthur had already considered that. "You pay a visit to Dieter von Hauer."

"When?"

"Tonight."

"Why?"

"Because Dieter von Hauer is the man who was involved with Frank Vulcek."

123

Garner made a face. "I think I should pay Toller a visit."

"Goddammit, Frank! Why must you be so fucking belligerent!?" Arthur froze in place, startled with his own words. They all noticed Arthur had just called Garner *Frank*.

Arthur sat down and calmed himself. "Mr. Garner. I want you to pay von Hauer a visit tonight, and I want Clarence to go along with you." He looked up, pleased that Garner did not protest this time. "It was von Hauer who first approached you several days ago."

"Yeah," agreed Garner. "But it was Toller who murdered Frank Vulcek and Helga Schleier."

"That hasn't been established!"

"Toller's man admitted it."

"He would admit anything with a gun in his face."

"You said it was a possibility."

"Yes, and we'll treat it that way until we have further evidence." Arthur's face was red from anger. "We'll start with von Hauer. If both he and Toller were seeking the same information from you, I want to know why. If what you say is true, the two men you killed were not supposed to know von Hauer, not even go near him. Don't you think that strange?"

"What am I supposed to do tonight, beat the information out of him?"

"You may have to be persuasive. I'll leave that up to you."

"I'd rather beat the hell out of Toller," snapped Garner.

"Goddammit!" shouted Farrington as he jumped out of his chair. "We'll start with von Hauer! Just find out what his connection is with Toller!"

Arthur was fuming, but took a moment to cool down. "Mr. Garner. Please see Miss Feldman home. Wait twenty minutes before leaving her apartment. That will give Clarence enough time to get over to von Hauer's house. He'll back you up."

"How'll I find the place?"

Arthur handed Garner a slip of paper with the address. "Take the Autobahn across the Main and follow the Offenbacher Landstrasse. It's about a fifteen minute drive."

124

Garner studied the address, stuffed it in his pocket and took Trudi by the arm. "We should be going to see Toller," he mumbled as they exited the room.

"Arthur," said Clarence as soon as the two were gone. "You know damn well Toller and von Hauer are in this together."

"Of course I know!" barked Arthur. "What did you want me to do, send him to see Toller? He'd probably kill him on sight."

"No," Arthur went on. "Garner will be better off dealing with von Hauer. At least he doesn't have a record for murder."

"You should have told him about Toller," Clarence insisted.

"Do you think for one moment he'd hang around if he knew what we now know about Toller? He'd be on the first plane out of the country for sure!"

"Where's he going to go? You said the FBI was waiting for him back in the States."

Arthur threw up his hands. "Clarence, nobody was ever caught, and the FBI never did have anything concrete on him from the very beginning. It was all speculation, all circumstantial. If he goes back to the States, he's a free man."

Clarence Tripson stared in disbelief. He never thought Arthur was a very convincing liar, but he had just convinced Garner and himself. "Arthur, you're using this guy!"

"Of course I am. Goddammit, we need him!"

There was a desperation in Arthur that Clarence suddenly did not like. "Arthur. You've got to tell Garner what Vulcek's real assignment is."

"Clarence, I have enough problems to contend with without your advice. Don't you see how valuable he is? He's our best link. He's digging up names of people we never knew about. Kendrid is ecstatic with the new information."

"But Arthur," Clarence pleaded.

"Clarence, look at the results we're getting! The ends justify the means."

Clarence shook his head. "If he discovers Vulcek's real mission, he'll hightail it."

"I don't think so." Arthur had a big smile of superiority on his face. "Haven't you noticed? Trudi's in love with him and he's in love with her. That's something I hadn't counted on."

Arthur made a fist. "He's mine, Clarence, he's mine."

"Arthur," said Clarence. "I think you're making a big mistake." He got up and headed for the door. "I better get out to von Hauer's place. Somehow, I think Garner's going to need help."

He left the room.

Arthur sat in his chair and felt his nerves crawl. He knew that the microfilm supposedly contained a man's name, but whose name, even he didn't know. The name was to be delivered into the hands of operatives in Prague, and obviously, it was a name that Toller and von Hauer wanted. What either of them would do with the name was pure speculation at this point, but it was a good bet that Toller was somehow connected with the KGB.

And now, Arthur's superiors in Langley suspected that Frank Vulcek may have been a double agent. But if he was, and if Toller was associated with the KGB, then why did Toller murder him?

Arthur whirled his chair around, plagued by his own questions. "Jesus Christ!" he exclaimed as he slammed a fist on the desk.

CHAPTER SIXTEEN

Garner located the address where Dieter von Hauer lived and parked a block away on a side street. The home was small, but the brick face and the quaint yard circled with a low wrought iron fence gave it some class.

From where Garner stood in the shadows of some pines, he could see a light coming from somewhere inside the home.

As he jumped the fence, he wondered if Clarence was nearby. He crossed the driveway and walked along the sidewalk in the grass, careful not to make any noise with his approach.

The doorway was shadowed in the night, but as he neared, he could tell the inner door was slightly ajar. He glanced about the yard, then lifted the Beretta from its place and opened the outer screen door. He pushed the inner door open a little wider and peered inside. A foyer opened to the living room, and somewhere from a doorway to the left, a light shown through.

He listened for a few seconds and thought he heard a drawer open. Papers shuffled. He silently crossed the living room and could now see through an open door into what appeared to be a den or library.

A drawer slammed shut. He let his eyes adjust to the dark, then made his way a little closer and nudged the door open a bit further. The man sitting at the desk was definitely von Hauer. The long face and pointed beard easily gave him away, but it wasn't Dieter who was making the noise, since a trickle of blood leaked down from his right temple.

Garner felt his heart pounding. Whoever killed Dieter was just beyond the wall in the room. He slowly lowered his body and was lucky that he did. Two muffled shots from a silencer sent splinters ripping through the door frame inches above his head.

127

Delray K. Dvoracek

He dropped down flat just as a lamp crashed to the floor setting the room in darkness. Garner kicked the door open and saw the curtain swaying at the window, and now he could hear running footsteps on the grass outside. He was up and jumped out the window in time to see the man running on the far side of the yard. He was nothing more than a shadow, but Garner snapped off two shots at the figure and saw the man go down.

He heard the man cry out. "Don't shoot, for Christ sake! It's me, Clarence!"

Off to his right, Garner glimpsed a second figure as he leaped the fence. Garner stormed after him, but by the time he cleared the fence, he heard an engine race from a vehicle a short ways away, and in moments, the car was gone.

Garner ran back to Clarence. "Are you all right?" he asked as he helped him to his feet.

"You're a lousy shot," Clarence scowled.

"You're lucky," retorted Garner. "I was shooting for your legs."

"Yeah," grunted Clarence as he pulled up a pant leg. The moonlight was just sufficient enough to see the back of his calf where a bulled had nicked him on the outer flesh. Blood from the wound was already filling his shoe.

"We better call Arthur," said Garner as he helped Clarence back to von Hauer's house.

* * *

Within minutes, they heard police sirens. In no time at all, three police cars had showed up and policemen lined the front yard, warding off the curious few, who had gathered. Two Vopos were on guard at the door when Arthur Farrington finally arrived.

"Good God!" he said when he entered the library. He pulled a handkerchief out and covered his mouth, his face already white.

"Shot at extremely close range," said Clarence. He spun Dieter around in the swivel chair and stuck his thumb above the bullet hole in his head. "You can see the powder burns."

Farrington cringed and turned his face aside, fighting back an urge to vomit. All the while, Clarence was smiling, enjoying his little game of show and tell.

Farrington crossed to a corner chair and sat, his face milky white. "Is that the same man that first approached you at your apartment?" he asked Garner.

"I think so." answered Garner. "Too bad he can't walk. I'd know for sure."

"Is he the same man you saw in the parking lot at the Golden Horse Gasthaus?"

"No. That was Toller."

Farrington burped and motioned to the dead man. "Who do you think killed him?"

"Toller," answered Garner. Clarence nodded in agreement.

Arthur seemed to gain his composure. "Or one of his men," he added to Garner's speculation.

"But why?" asked Clarence.

Garner made a stab in the dark. "Maybe it's because Dieter found out Toller murdered Vulcek in the first place."

"It was never established Toller was the murderer," said Arthur.

Garner grinned. "So he *was* murdered?"

Arthur's face went blank. He didn't intend to divulge that information. "We don't have solid evidence it was Toller."

"Jesus Christ, Arthur," Garner spit out. "He killed Vulcek, and then tried to kill me when he thought Vulcek was still alive. It doesn't take any brains to figure that out."

Farrington puffed up his cheeks and blew out some air.

Garner gritted his teeth. "Arthur, I've been stabbed, beaten half to death, and tonight I just got shot at. I am getting fucking tired of being used by you."

Arthur sank back in his chair knowing Garner was going to tell him to take the Prague assignment and stuff it. That's exactly what Frank Vulcek would have done if he were alive and masquerading as Phillip Garner.

Garner glared at Arthur. "You knew Vulcek was murdered, yet

129

you sent me all over this goddamn city without telling me I'm a target."

Arthur slouched, again feeling the world collapse around him.

"If you're going to keep this Prague assignment alive, you better damn well keep me alive!"

Arthur's eyes sparkled. Phillip Garner must still believe that he could not safely return to the States without repercussion, which meant he still had strings tied to him. Inside, Arthur was exuberant, but he dare not show it. He stood and defiantly walked around to the front of Dieter von Hauer and bent down close to the dead man's face. He did not raise the handkerchief to his mouth, although he felt an urge to do so. Right now, he needed desperately to be tough, to be in command. He was preparing himself to lie once again to Phillip Garner.

"All right," said Arthur in a firm voice. "I knew Vulcek was murdered, but I couldn't tell you that in the beginning. I now believe that Toller killed Vulcek and Helga Schleier, but it's only speculation at this point why."

He looked directly at Garner. "I believe Toller wants the information on the microfilm just like Dieter von Hauer did."

"What's on the microfilm?" asked Garner.

"A name."

"What do you mean?"

Arthur hesitated. "Look, there's a Russian scientist who will be in Prague in the next few days."

"What's so important about him?"

"He wants to defect."

Garner was stunned "Well, why do you need me? Or Frank Vulcek? Why can't someone else deliver the microfilm?"

"Because Frank was the only person who knew the defector by his face. We don't even have the defector's name."

"What?" asked Garner. "Are you telling me you don't even know who Vulcek was dealing with?"

"The defector made contact with Frank in Prague about ten weeks ago. We have reason to believe he is high up in the Russian scientific community, a missile expert."

"How do you know that?"

"Frank returned with some classified documents that our people verified as legitimate."

"And Frank didn't give you a name?"

Arthur grunted. "Why do you think we're so desperate? Frank made a deal with the defector not to divulge his name or face until a means to defect was set up. And when Frank gave his word, he kept it.

"Two weeks before Frank died, we got a date that the defector would again be in Prague, and we made arrangements for Frank to meet with him a final time.

"In the meanwhile, Frank had some leads on people who wanted the defector's name, so we made arrangements to deliver a piece of microfilm to Prague with a false name on it simply to trace where it went."

Garner was puzzled. "I don't understand. Whose trail were you supposed to follow?"

"Obviously Toller or von Hauer or both, two people we never knew about until you took over Vulcek's identity."

Garner motioned to Dieter. "This guy's a dead end, so that leaves Toller."

"I'm afraid so," Arthur reluctantly agreed. "We'll have to pay him a visit after all. He's the only link we have left. I'm sure he's involved, and if he is, he must have a contact in Prague. We want to know who that contact is."

"So I'm delivering a piece of microfilm with worthless information on it."

"That's right."

"What about the defector?"

"That's over and done with. Since Vulcek was the only person who knew him, that's a dead end, too. We enlisted your talents just to discover where the microfilm would lead us."

"What if Toller asks for the defector's name?"

"Tell him the name's encoded on the microfilm and you can't

read it. Frank wouldn't give anything away until he had a deal in his pocket."

"What kind of deal?"

"Money," answered Farrington. "What else?

Garner found that strange. Trudi said money didn't motivate Vulcek. "You think he was double dealing?"

Arthur shrugged. "We never knew for sure what he was up to. He was always so secretive, and he never told us anything until the last damn minute."

"What's Trudi's role in all this?" asked Garner. "Is she supposed to go to Prague, too?"

Arthur prepared himself for another lie. "No. She isn't part of the Prague assignment. Her only role was to help you acquire your new identity."

"When do I see Toller?"

"Tomorrow night. Toller has a meeting with several of his colleagues in the evening. He should return home about midnight. It would be the least likely place he would expect to encounter you.

"There are some obstacles, however," Arthur continued. "Our surveillance tells us there are at least two men guarding the grounds at night. We have a plan that will get you inside, but once you're on his estate you'll be on your own."

"You figured this out a long time ago, didn't you, Arthur?"

Arthur had a sheepish grin on his face as he hunched his shoulders. "It crossed my mind we might have to send you to see Toller." He eyed Dieter. "We wanted him first."

Garner was calculating the risks. "If I get inside Toller's house, I might just shoot the son-of-a-bitch. What would you say to that?"

Arthur heaved a sigh. "We're hoping that won't happen, but if it becomes necessary, then shoot the son-of-a-bitch."

Clarence rolled his eyes when he heard that.

"And if Toller asks where you're staying in Prague, tell him the Tatran Hotel. That was Vulcek's favorite place."

"The Tatran."

They heard voices coming from the front of the house, and

suddenly Inspector Gastmann was standing in the doorway of the library.

He glanced at the dead man and grunted. "Well, Arthur, what is it this time?"

Delray K. Dvoracek

CHAPTER SEVENTEEN

Farrington told Garner to sit tight for twenty-four hours, so that's exactly what he did. He spent a sleepless night in his apartment and the rest of the day with Trudi at hers. Making love had usually been a nighttime activity for him, but he made an exception on this day, all in the line of duty.

Garner told her of the plan to visit Toller, to which she strenuously objected. "That's insane!" she had told him. Maybe it was an insane idea, but Garner was looking forward to meeting the son-of-a-bitch that murdered Frank Vulcek and sanctioned the same for himself.

Garner was now sitting on a low hill among some trees and shrubbery. He glanced at his watch again. Twenty minutes ago, just short of midnight, he saw the limo enter the estate and park in the garage. He guessed it was Toller returning from his meeting.

Garner had an excellent view of the grounds. A bare hundred feet away was the six-foot wrought iron fence that surrounded the estate. Garner suspected Toller might have guard dogs inside, but he hated dogs, hated animals of any sort. At least, that's what Arthur had told him.

The cool night air bit at him as he peered through the infrared glasses at the huge, Bavarian styled home. He had been watching the grounds for the past half-hour and had figured out the routine of the two men who were patrolling the area. The man to his left, no more than fifty yards distant now, was headed back toward the house. Only minutes earlier, Garner had watched the man relieve himself right in front of him by the fence.

The second man was to his right, perhaps seventy-five yards distant. Both were wearing dark clothing, and to Garner's amusement, they were wearing ties under their jackets, a quirk Toller

134

demanded, according to Arthur.

Toller liked everything around him nice and tidy, yet underneath the man's outer shell lingered a deadly scorpion. Arthur had linked Toller to the syndicate in West Berlin. His activities on the other side of the wall were not entirely clear, but Arthur had an operative in East Berlin who had been busy checking out Toller, and now, more than ever, Arthur was sure the man was a major link in a chain of espionage.

Garner recalled Arthur's instructions; *Find out who the contact is in Prague, and then get out of there.*

That was easy enough for Arthur to say; Toller hadn't tried to kill him.

A faint buzz sounded from inside his coat pocket. Garner triggered a button on the two-way radio and listened while Arthur spoke.

"Right." Garner shut off the communicator and checked the positions of the two men on the other side of the iron fence. Within another minute, a driver would purposely crash an automobile into the fence at the front of the estate. The fence was motion-sensitive and would set off an alarm inside the house. It was then that Garner was to make his move.

It wasn't long when Garner heard the squeal of tires on pavement. He saw the car crash into the metal fence, and immediately, a faint alarm sounded from a faraway speaker.

When the two night guards ran for the front of the house, Garner made a dash for the fence. He hooked a shoe in the bar at the bottom, then pulled himself up. In seconds, he was over and dropped to the ground.

The alarm was still sounding as he ran across the grass to the rear of the house. He chose a window that had no light coming from it and banged an elbow through the glass. He listened for a few moments, then reached a hand through the broken glass and unlatched the window. In moments, he crawled inside. Seconds later, the alarm shut off and he smiled to himself. He had beat the alarm.

He remained still until his eyes adjusted to the dark. A large bed with a tufted quilt and pillows sat against one wall. He looked around at the other furniture and guessed he was in a master bedroom.

He crossed the carpet to a door that led to a hallway. An opening at the end of the hallway revealed a larger room, and now, from somewhere, he heard a voice talking into a telephone. A half-minute passed until a man in a gray suit appeared at the hallway opening. He walked a few paces in Garner's direction, then abruptly turned through an open doorway, and seconds later, his footsteps slowly faded. When Garner heard a door open and shut, he figured the man had exited the house.

Garner left the bedroom and made his way to where the man had come from. He was in a drawing room in which a bar with glasses behind it stretched along one wall, and to the side on a stand were a number of liquor bottles. The only light that angled into this room came through a set of French doors, which opened to an adjoining room. Toller had good taste, thought Garner, as he inspected the elegance around him. Every piece of furniture was colorful, expensive looking. Huge paintings filled the wall spaces, and a collection of beautiful flowered vases displayed the inside of an immense glass cabinet. Everything in the room was positioned with a keen sense of order.

When the front door opened, Garner could hear voices again. He crossed into a shadowed corner keeping the Beretta firmly in his grip. The voices grew louder, and suddenly a woman entered the room and went directly to the bar, where she began mixing some drinks.

His adrenaline was flowing. If she turned around, she would see him. His mind raced, and then a man entered the room, and he, too, crossed to the bar. He was dressed lavishly in a dark blue suit. Even in the dim light, his patent leather shoes gleamed brilliantly, and he had thick, blond hair.

Garner watched as he came up behind the woman, a beautiful dark haired lady, and slipped his arms around her. He kissed her on the neck and at the same time cupped both hands on her breasts.

She chuckled. "What if Max comes in?" Garner heard her say.

He answered something back, but Garner did not catch what he said. When the two turned around, both holding their drinks in their hands, Garner had the Beretta pointed at them.

Garner expected Toller to be nervous, but instead, he had a wide grin on his face, and he spoke in a rather soft voice. "Well, Herr Vulcek. How nice of you to pay us a visit." He nodded toward the front door. "The car crash outside? A very clever entrance. Very clever, indeed."

Garner couldn't believe how calm Toller was. If the man had any fear at all, he wasn't giving the slightest indication of it.

A door opened and closed somewhere off to Garner's left, and then, quite casually, another man entered the room. He stopped when he saw the Beretta pointed at him.

"Tell your friend to lift his gun out easy like and drop it to the floor," Garner commanded to Toller.

Toller simply smiled. "I heard you got messed up a bit. And you don't sound the same. Piece of glass in your throat or something?"

The man was certainly cocky and cool, Garner was thinking. "The gun," repeated Garner as he motioned toward the man.

Toller nodded. The man with the pocked face lifted the gun from its place and tossed it at Garner's feet.

"Allow me to introduce my friends," said Toller. "This is Crystal, my secretary, and this is Max, one of my many personal bodyguards."

Garner read the hidden meaning in his last words.

"Would you care for a drink, Frank?" He turned to Crystal and asked her to pour him a straight brandy, and then he was back at Garner. "That is the way you like it, is it not, Frank?"

Garner nodded.

"Good. I like a man who sticks to his habits." She poured the brandy, nervously walked toward him and set it on a coffee table in front of him.

"Shall we sit?" Toller asked as he and Crystal eased themselves onto the sofa. Max sat in a leather-backed chair, his hands planted on the armrests.

Garner stepped closer. "You seem to be in good humor, Manfried."

"Why shouldn't I be? You obviously haven't come to kill me."

The girl stirred, her face flat and fearful with the comment.

"What makes you so sure?" snapped Garner.

"You could have eliminated me much earlier. Yesterday, or a week ago. No, I detect some other motive for your presence."

He was talking about the deal that Dieter had mentioned. "What happened to your colleague, Dieter?" Garner asked.

Toller maintained a straight face. "There are some matters that are best discussed outside of mixed company, don't you agree?"

It was a good answer, thought Garner. The girl was obviously scared, and it was a good bet that she knew nothing about Dieter's murder.

"Come, Frank. You haven't had your drink yet. You want to be sociable, don't you?"

Garner picked up Max's weapon and put it in his pocket, then took the brandy from the table and tossed it down.

He motioned for Toller to get up. "Tell your friends to stay comfortable."

"You heard him, Max," said Toller as he rose from the sofa. Garner followed him through the house to the front door.

The two descended the few steps to the outdoors into a cool and welcome breeze. As the two walked along the circle driveway toward the front gate, swaying pine trees filled the air with creaking sounds.

"Let's start with Dieter," said Garner.

Toller obliged him. "I would imagine that if Dieter is dead, it's because he knew too much. That's why people usually die, isn't it?"

"Is that why you tried to rub me out?"

Toller stopped abruptly, his voice angry. "You know I don't like anyone fooling around with my personal affairs. I told you to stay away from Helga."

Good God, thought Garner. Did Toller kill Vulcek simply because he was associating with Helga? Would he kill a man for that reason only?

138

"But that's over now," said Toller.

"I should kill you, Manfried. Twice you've tried to kill me. Once in the car, once with your other two thugs."

Toller smiled. "However, you're alive and two of my men are dead. You seem to be ahead of me. Besides, with Dieter out of the way, we are now quite able to deal freely. It's too bad he didn't die a little sooner. It would have made things much simpler for us in the long run.

"Poor Dieter. We both know he loved money. He just couldn't seem to hold on to it. I'm guessing he committed suicide. Isn't that what some people do when they're heavily in debt?"

Garner almost wanted to laugh. "People who shoot themselves usually have a gun in their hand. Dieter didn't."

"Well, then perhaps he was trying to blackmail someone. Blackmail is cause to get oneself killed, isn't it?"

There was a hidden line in that sentence, too, Garner was thinking. Now he wondered if Vulcek and Dieter were in the process of making a deal, and if so, was that the blackmail Toller was talking about?

"I'm prepared to double the offer for the information," Toller said as he started toward the iron gates again. "Just give me the name of the defector and the fifty thousand is yours."

Garner tensed. He was making up anything he could think of now. "I never knew his name. The CIA just recently found a file on him. They know, I don't."

Toller stopped walking. "But you said you could get it."

Garner remembered what Dieter had first told him when they met. He used almost the same phrase. "You know these people in Washington. They wait until the last goddamn minute for everything."

"So you don't have it?" responded Toller. "When?"

"I'm leaving for Prague tomorrow. I'm supposed to get the name while in flight on the aircraft."

"Shit," said Toller. "Is it on microfilm?"

"Yes, and it's encoded. I can't even read it."

139

Toller was still for a moment. "I think our people can break it."

Garner's mind was whirling. *What did he mean by our people?*

"I'll line up a contact in Prague," said Toller. "Where are you staying?

"At the Tatran Hotel."

"I know it." He thought a moment. "Who are you supposed to deliver the microfilm to, and when?"

"I was told to sit tight for a few days in Prague. So I don't think everything's been worked out yet. Could be day one, could be day seven."

Toller nodded. "That's good. Mid-morning the next day after you arrive, take your time walking to the Karlovy Most. There are a couple of benches off the east tower. Enjoy the view of Hradcany Castle until my contact arrives."

"How will I know him?"

"You'll know him."

Garner nodded. If Vulcek would know him, he didn't dare ask. He also recollected seeing a photo of the Karlovy Bridge, and though he did not know the exact location, that was information Frank would have known.

"How were you supposed to get the defector out of Prague?" asked Toller.

"I don't know what the boys in Washington planned. All I was supposed to do was make contact with the defector so they could take over."

Toller nodded. "What will you do once the microfilm is in our hands?"

"Disappear. I've got friends in Prague and a lot of other places. Which brings me around to the money." It seemed the likely thing to ask.

"It will be arranged."

As they neared the gate, Garner caught sight of a shadowed figure off to one side.

"Don't worry about Helmut," said Toller. "If I wanted you dead, all I had to do was nod my head. He's had a gun on you ever since we came outside."

Garner felt a lump in his throat. If their conversation had not gone in the right direction, he'd be a dead man now.

Garner slipped the Beretta into his holster, then took the other weapon from his pocket and handed it to Toller. "Give back Max his toy."

Garner turned and headed for the iron gate not at all sure Toller wouldn't put a bullet in his back.

"Frank," Toller called.

Garner turned around, expecting to see the automatic pointed at him.

"Don't cross me again."

Don't cross me, Garner said to himself as he walked out of the gate. Frank Vulcek had died either because he had taken away the man's personal possession, in this case Helga Schleier, or because Vulcek was making a deal with Dieter von Hauer. Or both. Either way, it seemed Vulcek was dealing cards under the table, something Arthur didn't know about.

A heavy hum filled the air as the iron gates closed behind him. Within moments, Garner walked by the scene where Farrington had arranged for a car crash into the fence. Several bars were bent, and broken glass was scattered on the ground.

His mind wandered away from the scene of the accident, and his thoughts kept coming back to the words, *Don't cross me again.*

* * *

Arthur Farrington was waiting for him when he reached his car.

"How'd it go?" he asked.

He had had to make up half of his conversation with Toller, but he answered straightforward. "I'm supposed to make contact in Prague."

"Who's your contact?"

"Someone is supposed to meet me at the Karlovy Bridge. He didn't give a name."

"Damn," said Arthur. "I don't suppose you asked."

"Would Frank have?" snapped Garner.

"No," answered Arthur. "You're right. Frank might have guessed who the contact was."

"That's what I figured. Arthur, I have a few questions."

"I haven't got time for them." He switched on a dash light and produced a briefcase. "Your round-trip plane ticket is inside along with two hundred dollars in Czech Crowns. The microfilm is behind a lining in the back of the case. Take your passport and one change of clothing, since you'll be in one day and out the next. You'll also find a map of Prague. Frank knew the city quite well, so you better memorize some of the main streets, especially in the Old Town area of the city. Vulcek traveled as a representative for crystal glassware many times before. You'll find a list of businesses he usually called on. Memorize a few of them. If anyone asks, that's your cover. Is that clear?"

"How do I get this through customs?" Garner said as he lifted the Beretta from his shoulder holster.

"You won't need it."

"I'm taking it with me."

"You won't need it."

"Without the Beretta, Frank Vulcek doesn't go to Prague."

Arthur sighed a breath of resignation. "We'll meet you at the terminal and run you around security. When you arrive in Prague, look for a small man in customs with a big nose. His name is Dubskij, and he'll be wearing a nametag. Put some money in your passport when you hand it over. You will have no trouble."

"What about the contact?" asked Garner.

"We'll have a couple men on you from the moment you arrive in Prague. They'll follow you and watch the microfilm exchange hands."

"Is the contact the man you're after?"

"Chances are he'll deliver it higher up. We'll take care of everything. Don't worry, we'll be watching you like a hawk."

"Like Clarence watches me?"

142

Arthur did not appreciate the sarcasm. "Mr. Garner, Clarence is not a hawk. He's a pigeon. The people who'll be watching you in Prague are professionals, something Clarence will never become."

"And that's it?"

"That's it."

"What about Trudi?"

"What about her?"

"I want to see her before I leave."

"You are to contact no one between now and when you leave. Is that clear?"

"I want to see Trudi."

"She's in Fulda today and tomorrow. She has a cover, too, you know. You ought to be able to get along without her for a few days."

Garner thought Trudi would have something further to do with the Prague assignment, but he guessed wrong.

"Two days from now, you're a free man."

"Incidentally," said Garner. "Toller is paying fifty thousand for the information."

Arthur stirred. "So, he was planning on selling the name. Dollars or Marks?"

"One or the other. What do I do with it?"

Arthur smiled. "Consider it a bonus." He stepped out of the car and offered a hand. "Good luck."

Arthur watched as Garner drove away, then returned to his car where Clarence was waiting for him.

"Everything go all right?" asked Clarence.

"Better than I expected. Give me an update on Trudi."

"She crossed the East German border two hours ago. She should be in Dresden by now."

"Good, very good," said Arthur.

"Everything's in order. I don't think we have to worry about her. She's very capable."

Arthur nodded. "Phillip Garner is capable, too, quite capable. The man amazes me." Arthur started the Volvo and drove off.

CHAPTER EIGHTEEN

One of Arthur's men met Garner at the airport and helped him circumvent security so he could carry the weapon with him. He entered the aircraft with the ease and comfort of a man on a business trip for which he had travel papers, and that was how he was now looking at himself.

He remembered his first plane flight as Frank Vulcek, when he had crossed the Atlantic. The apprehension then was justified, but now things were different. The tough part was over. All he had to do now was deliver the microfilm to the contact in Prague, and the next day he would be back in Germany.

He searched the briefcase lining and found the microfilm, like Arthur said, a fine, black strip no larger than a small band aid. It matched the black lining in color, and even if anyone had discovered the hiding place, one would have had to search, as Garner had, before he spotted it. He also had packed a change of clothes in the case, exactly as Farrington had instructed.

All along, Garner believed anybody could have delivered the microfilm, but now that he understood the relationship between Vulcek and Toller, he also understood that only a Vulcek look-alike could carry out the assignment. The contact in Prague as it turned out, was somebody he was supposed to know, so another agent wouldn't have worked out.

He was concerned about Trudi. Her disappearance from his life was all too sudden. Perhaps he was selfish. He wanted to see her again before he left for Prague, but Arthur was against it. Once he returned, however, Arthur had no power over him.

He eased back in his seat, his thoughts on making love to her. She had become very special, and the thought of leaving her behind wasn't sitting well with him.

The Prague Double

The intercom inside the aircraft came on and a stewardess announced in Czech that they would soon be landing at Ruzyne Airport in Prague. He understood a lot of the Czech since it was similar to Russian.

Russian? That was another unanswered question. So far, he had not even had to use a word of it, yet that was another facet the men in Langley had been emphatic about. It was imperative that the double for Frank Vulcek needed to speak Russian. He reasoned that the possibility existed that he might run across a person who knew that Vulcek spoke Russian. If he couldn't respond in that language, his role might have been compromised.

Suddenly, the lights of the airport were flashing by his window, and seconds later, he felt the wheels hit the runway.

Ten minutes later he descended the ladder to the tarmac and marveled at the simplicity of the airport terminal. It was small but clean and well lit like any European airport. The air was fresh and cool, but not cold.

He was feeling good. The assignment was almost over, and he had not really contemplated what he would do with the money the CIA was giving him or the money Toller was paying. He might invest in a new plane.

In the distance, several small aircraft were parked on the tarmac, and suddenly the urge to get back into the pilot seat grabbed at him.

He entered the terminal and followed the crowd of passengers down a corridor to the customs area. Three booths were now ahead of him, but none of the men in them resembled Dubskij, the customs official Arthur had told him to locate. He lagged behind, letting other passengers slip ahead. Several other officials in dark colored uniforms were on the far side of the booths, but none of them was Dubskij. A sense of panic struck him. There was no way he could get the Beretta past any of these customs men if he were searched.

"*Idi, idi,*" he heard someone prod from behind him. He was only two people away from being searched, and the little wiry man with the big nose was nowhere in sight.

Abruptly, a man grabbed his arm. "Mister Vulcek, come with me please."

It was Dubskij!

He followed the man around the customs agents without bother, and in seconds he was led to an outside door. After he slipped a few bills into the man's hand, he received a pleasant nod in return and suddenly found himself at a taxi stand.

He stood for a moment in the open air letting himself relax when a taxi driver came up to him. "Taxi?"

"Yes," answered Garner. "Tatran Hotel."

"*Ruzumite Cesky?*" he asked in Czech.

"*Nyet,*" Garner answered in Russian.

"*Ah, Russkij, khorosho. Ya takzhe.*" The cabby was now talking in Russian. "*U vas bagazhi?*"

"No, just my briefcase."

Garner followed the man to his cab. He was short and stocky with a bushy mustache and heavy black eyebrows like Brezhnev.

He looked every bit a cab driver, complete with a black cap and jacket that matched the color of his taxi.

"Tatran Hotel," the cabby repeated as he nosed the taxi out into traffic. "Very old hotel on Vaclavske Namesti in Stara Mesto, old Prague. You will like it very much. First trip to Prague?"

His Russian was good, but he had a slight accent. This was Garner's first trip, but obviously Frank Vulcek had visited the city before. "No. I've been here before," he finally answered."

"Business trip?"

"I'm a sales representative for crystal glassware." The cabby started ambling on about glassware, stating he himself had purchased some fine Rosenthal for his wife, and then he talked at length about the abundance of Bohemian crystal for which Prague was famous.

Then his jabbering turned to the various sights they were now passing as the taxi whipped along the highway into Prague. He advised Garner to visit the Karlovy Vary, a health spa located on the Tepla River some distance from Prague. He also recommended a tour to the zoological gardens and a visit to the Hradcany Hill, the President's Palace. He had virtually become a tour guide for Garner.

The cab suddenly seemed to plunge into the city, and soon they were crossing the Jiroskuv Bridge. "The new part of town is on the right," said the cabby, "The old part is on the left. We go left."

Garner marveled at the gothic and baroque architecture of the massive and bulky buildings. The sidewalks were not nearly as crowded with people as he expected, but after all, it was night. Trolley cars seemed to be in view no matter where he looked.

The streets were not noisy like in Frankfurt at midnight, and there was a feeling of a slower, even pace about the city, which was very agreeable to him.

The driver swung left onto Vaclavske Namesti and sped down the cobblestone street alongside a trolley with the number 23 on it. "Construction," he said as he wove around some barricades. "Two months from now, there will be no street cars on this street. We're expanding the Metro."

Garner saw the Tatran Hotel sign, and in seconds, the driver whirled around and stopped in front.

Garner paid the man and added a fair tip.

The Tatran was located almost in the heart of the old part of the city. Garner had memorized a few streets of the city the night before, but the view he was now taking in was spectacular. Every building in this part of town dated back five hundred years or more.

He entered the Hotel to what looked like a club more than a lobby. A few people were sitting at the bar and a couple tables were occupied, but it was quiet.

He spotted the check-in counter off to the side where an older gent, whose white hair consisted of a few tufts on each side of his head, was reading a newspaper. "I need a room," Garner said in Russian.

"Name please?" the man responded in Russian.

"Frank Vulcek."

The old man ran down a list of names in front of him.

"*Tak i nyits*," he said in Czech. He looked up at Garner. "*Ruzumite Cesky?*"

"*Nein, Ich kann nicht*," answered Garner. He realized he answered in German.

Now the old gent answered in perfect German. "*Das ist Schade.*" *That's too bad.* He paused. "*Ihr Nahme stent hier nicht.*" *Your name isn't here.*

Delray K. Dvoracek

Garner reverted to German. "I don't have a reservation."

A smile sneaked into his wrinkled face. "Ah. That's why." He produced a form and had Garner sign his name.

"Funny you don't speak Czech," mumbled the old man again. "You have a Czech name. Everybody with a Czech name should speak Czech." The man chuckled with his own sense of humor and handed over a key. "Room 218."

Garner walked up the spiral staircase to the second floor and found his room. It was a little on the small side and far from plush, but it was comfortable. He removed his coat and sat on the edge of the bed, then retrieved the Beretta and shoulder holster from his briefcase and stuffed it under his pillow.

While he showered, his mind was on the two men who were supposed to be tailing him when he delivered the microfilm in the morning. He hoped they were better at their work than Clarence, but if they weren't, that was their problem.

He never realized how tired he was, and within minutes of hitting the pillow, he was out.

* * *

He woke to the sound of a voice. His eyes were open, his mind alert, and when he heard a key slip into the door, he quickly had the Beretta in his hand. When an elderly lady dressed in white appeared, he shoved the Beretta under the covers.

She stared at him a moment, then began jabbering in Czech and grabbed a do-not-disturb sign off the inside door handle and stuck it on the outside. She was still chatting in a not too friendly voice when she slammed the door shut.

Thirty minutes later he was in the dining area where he ordered breakfast, and a half hour after that, he was headed in the direction of the Karlovy Most. He had memorized, he thought, a way to the bridge, but the tall baroque buildings and their picturesque fronts intrigued him, and he found himself wandering through narrow passageways where only pedestrians were allowed.

Every street, it seemed, was layered with cobblestone, and the sidewalks, barely wide enough for two people to pass, looked as if they were terrazzo, and they were angled heavily toward the street, which gave him the feeling of walking with a limp.

Every other shop seemed to have Bohemian glassware displayed in their windows, and leather goods and doll puppets as well as a variety of clothing stores fronted the narrow street.

As he ambled along, he guessed whoever he was supposed to contact was probably observing him right now. Equally amusing, two of Farrington's men were also supposed to be watching him.

People were hustling in every direction, a complete turn-about of the night before, and in this area, no trolleys, cars or buses were allowed, and only occasionally did he see a taxi.

At a corner kiosk, he stopped to examine the newspapers. Czech newspapers, Pravda and Zvesda and other Russian newspapers, and a few East German papers heaped the racks, but the Frankfurter Zeitung was obviously missing.

He purchased the Berliner and only glanced at the headlines, then stuck the paper under his arm and moved on.

The cobble way opened to the Old Town square where the Town Hall and its miniature statuettes adorned an age-old clock. One of the statues was the grim reaper. Garner hoped that the carving was not an omen.

He crossed the square past the Tyn Church into another maze of winding streets and walked on until he reached the Bridge Tower of the Karlovy Bridge. The Vltava River in all its quiet-flowing luster separated the Old Town area from the quarters on the far side. Above, in the distance, the picturesque President's Palace on Hradcany Hill stood ominously like some guardian of the city. He was taken in by the spectacular view, and for a few moments, he even forgot why he was here.

He passed under the arch of the east tower and descended a set of cement stairs off to his right to a walkway below. Two long benches faced the Vltava where a few people were sitting quietly enjoying the sunshine of the morning.

He cautiously approached, carefully scrutinizing the faces of those who occupied the seats. Toller said he would know the contact, but of course, he was talking about Vulcek. Vulcek would know. Garner did not recognize any of them from the photos he had reviewed in Langley.

He chose the end of a bench, sat down and crossed a leg. The brick arcades that supported the upper structure of the cobblestone bridge must have been an architectural marvel when they were constructed. Statues hovered menacingly every so many feet on this side.

Toller was right when he told him to enjoy the President's Palace across the way. Spires poked up here and there, and the colors of the houses below with their red roofs offered a splendor he had never experienced.

A few boats moved lazily up and down river, but now Garner's attention focused on a man coming down the cement steps from the tower. He walked slowly in Garner's direction but passed by and disappeared into a shopping area beyond.

A man sitting off to his left pulled a candy bar or something from his pocket, and after he broke off a chunk and threw it in his mouth, he got up and left. The only other person on the bench now was a lady with a buggy in front of her. Inside of a few minutes, she, too, got up, and, pushing the buggy, headed off along the riverfront.

A small crowd of people on the bridge were now hurrying in this direction from the far side. In the lead was a younger woman heading his way, but it was not until she escaped the bridge wall that Garner noticed the two small children at her side. The last to cross in this small group was an older man, his cane clicking methodically against the cement as he made his way, every step seeming to be an effort.

The woman and two children passed on under the tower, but the older man with the cane was now holding the handrail as he labored down the steps. He was coming toward Garner, but then at the last moment, he walked around the bench and stopped.

Garner again was searching the bridge, and then a strange silence overtook him. The man who had been walking with the cane was to his left and behind him standing perfectly still.

He was not near as old as Garner originally thought. He had thick, curly brown hair and a bushy mustache, and when he gave a casual glance in Garner's direction, it was obvious that he had a glass eye. It did not coordinate with the other.

He suddenly spoke in perfect German, his gaze overlooking the Vltava. "The view from here is beautiful, is it not?"

The man maneuvered around the end of the bench with some effort and sat a few feet away from Garner. He loosened the belt from his tan coat and moved a hand down to his knee where he unsnapped a brace hidden by his pants. He lifted his leg and swung it backwards into a normal sitting position.

Garner's gaze was on the Vltava, but his mind was working on the face of the individual, his thoughts racing through the photos he had viewed back at the CIA complex.

"You always liked Prague, didn't you, Frank?" The curly haired man was smiling, his bad eye motionless, his good eye wandering.

Garner pressed his memory. He mentally removed the man's mustache, cropped the hair, and imagined both eyes coordinated. He should know him and cursed himself that he could not place the man.

"Come on, Frank, how could you forget all those good times in Hamburg? Or is it the eye that disturbs you. Or my wooden leg?"

Hamburg! Garner's mind triggered with the mention of the city. "Eric," he said casually. Garner remembered the photo-graph, and the information on the man was slowly formulating. Vulcek had pulled Eric Kopal from a wrecked car in Hamburg three years ago. The man was a freelancer, a man who had many contacts, some good, some bad.

"I never heard what happened to you after the accident," Garner finally said.

Eric smiled and looked directly at Garner. "I didn't know for sure it was you. These damn cars did a number on both of us, didn't they?"

Garner's mind whirled. Eric knew Vulcek had had a car accident!

"I never had a chance to thank you for saving my life," offered Eric. "But then, I guess I became rather useless." He tapped the cane against the wooden leg.

"I'm sorry, Eric."

Eric smiled. "No need to be. The hazards of our profession." He chuckled genuinely "I heard you had to get a new voice box. They patched you up pretty well, considering. At least you've got both eyes and legs."

Eric's gaze was out over the Vltava again. "I've always liked Prague. I should visit more often." He tapped his cane on the cement. "This is my favorite spot. Beautiful view from here."

The man seemed to be searching for conversation. Garner tried to accommodate him. "How's it going for you?"

"I don't work much anymore. I pick up a job here and there, those that I can handle. It isn't like the good old days."

Garner didn't know how to respond.

Eric hunched his shoulders, still facing the Vltava. "It's a living." He was silent for a bit, and then, "I never figured you to change sides, Frank. I always thought you were legit."

The comment was delivered as if Eric believed Frank Vulcek had always been on the side of the CIA. Garner's mind whirled. Was Vulcek a double agent or not?

"Times change a man," Garner replied with what he considered an appropriate answer.

Eric nodded and leaned on his cane. A breeze came up whipping his curly locks of hair. "Have you got the microfilm with you?"

"Have you got the money?"

Eric chuckled. "Frank, you know I'm not the accountant." He reached into his pocket and came up with a slip of paper that had an address written on it.

"Tonight at ten."

Garner studied the address. "I don't know where this is."

Eric pointed across the Vltava to his left. "It's beyond the Strahov Stadium on the hill. Any taxi driver will find it easily. Brodik will be with me. Do you know him?"

"No."

"He's the money man, but watch him." His one eye floated as he looked at Garner. "You know what I mean."

Garner guessed what he meant.

"Until tonight, then," said Eric. He moved his wooden leg

146

forward, notched the brace in place and struggled to his feet. "It's a beautiful day," he said as a warm smile covered his face. He walked off, his cane clicking with each limping step.

Garner watched as Eric once again struggled his way up the cement steps to the Karlovy Bridge and started across. The tapping of his cane slowly disappeared, and after another minute or so, he was swallowed up in the crowd of people on the bridge.

Garner could not help but feel pity for the man. He did not even know him, but in the short few minutes he had spent with him, he somehow thought he had just met the only real friend Vulcek ever had.

Garner walked up the steps to the bridge tower where he thought he heard a Dixieland band playing. Strangely enough, five men were off to one side a quarter of the way across the bridge. A trumpet and tuba were blaring away, and then a banjo joined in. In the background was a rolling sound like a drum, and then a clarinet took over the lead.

They were good, and while he listened, he spotted Eric in the crowd. He, too, was listening to the music, and then he moved on. Garner headed back into the narrow streets of the old part of the city, and soon the rhythmic sound of the band faded. All the way back to the hotel, his mind was on the name *Brodik*. He didn't recognize the name, and it was quite possible that Vulcek didn't know him either.

At the hotel entrance, he stopped and glanced about him somehow expecting one of Farrington's men to show up. He whiled away some boring hours in the club of the hotel and spent part of the day walking the streets nearby, fretting, and hoping someone would contact him, but no one did.

CHAPTER NINETEEN

It was 9:30 that night when Garner hailed a taxi in front of the Tatran. The route took him back across the Jiroskuv Bridge into the southern section of Malo Strana. The driver left the main road, and now the wheels of the taxi rattled on the cobblestone. The driver wound his way through a maze of streets in this older section of the city, climbing upwards around a series of sharp curves until he reached the top. Moments later, they drove past the entrance of the Strahov Stadium, a massive structure that could seat a quarter of a million people.

No activities were going on. At the next corner, the driver paralleled the north portion of the stadium. After a half kilometer, he halted at an intersection dimly lit by a single lamppost.

Garner paid the driver and felt a sudden loneliness as he watched the taxi drive off. A few homes and some shops lined the streets, but their doors were closed and he could see no lights. Behind him, the nightglow of the city lights streamed upwards, but here, it was as close to dark as one could find.

A car was parked along the sidewalk, but no one was inside.

A set of car lights beamed on him coming from the same direction he had arrived a minute before. Before the vehicle reached the intersection, it turned off and labored its way up a hillside out of earshot.

He looked around, strangely caught up by the shadows invading every building and doorway. The chimes of a bell sounded from a long distance away, and then another bell tolling ten o'clock resounded from somewhere to the north.

When his eyes adjusted, he noticed a small black sedan parked in the shadows of a huge overhanging tree a half block away. He wasn't sure whether the vehicle had driven up while he was listening to the bells or whether it had been parked there all along.

This area was remote, and now the words of caution, which Eric Kopal had given him, were firmly in his mind. *Watch out for Brodik.* He could feel the weight of the shoulder holster under his jacket, which gave him a sense of reassurance.

A car door thumped shut, and now a tall man was walking toward him in the shadows. He was wearing a light raincoat but had both hands exposed when he stopped only a few yards away from Garner.

Garner felt his nerves beating at his chest. "Brodik?"

"Yes," answered the man. "Have you got it with you?" He spoke in English, but with a heavy accent.

Garner strained to see the man's face, but it was too dark. "I've got it," he answered. "Have you got the money?"

The man pulled an envelope from his raincoat and handed it over. Garner lifted the flap and saw that it was filled with bills.

Garner handed him a small envelope that contained the microfilm. The man took the film from the envelope, then produced a small flashlight and examined it for a few moments.

He put the film back in the envelope and stuffed in his coat pocket. Then, unexpectedly, the man flashed the light across Garner's eyes, blinding him momentarily.

"Thank you, Mr. Vulcek," he said. "And now I'll take the money back." Garner's eyes cleared to see a pistol with a silencer pointed at him.

Adrenaline raced through his veins, and when two shots rang out, he fell to his knees, shaking, but he was alive! Brodik was carrying a silencer, yet Garner had heard loud gun fire. Suddenly the figure in front of him slumped forward face down on the cobble street. His weapon clattered against the stones and came to a rest a few feet from Garner.

The lights of a car down the street were suddenly on as the vehicle raced forward and came to a halt next to Garner and the dead man. Garner had his Beretta aimed at the shadowed man in the driver's seat, but when the man stepped out, he recognized the bulky figure.

"Help me get him inside!" Eric commanded. In seconds they

grabbed the man by the arms and feet and shoved him into the back seat.

The motor roared as Eric sped along, maneuvering the vehicle around curves with the finesse of an experienced racecar driver. Garner stared blindly ahead, confused, shocked by what had happened.

At an intersection, Eric turned the lights out, and without braking the vehicle, he swerved down a steep hill, jammed on the brakes and slid to a stop.

Above on the main road, another vehicle sped by, and when it was out of sight, Eric spun the car around, drove back up the incline and headed the opposite direction.

"You were being tailed," he said.

Garner guessed the other vehicle was assigned by Farrington, but he remained silent. "I don't understand. What the hell's going on?"

"I had an idea Brodik was going to kill you. The son-of-a-bitch." The bitterness charged out of the man, not at all like the person Garner had spoken to that morning.

"I don't understand," said Garner. "Whose side are you on?"

"What difference does it make? He's dead now. Does he have the microfilm?"

"Yes."

"Get it."

Garner reached over the seat, searched the man's pocket and found the envelope. "Who was he?"

"The worst kind. Worse than a thief among thieves. For over a year now, I have been working with the bastard. Whenever a sizeable amount of cash was involved, he would make the exchange, then kill the victim and pocket the money."

"Why did you work with him if you hated him so much?"

Eric slapped a hand against his wooden leg. "I told you. One has to make a living. I still have some ethics about my work, but Brodik had no respect for human life, no respect for anything. That's why I killed him. Besides, I owed it to you, whoever you are."

Eric glanced at Garner, and then his eyes were on the road again. "I know you aren't Frank Vulcek," he said. "You made too many mistakes. The first one was this morning when you didn't offer to shake my hand. Frank would have, but I forgave that incident, thinking perhaps the car accident might have given you some other problems. You also asked me where the Strahov Stadium was located. Frank would have known.

"However, tonight I knew for sure you weren't Frank. Frank would have had a gun pointed at Brodik first. You were not cautious enough, even though I gave you a warning."

Garner resigned himself to his discovery, yet he felt no fear of the man.

"And the final error," went on Eric. "No one ever tailed Frank. He could take care of himself."

"You saved my life and you don't even know who I am."

"I don't want to know what game you're playing. I'm just paying back the favor I owe Frank. That's all."

Eric slowed the car and turned off onto a gravel road. After a few kilometers, he dipped over a hill and came to a stop.

"Let's get rid of him," he said.

Garner opened the car door and dragged the man from the back seat. Eric came around to his side, hobbling, laboring without his cane, and helped Garner with the body. They carried Brodik through the ditch to a steep embankment where Eric rolled Brodik's body over the side, and a few seconds later, Garner heard his body thump in the brush below.

Eric hobbled back to the vehicle. "It'll be sometime before Brodik is reported missing, and even then, he won't be found for a few days."

Eric turned the car around and headed back to the highway. When they came over a crest in the road, the nightlights of Prague down below loomed magnificently.

Garner was confused by the man sitting next to him, wondering how his relationship with Eric would end.

They crossed the Vltava and passed through the peninsula of Holesovice and then crossed the river again.

Garner wasn't exactly sure where they were, but now the old part of the city was recognizable. Eric turned off the main road onto a narrow street, drove a few blocks to an intersection and came to a stop.

"I've got the microfilm and you've got your money," said Eric. He pointed ahead. "Your hotel is three blocks that way. Just follow the trolley tracks."

Eric breathed deeply and blew out some air. "What really happened to Frank?"

"He was killed in a car accident. I was hired to take his place because I look like him."

Eric nodded. "When I first saw you, you fooled me. Who are you working for? The CIA or the KGB?

"The CIA. Why do you ask?"

Eric chuckled. "The name on this microfilm is headed for the KGB. Didn't you know that?"

"We suspected it might be."

"Who's tailing you?"

"I don't know for sure. I assume someone from the CIA."

"Why are they following you?"

"They want to know where this film ends up."

Eric laughed again. "Tell them Anton Brodik. They'll know him."

"But you're going to deliver the film higher up."

"Of course. Sorry I can't tell you who. That's part of my contract. I may be working for the other side, but I made a deal, and my word is good."

"You killed Brodik."

"He's expendable. Nobody liked him, so I'll make up an excuse tonight when I deliver the information."

Garner grabbed the door handle and then turned to Eric again. "You knew Frank well. Do you think he would ever sell out?"

Eric grunted. "No. He may not have been very orthodox in his methods, but he wouldn't switch sides. I don't know what you're up to, and I don't really want to know how you got raked into this mess, but these are big boys you're fooling around with. You realize that, don't you?"

Eric had hit it on the head. "Do you know a man named Manfried Toller?"

152

Eric raised an eyebrow. "Who do you think I'm working for?"

Garner's face froze.

"He's another Brodik," said Eric. "A parasite with an obsession to possess everything and everyone. Watch out for him."

Eric didn't have to tell him that. Garner stepped from the car and closed the door. For the first time since the Prague assignment began, his conscience was bothering him. Eric Kopal had just saved his life, and now he had just handed him a piece of microfilm with worthless information.

Garner bent down through the window. "Eric, once you pass on the microfilm, get out as soon as you can."

"I intend to."

"I mean, disappear immediately. You gave me a warning, and I'm returning the favor."

Suddenly, the money in the envelope meant nothing to Garner, and he threw it in the front seat of the car. "Take it. I don't want it." He turned and walked off in the direction of the hotel.

"Wait!" he heard Eric holler, but he kept walking and had gone a half block before he finally heard Eric's vehicle speed away.

As far as he was concerned, he had delivered the microfilm, and the Prague assignment was over.

CHAPTER TWENTY

It was six in the morning when Garner approached the front desk carrying his briefcase. His flight from the Ruzyne airport terminal was at 9:15, so he had plenty of time.

The same old gent, who initially checked him in, was behind the counter and using the phone, so Garner casually looked about the lobby and waited patiently for him to finish. Only a handful of people were present. Though he was being as unobtrusive as possible, his gaze kept coming back to a man sitting in a corner reading a newspaper. Garner looked away, but in a mirror on the opposite wall, he saw the man's reflection and he was looking back at Garner. When Garner turned around, the man buried himself in the newspaper once again. If he was one of Arthur's tails, he should be following Eric Kopal, Garner was thinking.

He happened to looked up at the key box to his room and saw a slip of paper in it.

The old gent finished his phone call and turned to Garner. "May I help you?"

"There's a message in my box."

The man handed it over, and after Garner read the message, he glanced about the room again. The man behind the newspaper was gone. Garner reread the contents of the message, then looked up. "I'm staying," he said to the old man.

"What's that?" The old man apparently didn't understand him.

Garner's mind was working furiously reviewing the contents of the note. He changed his mind. "I'm leaving."

"Very well. I thought you said you were staying."

The old man began searching through a file just as the phone rang. As he answered it, Garner took the note out of his pocket and reread it.

"Herr Vulcek?"

"What?" When Garner looked up, the clerk handed him the phone. Garner wondered who would call him and know him by the name *Vulcek*.

"*Hier spricht Vulcek*," he said in German. He listened closely, then looked through the front window of the hotel and spotted the gray sedan along the curb. He hung up the receiver and turned to the clerk. "I'm staying."

"I beg your pardon?"

"I said, I'm staying."

"Oh," responded the man. "For a moment I thought you said you were staying."

"I *am* staying!" he practically shouted, and as he looked around, those few people in the lobby were staring at him. He hurried out of the hotel onto the street and went directly to the gray sedan.

The door opened, and to Garner's surprise, the man behind the wheel had heavy black eyebrows and a black bushy mustache. He was the taxi driver, who had given him a ride from the airport to the Tatran Hotel the day before.

"Hello, Mr. Vulcek. Or do you prefer Mr. Garner?" he asked in accented English. Garner remained outside the vehicle, confident but curious. "Who are you?"

"Jan Bertok. Please get in. I work for Farrington."

"How do I know for sure?"

"We have been watching you since you arrived."

"Is that right?" snarled Garner. He tested the man. "Where's Farrington now?"

"I suppose in his office in Frankfurt," came the matter-of-fact response.

"Who works for Farrington?"

"Clarence."

"Describe him."

"About my age, gray hair, mustache."

"How did Clarence break his finger?"

"I didn't know he broke a finger, but I heard you shot him in the leg."

That amused Garner. When he entered the car, he noticed the

man in the back seat was the same person who had been reading the newspaper in the hotel.

"This is Emil Prazak, my partner," said Jan. Emil reached a hand across the seat. Garner hesitated, then shook it. The man had curly hair, thick like Eric Kopal's, but his eyes were very dark, sunken almost.

"And as I said, I am Jan Bertok." He too offered a hand. "You had a little trouble last night."

"Did you see the action?" asked Garner.

"We saw the man fall to the pavement. Did you kill him?"

"No. Eric Kopal did. Do you know Eric?"

"Yes. Who was the victim?"

"His name was Anton Brodik. Do you know him?"

"That bastard. So, he's back in Prague." Jan gave a chuckle.

"Permanently it appears." His thoughts came back to Eric Kopal. "Why would Eric shoot Brodik?"

Garner quickly briefed the two men on what he had learned, that Vulcek had evidently known Kopal in Hamburg, and he told them that Eric knew he wasn't Frank Vulcek. The two were both surprised when he told them he had given Eric the fifty thousand in cash.

"What the hell," Garner said. "He saved my life. That's worth fifty thousand, don't you think?"

Jan tapped his ring finger impatiently against the steering wheel. "We were hoping Eric Kopal might lead us to the eventual destination of the film."

"You don't know where the film went?" Garner asked.

Jan threw his hands up. "How could we. You and Eric disappeared. We couldn't keep up with you."

Garner was dumbfounded. First Clarence hadn't been able to tail him properly in Frankfurt, and now these two men had failed to trace the microfilm to its final destination. He had thought maybe the two might pick up Eric's trail when he dropped him off last night, but of course, they didn't know when or where Garner would show up.

"We didn't expect to chase you all over Prague," Jan apologized. He was direct, angered with himself. "We were not prepared for that, especially with Eric driving. He hasn't been working much lately, but it does not surprise me he was your contact, since he apparently knew Vulcek. You said he recognized you?"

"I said he knew I wasn't Vulcek. He doesn't know who I am, and he didn't ask."

Jan gritted his teeth and slapped his forehead. He was suddenly jabbering to Emil in the back seat in Czech. Then his attention was back on Garner. "Oi, oi. Arthur will not like this. We've lost him. We do not know where the microfilm went."

"I can tell you where to find Eric," said Garner.

Jan and Emil both raised their eyebrows.

Garner handed over the note the clerk had given him. On it was an address where Eric had asked Garner to meet him at ten o'clock tonight.

The two men were talking excitedly in Czech again.

"Ah, this is excellent!" exclaimed Jan. "This address is in the north of the city, somewhere around Prosek. You meet him tonight and we will cover you. This may still lead us to the final destination of the microfilm."

"Uh-uh," said Garner. "You two go see him. I've got a plane to catch."

Jan's expression didn't change. "And how do you expect to get out of the country without your passport?"

"I have a passport," said Garner. He flipped open his briefcase and rummaged through it, then searched his pockets.

Jan hunched his shoulders. "We took the liberty of removing it from your briefcase yesterday when you were gone."

"Why?" Garner spit out.

"Insurance, you might say. We did not want you to leave until we traced the microfilm."

"Arthur said when I delivered the film, I could fly back to Germany. I delivered it."

"But unfortunately, Arthur is not here," said Jan.

Garner turned his gaze to Emil in the back seat. He just grinned.

"It is a very simple matter," continued Jan. "You meet Eric Kopal tonight, we follow you, tomorrow you go home. Okay?"

Garner was trapped, and he knew it. This Prague assignment was becoming a never-ending game.

CHAPTER TWENTY ONE

That night, a taxi dropped Garner off under a lamp pole a few blocks from where he was supposed to meet Eric Kopal. He swore silently as the taxi disappeared into the dark. He swore because he had looked into the key box and found the note. He swore because Jan Bertok and Emil Prazak had sneaked into his room the night before and taken his passport. He swore because right now he would be in Germany if he had been wiser, more careful.

The day had given him time to reflect. If nothing else, he almost felt he owed it to Eric to meet him. Eric was a man of integrity, and so far, he was the only person who had been straight with him during this entire ordeal.

He checked his watch. He was twenty minutes early. Tonight he would be cautious. He would locate the address and stake out the meeting place for himself.

He wondered why Eric wanted to see him and hoped that he simply wanted to return the money. He wouldn't take it back, but then, the main reason he was even here was so Jan and Emil might receive a lead concerning where the microfilm went.

As he crossed the street, the heavy odor of chemicals penetrated the night air. Trudi's cover had something to do with a chemical factory in Fulda, he recollected. Some coincidence.

Some distance away, a large building with a row of glass-paned windows was glowing at this late hour. A constant hum came from the factory, but as Garner moved on, the hum began to fade into the night. He guessed he was in an industrial district of some sort.

Garner was now walking along a series of wooden buildings, boarded-up warehouses, he surmised. A high, wooden fence began at the end of the buildings and ran the length of the block.

He located a gate on which the address he was seeking was written in crude letters. This whole area was remote, dark, isolated like the meeting place the night before.

The only sense of relief he felt was that Jan Bertok and Emil Prazak were in the near vicinity, or at least he hoped they were. Two cars were parked on the opposite side of the street, but neither was gray in color like Jan's auto.

He pulled the Beretta from its place and held the gun firmly, then pushed the wooden gate open and slipped inside. To his surprise, a junkyard full of cars lay before him. Metal heaps sprawled haphazardly as far as he could see, but a pathway led straight ahead.

The only thing he could hear now was the faint hum coming from that same distant factory. On the far side of the lot above the fence, a faint glow of lights shown from some other building.

Then suddenly in the building off to his left, a door opened and a shadowed figure appeared. Garner knew it was not Eric. He raised his gun.

"Mr. Vulcek," he heard the man say. "Please drop your weapon and step forward." There was no mistaking the Slavic accent attached to the man's broken English.

"Drop it," repeated the man, "or Sergei will drop it for you."

Garner stiffened with the command. Sergei? Was there someone else in the lot? And then from somewhere behind him, he heard the distinct click of a hammer being pulled back on a revolver.

"*Brosij!*" came the command from behind him. A wave of nausea ran up the back of Garner's throat. The man had told him to throw down his weapon, and the command came in Russian!

Fear shook its way through Garner's system as he dropped the Beretta. Immediately, a man approached. He towered over Garner and looked as wide as a bull at the shoulders. He had tiny eyes, black straight hair and a bulbous nose pressed into a fat grinning face, all definite Mongolian features.

The giant grunted and jabbed Garner in the back with his revolver. As Garner moved toward the figure in the doorway, he could see the reflection of light bounce off his round glasses, and in his hand he was holding what looked like a Luger.

"Come in," the little man commanded, but Garner hesitated too long. The Mongolian jammed the gun into his back sending a stabbing pain between his shoulder blades.

They led him up a flight of wooden steps to a dimly lit hallway. A door slightly ajar at the end of the hall was the source of light, and when Garner entered, he gasped. Eric Kopal was strapped to a chair, his face mercilessly beaten bloody. His glass eye was flipped in the socket so only the white showed. On the floor next to the chair lay his wooden leg, leaving his one empty pant leg dangling grotesquely over the edge of the seat.

"My god!" said Garner. He lifted Eric's head and brushed the man's hair back.

Eric could barely see. "I'm sorry," he said weakly. "They made me tell where you were."

Garner whirled around at the little man. "You son-of-a..."

The Mongolian slammed a fist into Garner's stomach before he could finish, and as he doubled over, a knee smashed against his face. He reeled and fell to the floor, shaking, gasping for air.

The little man was right in Eric's face. "Now," he said to Eric. "Perhaps you will talk or Sergei will make a cripple out of your friend just like you. We could start with his eye, or maybe tear off a leg. All we want is the name."

Garner could not believe the courage that Eric managed to display. He spat and hit the little man squarely on his glasses. The big Mongolian swung at Eric with both hands clasped together. The blow was so fierce, that his head snapped and his glass eye flew from the socket, banged against the wall and rolled to a stop only inches from Garner's face.

The little man jerked Eric up by the hair and leaned in on him. He stopped, startled, then turned to the Mongolian and sneered. "Durak, ty!"

You fool! were the Russian words. The little man shook Eric again and slapped his face a few times, but Eric had passed out.

The little man's attention was now on Garner. He adjusted his glasses and then spoke in slow, chilling words. "There was supposed to be a name on the microfilm, but there was nothing. Perhaps you can tell us the name."

"I don't know what you're talking about," said Garner.

"Come, come," said the man. "We tried to decode the message, but it doesn't break out. Obviously, your people have changed codes. We would like the name of the man."

Garner's heart was beating like he had just run a hundred-yard dash. "I don't know anything about codes. I was just supposed to deliver the microfilm, that's all."

The little man nodded and the Mongolian took over. He kicked Garner so hard in the chest that the pain shot through him like a bolt of lightning. He writhed, gasped for air, jerked his legs, forcing the wind back into his lungs. When it came, the little man was bent over him again.

"The name on the microfilm. I want it."

Garner's breath was practically gone. "For God's sake, I don't know!"

The giant jerked him up by the lapels, and although Garner swung two weak punches, the effort was futile. The man's big hands closed in around his throat choking off his air. His feet dangled helplessly, and he felt as if his eyeballs would pop out of his head.

Then Garner heard the two *zip-zip* sounds, and the hands around his throat slackened as the giant fell forward and slammed to the floor. Garner saw the two bloody bullet holes in the middle of his back.

Garner wavered and fell against the wall as two loud shots rang out. The little man had fired wildly and then disappeared through another door in the room.

Garner, half dazed, searched the Mongolian's pockets and found his Beretta.

"Garner! Are you okay?!" It was Jan's voice coming from the hallway.

"Yes!" hollered Garner. "Get the other one!"

Garner struggled to his feet and stumbled to the doorway where the little man had escaped to a narrow corridor leading to the center of the building. Garner moved as quickly as he could, and when he reached the end of the corridor, he peered around. A bullet splintered the wood near his face.

He heard footsteps running. He dashed across an open space to behind a wooden bench and kept low as he crawled the length of the structure. A door banged off to his right. Garner ran to an open window and looked out. The man was running along an outside catwalk and was no more than thirty feet away when Garner fired. The man yelled when the bullet struck him in the back. His forward motion propelled him over the catwalk, and when the man's body landed, Garner heard the crunch.

By the time Garner made his way to the end of the railing, Jan and Emil had reached the body down below. The man was sprawled like a huge rag doll on the roof of a junked car.

Garner rested for a few moments, letting his body work off the shakes, and then, slowly, he groped his way back along the catwalk. When he reached the room, Jan was untying Eric and Emil was bent over the Mongolian. "This one's dead, too."

"Are you all right?" Jan asked Garner. There was no panic present in his face or his voice.

"I'm all right," said Garner. But he was not all right. He could hardly control his trembling. His stomach ached, and his chest felt as if it had been kicked through his spine.

Jan pulled the remaining ropes off Eric Kopal and stretched him out on the floor. "Let's get out of here," he said.

"Not without Eric!" Garner charged.

"He'll be all right. They will find him."

"We're taking him with us!"

The glares that Jan and Emil gave him did not deter him. Garner grabbed Eric under the arms. "Get his leg!"

He struggled to lift Eric. "Goddammit, help me!"

Jan and Emil stood helplessly by, and finally Jan knelt down and stared into Garner's face. "Phillip, he's dead! Eric's dead!"

Garner shook Eric, and shook him again. Then, realizing that he was gone, he ever so gently laid him back down.

"We've got to get out of here," said Jan." He and Emil hurried out of the room, but Garner stared into the bloody face of Eric, his mind blank.

Jan returned to the room. "Goddammit, Phillip, he's dead! Let's go!" Jan spun Garner around and slapped him across the face, finally shaking Garner's mind back into reality.

The Prague Double

They left the room and scrambled down the stairway to the outside where Emil was waiting with the car.

"Holy Jesus," Garner lamented as they drove off. "Holy Jesus."

* * *

They had already driven several kilometers. Garner was sprawled in the back seat, his body wilted, his strength exhausted. He had been listening to the two men whose conversation was mostly in Czech, and though he didn't understand most of what they were saying, he didn't care. He only wanted to sleep, but his aching body refused him the pleasure.

Jan leaned over the seat. "Why did they kill Eric?"

"They wanted the name on the microfilm."

"There was no name."

"I know. If there had at least been a fictitious name on it, he'd probably still be alive."

"He was working for the other side," Jan said.

"At least he had some integrity."

Emil entered the conversation. "You think we don't?"

"You had me deliver a useless piece of information."

"Delivering useless information in this case turned up some new faces."

"Who were the two men?"

"Russians," said Jan. I didn't know the big guy, but I have seen a photograph of the other man somewhere. We'll identify them."

"Are they KGB?"

"I doubt it. More than likely freelancers. The Russian Security Service doesn't like to do the dirty work. With Brodik out of the way, the Russians must have sent in these two. Judging by their tactics, they obviously were not professionals, but rest assured, they will lead us to a network of individuals we never knew about."

Garner couldn't believe the calmness with which Jan and Emil were reacting. They were talking about espionage as if it were a job on the assembly line of the Ford Motor Company. He wondered what motivated men like these to undertake such blind duty.

163

"What about Vulcek?" asked Garner.

"What about him?"

"Who's side was he on?"

Jan seemed amused. "Ours, of course. He had everything he needed with the CIA. He wouldn't sell out."

"Arthur thought he might."

"Sometimes Arthur can be absolutely brilliant, and other times he's full of shit. He was always looking on the dark side of Vulcek, because he never liked him. No matter what Arthur thought, Vulcek was a good operative."

"But there was fifty thousand Marks involved."

"Was," said Jan.

Garner sat back angered when he thought about the money. Fifty thousand Marks was the equivalent of about twenty-five thousand dollars, and it was probably in the pockets of the two dead men back at the junk lot.

The car turned off the highway and onto a gravel road, and within a few kilometers, they crossed a narrow bridge that led to a small farmhouse. A light shone dimly from within when they pulled to a stop in the yard.

"This is a safe house," said Jan. "It is better if you spend the night here and do not return to the Tatran Hotel. We'll be in contact."

When Garner crawled out of the back seat, the pain in his stomach was wracking. Just as the sedan turned around, Garner hollered, "Hey, goddammit! Where's my passport?"

But Jan kept on going, and when the sound of the engine faded, Garner headed up a stone sidewalk to the farmhouse, his mind refusing to think anymore.

He had absolutely no idea where he was, and he didn't care. He only hoped they had at least left him a bottle. A stiff drink or two after tonight was certainly in order.

When he pushed the door open, two glasses and a bottle were on a small table in the center of the room, and beyond he saw her sitting on a sofa. She was bundled up in a white robe with her feet tucked underneath her.

"Hi, Phillip," she said.

CHAPTER TWENTY TWO

He jerked up out of his sleep, momentarily unaware of his surroundings. The sun shimmered through the window where a gentle breeze lazily shuffled the sheer curtains back and forth like waves lapping on a shore. Trudi was not at his side, but he could hear her rummaging in the kitchen.

He looked out at a farmyard of dilapidated buildings. Broken fence posts and drooping barbed wire lay almost hidden in the tall grass. He marveled at the green countryside of rolling hills, and near the bridge over which he had come the night before, two deer were grazing. Wherever this farm setting was, it was isolated in and among many trees.

A cloud layer was building on the horizon, and now he felt the chilly air, which hinted at an oncoming storm.

He was stiff as he made his way to the bathroom where he showered. A razor and shaving mug were laid out for him. He couldn't remember the last time he had used a brush to work up a lather. He had no marks on his face as he shaved, but the bruises on his rib cage and chest were agonizing reminders of the kicks he had received the night before.

When he finished shaving, Trudi was standing in the doorway.

"Hungry?" she asked.

He laughed. "You know, if we didn't eat together, we wouldn't see much of each other."

"Breakfast will be on the table when you're dressed," she said as she blew him a kiss and headed back to the kitchen.

While dressing, he noticed a couple loose sheets of paper alongside Trudi's purse. Curious, he read the first few lines of the official looking document. It was written in German, and he noted to whom the document was made out.

Delray K. Dvoracek
Gisela Schwaben, Hilfschemiker
Rohrkamp Chemikalien, GmbH.
Dresden, DDR

The named person was granted travel and authorization to attend a chemical conference at the Academy of Sciences in Prague.

His thoughts were back in Germany where he knew Trudi had been working in a chemical firm in Fulda. He found Trudi's passport in her purse and thought nothing more until he read the name under her photo. Gisela Schwaben! Her address was listed in Dresden, which was in East Germany! The reason for Trudi's unexpected arrival in Prague was slowly beginning to unfold.

He returned to the kitchen where he began devouring eggs, bacon and pancakes. As she poured him a cup of coffee, he casually asked, "Have you ever visited Prague before?"

"A couple times," she answered with a huge smile.

"As a member of the Academy of Sciences?"

The question did not jolt her, but her eyes dropped to the table. "No."

"Farrington sent you down here to soften me up for something, didn't he?" She did not respond. "Is that why you made love to me last night? Is that why you made love to me all along?"

Her eyes saddened, but he was not angry with her. If he had learned anything while masquerading as Frank Vulcek, it was that the CIA never let out any more information than necessary. It always came bits at a time.

He wondered what startling piece of information Trudi would supply him with now. He surmised her sudden appearance in Prague held some special purpose, but last night he didn't want to think about it. He hoped that if she had lied to him about the Prague assignment from the beginning, it was because Arthur had instructed her to do so. He could forgive her for that, but he could not forgive Arthur.

What more could happen? He had already run the gauntlet. "I was hired to deliver a piece of worthless microfilm to Prague," he said. "But there's more, isn't there?"

166

The Prague Double

Her face saddened some more. "Phil," she answered softly. "The original Prague assignment hasn't even begun."

Garner was lost for words, his thoughts all shattered.

"We never knew for sure what Frank was involved in from the beginning," she explained.

"I can believe that," he answered sarcastically.

She went on. "Up until a few days ago, none of us thought you would make it this far playing the role of Frank. Originally, we didn't even intend for you to bring anything to Prague. We just told you that to make the assignment look simpler.

"What we really wanted to know was who Frank was dealing with, and you found that out in a hurry. That's when Arthur began to piece everything together. At first he thought Frank was selling information to the other side, but now it appears Frank was trying to penetrate a group of individuals who were affiliated with the KGB. That's the way Frank worked. I didn't even know what he was up to, and I was sleeping with him."

Garner seemed to be looking right through her. "Nine people have already died over a piece of worthless microfilm, and one of them was Frank's best friend, Eric Kopal."

She cast her eyes away from him, and when the hum of an engine suddenly sounded coming up the road, she was at the window looking out. "It's Jan and Emil."

She abruptly left the kitchen and met them at the front door. Jan was carrying a suitcase and set it down when they took places at the table.

"Well, we have everything," said Jan as he patted the suitcase." His eyes were suspiciously on Garner and then back to Trudi. "Did you tell him?"

"Tell me what?" asked Garner.

"He doesn't know," said Emil

Jan was his straightforward self. "We need to get a man out of Prague."

Garner was not at all surprised, and then with all the cynicism he could muster, he said, "Why don't you give him my passport and fly him out."

Delray K. Dvoracek

Jan overlooked the snide remark, but Emil was grinning.

"It's not quite that simple," Jan explained. "First of all, he's Russian, and second he's a nuclear physicist—an expert on multiple warheads."

Garner's eyebrows shot up. "Anti-ballistic missiles?"

"Yes."

Garner's mind was back in Langley reviewing what transpired between him and the Russian, Dr. Kuranik. During their conversation, Kuranik had brought up the topic of missiles, and now Garner understood why, and the reason for his ability to speak Russian was slowly taking shape.

Jan went on. "We suspect this missile expert knows the placement of the Russian's underground track system. That is information we would very much like to have."

"And you need me to get him out?" asked Garner as if he were participating in a normal conversation.

"Of course."

"And of course you don't know his name, and you don't have a face. Only Frank Vulcek could identify him."

Emil grunted his pleasure at the response. "So you know?"

"Arthur told me that, and he also told me that getting the defector out was a dead issue." Garner shook his head. "I somehow knew it wasn't that simple. Just deliver some stuff to Prague, Arthur said. You people don't have a name or a face and neither do I, so how can I help?"

"Well, of course, the *muzhik,* as we call him, knows you, or rather he knows Vulcek," said Jan. Muzhik meant *peasant* in Russian.

He clarified. "That's our nickname for the defector since we don't know his real identity. But we know where to find him."

"At the Academy of Sciences convention."

"Of course," answered Jan.

Garner was amused. *Of course* seemed to be Jan's favorite words. He used them as if they were the solution to any problem, as if getting a defector out of Prague was all in a day's work.

"What makes you think I will help you?" asked Garner.

The Prague Double

Jan leaned forward and clasped his hands. "Well, Arthur asked me to remind you that after the assignment, you are a free man in the United States with many thousands of dollars. That is nice, no? He also said something about cleaning up your pilot background."

"In the United States, we call that blackmail," said Garner.

Jan grinned. "We use the same term in Czechoslovakia. It can be very useful at times."

His answer struck Garner funny, but it did not change the expression on his face. "And of course, getting this... *muzhik* out of Czechoslovakia will be a simple matter."

"No, it is not a simple matter, but things of this nature have been done before. Miss Feldman will get you into the conference. She will be representing the University of Dresden, East Germany, and you will be her escort."

"Her what?" Garner was confused.

"The East Zone doesn't permit any of its scientific members out of the country without an escort." Jan handed Garner a passport, and when Garner opened it, beneath his photo was the name *Nikolai Dovchenko.*

"A perfect forgery," said Jan, "And here are your travel papers as a Major in the Soviet Army. I am told your Russian is very good."

Garner's eyes remained frozen on the photo. "You can't be serious?"

Jan opened the suitcase he had brought, and inside was a Russian officer's uniform, complete with garrison hat and pistol belt.

"Good lord," said Garner as he eyed the red star on the officer's hat. Underneath the dress uniform was a pair of highly polished knee-high riding boots.

"And a set of military sun glasses," said Jan as he emptied the contents of a manila envelope. "Russian Rubels, coins, a pocket knife, key chain and a wallet complete with your credentials and photos of Dovchenko's family." He pointed out a small leather bound manual. "Brush up on your military courtesy."

Jan and Emil were on their feet, their raincoats draped under their arms. "Memorize everything," commanded Jan. "Your family, your unit, your military number. Rest assured, everything is in order.

Delray K. Dvoracek

There is a real Major Dovchenko. We have gone to great pains to detain him for the next week, so no one will suspect you.

"There will be dozens of military men dressed just like you at the conference. All military escorts consider this a rest and relaxation holiday. Do the same and have a good time. It will not be expected of you to participate in anything other than an occasional drink of vodka. Miss Feldman will fill you in on the meetings and itinerary of the conference."

Garner was still holding the tunic and breeches in his hands when Jan and Emil walked out the front door. Any thoughts of protesting the entire caper seemed futile. The two men were as sure of their plan as Garner was of becoming a part of it.

As the car pulled out of the driveway, Garner's eyes were on Trudi. She was willingly a part of the Prague assignment, a factor he had not considered until now.

"You knew all along you would have to do this?"

"Only if you went along with it."

"And you're not afraid?"

"I'm apprehensive, as we all are. No one will belittle you for being afraid. There may be problems, but Jan and Emil are very capable men. And unlike Arthur, they are field agents. They will be in this with us all the way."

"I don't have to go along with this, you know," he said.

"I know."

He turned his attention to the contents of the suitcase once again. Some additional pages were typed in with drawings of the military post Dovchenko was attached to. Detailed information outlined key buildings, streets, strategic points, areas nearby with names of villages and highway numbers. The last few pages contained the rank system of the Red Army, with colored detail of all military insignias and an unending list of military terminology, many that had never been a part of Garner's vocabulary.

"You people are insane," said Garner. "This will never work."

"It must work. The defector is an expert in multiple warheads, and the fact that he is here at the conference indicates that the warheads may be adaptable for chemical and biological warfare."

170

Garner's eyes went wide. "That's against the Geneva Convention."

"The use of it is," answered Trudi. "But not the development of it. We have similar capabilities. Chemical warfare is an insurance factor. It's to be used only as a retaliatory measure. The defector is invaluable."

Garner understood the urgency of the assignment, and he had no doubt that the defector could deliver a severe blow to the Soviet Union's national security and at the same time enhance the national security of the United States.

"You said everything has been worked out," said Garner. "I presume that includes an escape route?"

"Yes. I have something to show you." She extended a hand and led him out the back door. They descended a set of cement steps that opened to a pathway through the trees behind the farm home. After a hundred yards or so, they came to a clearing, and across from them, a clump of trees partially hid a structure of some sort, and as they neared, it became clear to him.

"This was a bunker for the Germans during the war," she said. "It was converted into a temporary workshop."

"For what?"

She liked the suspense. "You'll see." They passed the bunker and headed for a mound in the distance where a camouflage netting was strung above in the trees, and when they rounded the mound, before them was a single engine high-wing aircraft. It was expertly hidden, painted dark green and completely devoid of markings.

It all made sense now. The clearing they had crossed was the take-off strip.

"Can you fly it?" she asked.

"I can fly anything." He opened the door, slid in behind the wheel and made a quick inspection of the dash panel. He primed the engine, shoved in the carburetor shut-off and edged the throttle forward a bit, then triggered the master control switch and turned the key. Within a half dozen revolutions, the engine fired and the propeller was spinning wildly. Immediately, he shut down the engine and let the propeller spin to a stop.

171

She pulled a manual from under the seat. "They said you would understand this."

In the manual was a flight chart, and on the chart was a plotted route he was to follow. The route traced the Vltava River southwest toward the West German border at an altitude of 2500 meters, almost 8000 feet. He studied the flight plan more critically. At a point marked on the map, he was to cut the engines and glide the remaining ten miles across the Czech border. A landing strip to the north of Passau, Germany, had been circled with a pencil.

"They said we should cross the border as close to one-thirty in the morning as possible," she said. "Something to do with security."

Garner was scrutinizing the dash panel. The aircraft was a two-seater but it had been stripped of every instrument except the altimeter, airspeed indicator and gyrocompass. No radios, no vectoring equipment, no DMA—distance measuring equipment. He looked behind him. The back wall had been removed exposing the fuselage interior. He knew the reason why the aircraft had been stripped down. This was the means of escape for him and Trudi, and the defector would be the third passenger in an aircraft that was built to carry only two. That was the reason the fuel tank contained no more than eight or nine gallons of fuel. With the tanks only one-third full, the aircraft would be another ninety pounds lighter. He wondered how big of a man the defector was. If he was anywhere near two hundred pounds, the aircraft would never leave the ground.

He would have to fly visually at night with only a compass, which he had often done before. It would not be the worst set of flying circumstances. The only thing that would hamper the flight would be if the weather did not cooperate.

"Was Frank Vulcek a pilot?"

"No. We had an alternate escape route planned by vehicle."

Garner nodded. "And since I was a pilot…"

"Arthur suggested the alternative plan and everyone went along with it. Jan and Emil made the arrangements. It's faster and less dangerous."

"Who told you that?"

"Jan and Emil."

Garner had to agree somewhat. It would be a quick way out—as long as the defector didn't weigh two hundred pounds, and as long as the weather held.

Just as he mentioned weather, a few raindrops smacked against the windshield. He crawled out of the plane and slammed the door shut.

They just reached the bunker when the first onslaught of rain hit. Inside, he discovered the radios from the aircraft lying on a bench and other panels and parts of the craft heaped in a corner.

He wrapped an arm around Trudi and looked up into the menacing sky. Thunder rolled from miles away, and now the wind was whipping a cold breeze through the doorway of the bunker. Then, almost miraculously, the rain reduced to a drizzle, and after another minute, it stopped.

"Come on," said Garner. "Let's make a run for it."

Hand in hand, the two hurried over the clearing. Half way across, he scrutinized the open field, which represented the runway for the escape. Two hundred yards away or so, several trees had been cut away, and beyond was another clearing.

He understood now why the trees were chopped down. He would have to fly the craft through that narrow opening. From here, it looked barely wide enough for the wings to clear.

They hurried on when they heard a wall of rain coming, but it was suddenly upon them and they couldn't outrun it. As they trounced across the field, he loved the smell and freshness of the air, and for a moment he reflected back. When he was a boy, he had been fishing in the Missouri river and remembered how he had been caught in a similar downpour. He and a friend had walked two miles in the rain before they arrived home.

He still had his arm around Trudi, and now as he looked at her, her face was white and as fresh as the rain. Water streamed down the sides of her drenched hair, and he was thinking how beautiful she was, and he was trying to imagine what it would be like to have and hold her for a lifetime.

This game in which he had become entwined was suddenly deadly for both of them. He admired her courage and her steadfast loyalty to the Prague assignment, but he feared what the consequences might be. His worst fear was that somehow he might lose her.

She was looking back at him, her smile vibrant. He tightened his arm around her again as they neared the farmhouse. The thunder rolled in heavy rumbles now, almost constantly, and the rain kept coming.

CHAPTER TWENTY THREE

Jan wheeled the black limousine into the cobblestone square behind the President's Palace and headed for the gate to the palace grounds. A guard post on each side of the gate contained an armed soldier. Several other soldiers, both Czech and Russian, stood ominously in a line on each side of the arch, enlisted men with rifles, officers armed with pistols.

Jan gave some last minute instructions to Garner as the vehicle slowed to a stop. "When you walk, strut. When you are standing still, put your hands behind your back or hook a thumb in your belt, and plant your feet apart as if you own the building. You have a respectable rank. Most other officers will be junior in grade. If you must indulge in conversation with other officers, joke with them, but keep a straight face. They will respect you for it.

"Remember, the defector knows you by your face and Vulcek's name. Be alert but not conspicuous for anyone who approaches you. If he makes contact, it is imperative we know his whereabouts for the next forty-eight hours."

The Czech and East German flags on the front fenders flapped soundlessly in the mild morning breeze as Jan emerged from the vehicle. He walked smartly around the front in his chauffeur clothes, and when he opened the rear door, Garner was the first to step out wearing the rich, brown uniform of the Russian officer. He offered a hand, and Trudi emerged. She wore a dark matching coat and skirt, very plain, with a turtleneck sweater under the jacket. Her clothes did not match her beauty, thought Garner, but she did look German.

Jan climbed back into the vehicle, and as he drove off, Garner caught sight of the statue above the left guard post. A figure of a man with a raised dagger was about to plunge it into the wretched soul beneath him.

That was not a good omen.

Trudi took his arm. "Walk through the courtyard to the archway," she instructed as they paraded past the line of soldiers. A junior officer called the soldiers to attention when he saw Garner's rank. He saluted smartly and Garner returned it.

"So far so good," said Garner as they rounded a fountain.

They passed through the archway under a wing of the palace and entered another courtyard, where Trudi headed across guiding him with her arm.

"That's Vladislav Hall where the conference is being held," she said.

The bricks of the 16th century hulk were gray and black, tainted by years of pollution. The two entered through a passage with opened double doors and walked up elongated steps that were wide enough to allow a horse and carriage to pass through.

A small group of Chinese delegates was immediately ahead of them in a hallway that led to the main hall, but now, people were all around them. In spite of the crowd, his boots clicked loudly and re-sounded off the corridor walls as he strutted in the fashion Jan had instructed.

Garner's nerves were working on him as two Russian junior lieutenants approached from the other direction.

"Tovarish Major," they both greeted in unison as they touched the bills of their garrison hats. Garner nodded and returned a sloppy salute.

Do not be too military with your salute, Jan had told him somewhere along the way. *You have been in the military for sixteen years. It is a bother to salute.*

They entered the main hall where huge pillars on each side of the room were spaced evenly and reached upward for forty feet. For the entire length of the hall, giant chandeliers hung uniformly from the ceiling.

"This is late Gothic," Trudi informed him. Garner knew nothing about the architecture, but he did equate the size of the hall as about half that of a football field.

Tables sat in front of sculptured reliefs that adorned the vibrant pastel colored walls, and above the tables were placards indicating the various nations.

The Prague Double

Military men representing armies from numerous countries stationed themselves at strategic points, and chatter bounced irritatingly off cement walls unable to handle the acoustics.

Garner was wearing the lightly colored military glasses. Jan reasoned that wearing the glasses indoors would be expected from a man who had supposedly suffered such scars in an aircraft accident. If he were asked about the scars, he was to joke about them and belittle the Russian pilot who had crashed the plane.

There was no line at the East German table when the two approached. While Trudi presented her papers, Garner inconspicuously eyed the crowd. If anyone had recognized him so far, he had no indication of it.

Not far away, two Russian officers were engaged in conversation, and a small group of officers had gathered in another corner of the hall, their voices emitting an occasional outburst of subdued laughter.

"Tovarish Major?" The man behind the counter was addressing him. Garner reached inside his coat for his travel papers when the man interrupted. "That will not be necessary. I wanted to inform you that refreshments have been set aside in room 111." The man spoke perfect Russian.

Garner nodded courteously, took Trudi by the arm and led her away from the table.

"What did he say?" asked Trudi.

"He told me where they store the vodka."

He had no intention of joining one of the small groups of officers and instead headed toward the meeting room with Trudi.

When they turned down a corridor, they passed three officers standing along a wall. One of the officers spoke to Garner. *"Kuda zhe? Sobranie vam interesno ne budet."*

Garner had no choice. He excused himself from Trudi. *"Wir wollen uns spaeter treffen,"* he told her, and in moments, she was gone.

"Nyet, nyet," The Russian officer was saying. "You won't like the meetings. I'm sure you will enjoy the lounge much more."

The senior officer introduced himself as Major Tumanov and

introduced the two captains with him. Garner gave each a handshake, fighting to let his nerves cool.

"You speak German, I noticed," Major Tumanov said.

"Yes," responded Garner. "After being stationed in the East Zone for so many years, I sometimes think I am German."

"I thought you had an accent," responded the Major with a deep smile, his chubby face cocked at an angle. "I am Polish myself. But a German or a Pole in a Russian uniform is still a Russian, right?"

The small group broke out in laughter, and after a slap on the back, the four headed off in the opposite direction from where Trudi had disappeared.

There was no doubt in Garner's mind that the Major had frequented such conferences, and by the time they reached the lounge, Garner learned the officer was stationed with the Leningrad Embassy. He had been in the service twenty-two years, never married, and said he never would.

Garner was surprised the major had not asked specifically where he was stationed. He was prepared to discuss his army unit as well as his family, his job title, anything, but none of the officers seemed remotely interested.

The lounge was crowded with military officers, mostly lieutenants. *If you must indulge in conversation, joke with them*, Jan had said. What an understatement, thought Garner as a glass of punch was shoved into his hand.

"*Na zdarove!*" someone shouted. Garner raised his glass and only sipped at the punch. There was no liquor in it.

"Perhaps it is too early for you to drink," Major Tumanov quipped as he eyed Garner's glass. He was the only one who had not emptied it.

Garner looked at his watch. It was ten-twenty. "I usually start at eleven," he said, "But today I'll make an exception." He downed the punch, which was chased with a flurry of laughter.

* * *

Thirty minutes later, Garner could not believe he was still with the same group. They had covered a variety of topics, but he mostly listened. Finally one of the officers asked him what unit he was stationed with. He answered straightforward, "The 7th Guard Ground Forces out of Dresden."

Garner tensed when Major Tumanov said he had visited the 7th Guard Unit at Pirna on the Czech border. "Tell me," he asked. "Is the food still bad at the mess hall?"

"No," Garner quickly answered. "It's worse." The snappy answer broke up the group again, and the topic of conversation shifted once more.

Garner was drinking his fourth glass of punch, this one spiked with vodka, when a buzzer sounded outside the lobby.

"What? Already?" Major Tumanov checked his watch. "The orientation meeting must be over."

When the officers stood, Garner saw his opportunity. "If you gentlemen will excuse me I better find my little professor."

"I don't blame you," said the Major. "She's a good looking lady. I suppose I had better find mine. She also is good looking."

The other officers burst with laughter. One of them explained to Garner that the Major was escorting a *starushka*, which loosely translated in Russian meant *a little old grandma*.

"Well," said Garner as he stood up. "Let's hope your rubber doesn't break." He left them all doubled over from laughter as he walked out of the lounge.

He returned to the registration area, but he could not see Trudi anywhere. He let his thumb drop from his belt and strutted along the corridor, searching the crowd as he went. But his thoughts kept coming back to the lounge. He handled himself well, he thought, but he did not want to repeat the experience. How much could Jan expect of him? How much could he expect of himself?

Someone touched his arm, and he spun around relieved to find Trudi standing next to him.

"Why did you leave me?" He whispered in an angry tone.

She was smiling, but underneath her voice she was scolding. "You are not expected to attend the meetings. Did everything go all right?"

Delray K. Dvoracek

"I think so. You don't have any idea what I've been through."

"Don't turn now," she said, her eyes still trained on him. "Since I entered the room, there has been a man looking at you. He is in the dark suit near the Ukraine registration table at the moment. It may be nothing, but when I leave you, casually catch a glimpse of him."

"What does he look like?"

"Slightly bald, light build. I must leave you. I have a meeting in a few minutes."

"Trudi!" he said in a loud whisper, but she walked off. His mind was working furiously. When he turned around, he needed to give some indication that he recognized the man in case he was indeed the defector

A plan was evolving.

He turned innocently and made a few steps toward the Ukrainian registration desk. He was looking in a different direction, but his eyes, hidden behind the dark glasses, were now on the man, and he was definitely looking Garner over.

It was all guesswork now. Garner turned his head directly at the man, removed his dark glasses for a moment and then slipped them back in place.

Garner did not know if the man recognized him as Vulcek, but he turned and slowly headed for the outer corridor. He dare not turn around and simply hoped the man would follow *if he was the defector.*

He headed for the men's room, wondering whether the defector would even recognize him with his scarred face and dark glasses. It all seemed so chancy and improbable.

Once inside the lavatory, he made a quick inspection to see if any of the stalls were occupied. None were.

He walked directly to the wash basins where two other men were engaged in conversation. He removed his hat and began to wash his hands, listening as the two men spoke. They were Yugoslavian, he guessed, and neither was paying any attention to him. Moments later, they both left, and almost immediately, the door opened again. In the reflection of the mirror, Garner saw the man whom he thought may be the defector.

180

The Prague Double

The man glanced under the stalls like Garner had when he first entered, and then he came to the wash basin next to Garner. He turned on the water, but his hands were planted firmly on the edges of the basin.

"Excuse me," the man asked. "We have met before, have we not? May I ask your name?"

"Major Nikolai Dovchenko," Garner answered, throwing a raspy sound along with his voice.

The man gaped. "I-I'm sorry. I mistook you for someone else."

He turned to leave, but Garner could not let him go. "Perhaps you are looking for a man named Vulcek."

The man whirled around. "It is you! I wasn't sure. Your face, I..."

"I had a car accident." He removed his glasses and pulled his collar back to show the scar on his throat. "I don't look the same and I don't sound the same, but at least I'm still alive."

The man glanced in the mirror checking the door behind them. "I did not expect to find you in a Russian army uniform. Who was the woman with you?"

"She's working with me." He seemed satisfied with the answer. "Are you being watched?"

"Yes. Two men are with me almost constantly. I am probably already missed."

"Where are you staying?"

"At a military compound near Zbraslav. It is a kilometer from the chateau. Do you know it?"

"Yes." Garner didn't know the compound, but he knew Jan and Emil would.

"Then you know it is heavily guarded," said the defector.

"Let me worry about that," Garner said calmly. He was giving answers he could not remotely back up, but he had no alternative. "I must know where you are at all times within the next 48 hours."

The defector's hands trembled as he reached up and adjusted his tie. "I have an agenda, but it is in my briefcase." He swallowed nervously, his cheeks red from embarrassment. "I don't even know what..."

The door opened to the lavatory, and immediately the man had

181

Delray K. Dvoracek

his hands in the basin. Garner pressed the glasses back in place and was adjusting his garrison hat when a second person entered the room.

The defector glanced into the mirror at the figure who had entered and said, "*Minutuchku.*" *One moment.*

Garner tugged at his pistol belt as if making himself more comfortable. Obviously the man behind him was one of the men who was watching the defector. Garner turned and, maintaining a strut, walked past the individual near the door.

"Are you enjoying the conference, Tovarish Major?" the man asked in Russian.

"Frankly, no," said Garner as he stepped past. "I find it a complete bore."

* * *

Outside of Vladislav Hall, Garner strolled over to the retaining wall that lined the courtyard. From here, he had an excellent view of the city, now engrossed in sunlight and as beautiful of a sight as he had ever witnessed. He could easily pick out the Powder Tower at the east end of the Karlovy Most where he had first met Eric Kopal. He reflected for a moment. It was a terrible commentary on how senselessly the man had lost his life.

Garner did not want to return to the hall or the lounge, but rather opted to spend the time outside. It was evidently a good decision, since several other officers had made the same choice.

As he walked about, he returned salutes to numerous junior officers, and he cherished the freedom to walk off his anxiety, which allowed him time to think. He had expected the man that Jan and Emil nicknamed the *muzhik* to be staunch in appearance, abrupt, forceful in voice, but the peasant was a rather frail individual. He appeared nervous, and his voice was weak. But then, how else should the man have reacted? He was defecting, leaving the country he had lived in for some fifty years. A great deal must have been going through the man's mind. Garner couldn't remotely contemplate the man's motives.

And he cursed when he was unable to get the man's itinerary for the next few days, which meant he would have to make contact again.

His attention was suddenly directed to the front of the building. The meeting had let out for the afternoon break, and people were emerging in greater numbers now.

He spotted her looking out over the grounds, and then she saw him. She hurried over, wrapped an arm on his, and the two headed for the front gate.

Jan saw them coming, pulled up and came around to the back door. As they entered, he asked, "How did it go?"

"All right," answered Garner. "I met the muzhik." It did go all right, considering what he had been through.

"Tell me everything," Jan asked excitedly, once he had the vehicle in motion.

"The peasant is staying at the military compound near Zbraslav," said Garner. "Do you know where that is?"

"Yes, go on."

"That's all," answered Garner.

Jan turned his head. "That's all?"

"We were interrupted by one of his body guards. He has two with him almost constantly."

"Did the bodyguard suspect anything?"

"No."

"Are you sure?"

"Positive."

"Good. Describe the peasant."

"About five-foot eight, thin hair, dark skin, middle fifties. About a hundred sixty pounds."

"How did he react?"

"Nervous, excited."

"Did you convince him you were Vulcek?"

"I think so."

"Yes or no?"

Garner frowned. "I had to take off my glasses and show him the scar on my throat. He looked surprised when I first spoke. I don't know if it was the voice or not."

Jan nodded. "Describe the bodyguard."

"Shorter than the peasant, stocky, about forty. Black hair, square face and a nose that probably was broken at one time."

"Did you speak to him?"

"Yes. I told him I was bored with the entire conference."

"That was a very good answer." Jan entered a main street and increased his speed.

"What now?" asked Garner.

"We're headed for Dejvice. It is only a few kilometers from here. You will spend the afternoon with Emil."

"What about Trudi?"

"She must go back to the conference, at least for today." Jan seemed irritated. "We must know the peasant's time schedule. We will have to attend the palace reception tonight."

"What reception?"

Trudi clarified. "All members of the conference are invited to attend a social function at the President's Palace. It is a tradition. The peasant will be there." Trudi spoke as if she had expected all along that the two would have to attend the function.

"How do we get in?" asked Garner.

"It has been arranged," said Jan.

Garner leaned back in the seat, a knot forming in his stomach. He could have anticipated that. Jan and Emil weren't overlooking anything.

His mind was working ahead. More Russian officers would be at the Palace, and he was not looking forward to spending any more time with them.

"I met a Russian Major by the name of Tumanov," said Garner.

"Did you like him?" asked Jan.

The question amused Garner. "He was interesting. A Pole. I don't mind telling you that was the most uncomfortable part of the conference. I would rather meet with the peasant again."

"Do not be alarmed. Tonight at the President's Palace, everyone will be on their best behavior. Especially the Russian officers."

Jan weaved the vehicle up the sides of the huge hill. After several minutes, he slowed and turned down a secluded road, then pulled into the driveway of a home that was surrounded by a high wire fence entwined with vines. Thick trees on all sides kept the home even more secluded, and no other homes lay within a hundred yards either direction.

A garage door went up electronically, and once inside, the vehicle dipped down to an underground area that was large enough for Jan to turn around. He stopped and pointed to a staircase. "Up there. We will be back at exactly eight-thirty. Emil will brief you on anything you need to know. Any questions?"

"No," answered Garner. Trudi had been silent for most of the trip through the city. He kissed her, then slid out of the vehicle.

"Mr. Garner," said Jan through the window. "You are doing a very good job." He rolled up the window and drove out of the garage. When the garage door lowered, Garner made his way up the steps to the interior of the house and entered a large living room where Emil was sitting at a table, an open file in front of him.

"Welcome back, Major," he said to Garner. "Did you make contact with the muzhik?"

"Yes," said Garner as he sat in a chair opposite Emil.

"Very good," he answered as he turned the file around and opened it. Inside were several pages of photographs.

Garner knew what Emil wanted. He methodically examined the photos and had only gone through a few pages when he stopped. "This is the man," he said as he thumped a finger on a photo. "It's obviously a photo when he was younger, but it's him."

"Are you sure

"Positive."

Emil pulled the photo from its plastic casing and slid it into his pocket. "Make yourself comfortable. Do not leave for any reason, do not answer the phone or the door." Without further explanation, he was suddenly gone.

Garner did not bother to ask him where he was going since he knew he wouldn't get an answer anyway. He was catching on to the CIA's methodology.

When he heard a vehicle leave the house, he crossed the room and looked out the window to a backyard of trees and flowers and let his body and mind relax. He was in a comfortable home, spacious, immaculately decorated with antique furniture, everything exhibiting a feeling of wealth.

He walked through the house to a front window where he had a distant panoramic view of the city with all its towers and spires reaching upward into the sky. Massive buildings were jammed together forcing the streets to disappear. For a moment, his mind was engulfed in the splendor of the view, then abruptly, he returned to the table where an inviting tray of liquor bottles stood. He poured himself a drink and eased himself into a comfortable chair. His thoughts were back in Frankfurt wondering what Arthur Farrington was doing at the moment. Then his thoughts flashed to Manfried Toller, and he wondered if he would ever see him again.

CHAPTER TWENTY FOUR

That evening as they drove into the palace square, Jan once again offered some final advice. "The only way in and out of the palace is through these gates. There will be guards at all other exits. Be extremely careful when you meet the peasant. Do not accept any written notes from him. Memorize everything, where he will be in the next two days. Get times, places, anything that will be useful. And above all, act like you're having a good time."

When the vehicle pulled to a stop in front of the palace gates, the knot was back in his stomach. He hoped it would leave him once he was inside mixing with the crowd.

A doorman opened the back door for Garner and Trudi, and as soon as they emerged, Jan drove away to park.

The palace facade, brilliantly lit by numerous floodlights, loomed out at them as they crossed the square. They traced the same route on foot as they did that morning and entered Vladislav Hall. A long red carpet runner ran the length of the corridor this time, and at the end of it, a man dressed in historical clothing near a registration desk welcomed them.

Garner removed his garrison hat as he gave their names.

"Ah, yes," the host said as he checked their names off the roster. "Miss Schwaben and Major Dovchenko. Please," he gestured for them to move on to a coat check area.

After Garner handed over his garrison hat and Trudi's wrap, a second person ushered them into a line of people. They shuffled along shaking hands with a number of dignitaries and accepting welcomes in a variety of languages. All the while, he could hear a small symphony playing classical music.

The last couple in line complimented Trudi on her white, full-length gown. She was beautiful, Garner mused. Her earrings and brooch matched her beauty, and as she glided across the floor, she could easily pass for royalty.

Garner felt a bit more relaxed as he looked over the crowd. Several dancing couples had taken to the floor, their attire radiant and rich-looking. Others sat at tables on raised tiers, each table set with white linen and crystal glassware and adorned with a flower centerpiece. Everything sparkled from the brilliant lights of the overhead chandeliers.

A host approached the two and led them to a free table. As they walked along the edge of the dance floor, Garner was ever alert hoping to spot the *muzhik*.

"Do you like to dance?" whispered Trudi.

"No," Garner answered.

"Tonight you will. If we spend most of the night on the floor, you won't have to spend time talking to anyone."

He liked the idea, and after nodding to a passing officer, he whispered back, "I'll at least have to talk to the peasant."

"Do you see him?"

"No." They had no sooner located a free table when a waiter was at their side and took their order for drinks. As soon as he was gone, Garner again looked over the crowd. In short time, their drinks came and the music started afresh.

"Dance?" she asked.

"I'd love to."

* * *

They had just finished their fourth waltz in a row, and as they were walking off the floor, Garner spotted the peasant no more than twenty feet away talking to a Russian officer. The officer's back was to Garner, but as Garner and Trudi neared their table, he caught the profile of the army man. He was Major Tumanov, the officer he had met at the conference earlier in the day.

Garner squeezed Trudi's arm. "Do you recognize the Major?" he asked as they sat at their table.

"Yes."

Garner's gaze reached beyond the two individuals now, searching for the muzhik's bodyguard, but he did not see him. The knot was back in his stomach. He wanted the Major to leave before he approached the peasant, but the officer was pumping his hands up and down explaining something, and then, suddenly, he looked over the peasant's shoulder and spotted Garner.

"Major Dovchenko," he called out. He was headed for their table and bringing the peasant with him! "Major Dovchenko. How nice to see you again," he greeted in Russian. He bowed graciously to Trudi, and surprisingly bent over and kissed her hand. "What a lovely lady to escort about the ball."

"May I present Professor Anatol Sedovskij," he offered. "This is Major Nikolai Dovchenko, and this young lady is..."

"Miss Gisela Schwaben," Garner answered.

"The Professor is from..." Dovchenko stopped and turned to the man, not knowing where he was from.

"From Moscow," finished the Professor.

Garner felt his nerves beating away as Major Tumanov ambled on about the ball and the music, his cheerfulness not leaving him for a moment. Abruptly, and with the grace of a fairy-tale prince, Major Tumanov bowed and asked Trudi for the pleasure of the next dance.

He whisked her away to the floor leaving Garner alone with the peasant.

The awkwardness of the moment played in Garner's mind. He conveniently had an opportunity to talk to the peasant, but there were too many people nearby.

"Would you care to view the paintings in the east wing?" remarked the Professor, as he gestured to an open doorway leading to an outer corridor.

As the two circled around the dance floor, Garner could only believe that providence had crossed his path. Better yet, the Professor seemed totally at ease and made a few comments about the architecture of the castle.

A wainscoting of rich redwood circled the room, the carpet beneath their feet flowery and plush. Above the paneling, gigantic paintings filled the walls. Other people were in the room admiring the artwork, but none far enough away for the two to talk.

189

Delray K. Dvoracek

In front of a painting on which nobility were poised, the Professor began gesturing at the work as if he were discussing it.

"We are being watched at the moment," he said. "The man in the far corner near the door is the only escort with me tonight."

"I understand," said Garner, as they moved to another painting. "I need to know your whereabouts for the next 48 hours."

"I will not be here in 48 hours!" the peasant answered. "Tomorrow morning I deliver a lecture and in the afternoon I have two other meetings separate from the conference."

"Where are the meetings?"

"I do not know. The location is kept secret since the topics are classified."

"That makes it difficult," said Garner. He suddenly wished he hadn't said that.

The stress in the man's voice was so recognizable. "I must go! I have waited years for this opportunity! I will not have another chance like this. I must go!"

Garner had no other choice. He was forced to make a decision. "What's your schedule for tonight?"

"I will not return to the military compound until after midnight."

Garner bit his lip. He knew he had to fly the aircraft out so that he arrived at the border of Czechoslovakia about one-thirty in the morning. That would not give them enough time.

"Tomorrow's schedule. What time are the meetings?"

"At four and six in the afternoon."

"When will you return to the compound?"

"At midnight again. Our aircraft leaves for Moscow early the next morning. I am leaving the conference early."

Garner absorbed the information and decided. "You must be at the military compound no later than 10:30 tomorrow night."

"That's impossible! I cannot leave the meeting early!"

"You must." Garner was emphatic. "Feign sickness, make any excuse, but be at the compound at 10:30 tomorrow night."

The Professor licked his lips and grimaced as if contemplating the demand.

"Tell me everything about the compound," Garner asked, not

190

waiting for a response. "How it is guarded, where your room is..."

The peasant rattled off in a nervous tone. "There are two soldiers at the main gate. The barracks I am located in is directly across from it. An officer inside must let you in. Another door is operated electronically by the same officer in order to enter the main floor of the barracks. I am on the second floor in room 212."

"Are you alone in the room?"

"Yes."

"Are there other soldiers present inside the compound?"

"At least two platoons. They are billeted in another barracks and patrol the grounds, but I don't know their schedules."

Garner recollected that Jan said he expected the peasant would be staying at the compound, so he guessed that's where the abduction would have to take place.

"Be in the compound at 10:30," Garner repeated.

The Professor restrained himself. "There is no possible way you can get in!"

Garner was done trying to convince him otherwise. "Professor, your bodyguard is still watching us. We're going to walk right past him. I don't care what you talk about, but talk, and talk as if you are enjoying the evening. Do you understand?"

Garner didn't wait for the man's response. He turned, and immediately Anatol Sedovskij was at his side. By the time the two reached the doorway and were passing the bodyguard, Sedovskij once more was ambling on about the architecture of the building.

When they reached the ballroom, Garner offered a hand to the man. "Ten-thirty," he said under his breath.

The music had switched to Mozart, but Garner was not hearing one note of it. His mind once again was far ahead of his body.

When he returned to the table, Trudi was sitting by herself, but her face was not carrying the smile she had been wearing earlier in the evening.

He barely sat down when she spoke. "Remove your glasses, quickly!" she whispered.

He had the glasses off and placed them inside his tunic.

"Look over my shoulder to your left," she indicated. "In the corner. Is it him?"

Garner stiffened. He easily recognized the blond hair and squared-off face of the super race. "Manfried Toller! What the hell is he doing here?"

"He might have recognized you with the glasses on," said Trudi. "He might anyway." The nervousness in her voice had reached a peak. "He's been standing at the exit for the past several minutes."

Garner kept his back to the door. His thoughts were on the microfilm, and he wondered if somehow Toller had discovered there was no name on it.

"Did you get the information from the peasant?" asked Trudi.

"Yes." He looked around. "How do we get out of here without being seen?"

She leaned forward. "I've made arrangements for Toller to be interrupted. When I tell you, we'll get up and make our way quickly to the door."

Garner gave her a hard glance, wondering with whom she could have made arrangements, especially since he and Trudi were the only two in the building who were working on the Prague assignment.

She nodded her head to someone behind him, and a moment later, she stood up. Garner followed her along the dance floor, hidden from Toller's view by the crowd of dancers. She stopped twenty feet from the exit and after a few seconds said, "Now."

As the two headed for the exit, Garner saw Major Tumanov conveniently engage Toller in a conversation so that his back was turned to them.

They slipped past and hurried to the cloakroom while Tumanov carried on about something or other. When the girl in the cloakroom disappeared behind the racks to gather their items, Garner looked dumbfounded at Trudi. "Major Tumanov? How did you arrange that?"

She had a coy smile on her face. "Easily. He's one of us."

Garner practically choked. When the coat check girl returned, he tipped her, and they quickly made their way outside.

"Why didn't you tell me before?" he asked as they headed for the palace gates.

"Jan said you would be more alert if you didn't know."

"Jesus!" Now that he thought about Major Tumanov, it was he who made Garner feel comfortable among the junior officers, and the great fortune that he assumed brought him and the muzhik together wasn't providence at all. Tumanov had arranged it.

Garner could not help but hold these Czech nationals in high esteem. They weren't CIA operatives, but they certainly knew their work

Jan drove up, and when the two entered the limo, Garner sat back and stretched out. He had had enough surprises for one night.

CHAPTER TWENTY FIVE

In the morning, Jan drove Trudi back to the palace where she signed in at the conference. Officially, she had registered at the Olympik Hotel where she stayed the first night when she arrived. If she didn't sign in today at the Academy, someone would definitely check on her whereabouts, a risk Jan could not afford to take. He had arranged for an associate to pick her up later in the day to drive her directly to the farmhouse.

It was now four in the afternoon at the home in Dejvice. Emil Prazak had been standing in front of the bay window watching the street below for several minutes, and when he saw the vehicle approach, he turned to the others in the room. "Frantisek has arrived."

Garner crossed to the window and looked down at the car as it pulled up. Frantisek Plauder, known to Garner as Major Tumanov, was walking up the sidewalk. He had shucked the military uniform and was now wearing a long black coat and a homburg. He did not at all resemble the comical Russian officer he had earlier portrayed.

From below, Garner heard the man's footsteps as he ascended the staircase, and in moments, he walked into the room and came directly to Garner with his hand extended.

"Mr. Garner, I presume? Or is it Mr. Vulcek?" he said. "It is my pleasure to formally make your acquaintance." His English was flawless. He removed his coat and hat and joined Jan and Emil at the table. The thick black hair and black eyebrows were the same, but the man looked strangely different without a uniform.

"The plans are all formulated," he said. "Miss Feldman should be arriving at the farmhouse within the quarter hour. She is to confirm her arrival by telephone."

He looked at Garner. "Your identification of the peasant's photo was excellent. I have confirmation from Frankfurt that the defector is indeed Anatol Sedovskij, a top man in the Soviet Union's field of anti-ballistic missiles. He is without question an excellent find, and Arthur is most anxious to get him out."

Garner marveled at this new personality. Frantisek Plauder would have been the most unlikely man that Garner would have picked out of a crowd to be an agent. He was not only comical as Major Tumanov, but he was somewhat comical now, every word delivered with the crispness of a man who thrived on precise vocabulary and the wise use of it. The man was fluent in Czech, Russian, English and German.

Plauder was very pleased. "Mr. Garner, you have done an excellent job. If I hadn't known you at the conference, I would never have suspected you were impersonating a Russian officer. Last night at the palace you were superb. Brilliant performance." He chuckled, and then the serious tone was back.

"Regarding tonight..." He stopped. "Incidentally, Mr. Garner, you were absolutely correct. Our original plans dictated the defection to take place at the military compound. We were quite certain he would be billeted there. Yes, indeed. Demanding that the peasant be there at 10:30 was a stroke of innate intuition.

"About tonight's mission. We will drive to Zbraslav in two vehicles where we will leave one behind and continue the remaining few kilometers together. Jan will act as chauffeur, I will ride in the front with him, and you two shall occupy the back seat. The two soldiers at the gate are Emil's responsibility. Once inside the compound, Mr. Garner and I shall make entrance to the barracks where Mr. Sedovskij is domiciled. Mr. Garner, your responsibility will be to detain the military officer inside the first office. I shall brief you before we leave. While I locate Mr. Sedovskij, you, Jan, will set the charges on the staff vehicles parked outside."

Jan nodded.

"Charges?" asked Garner.

"Yes, charges. Perhaps explosives is a better word."

Garner wanted to laugh. The man was discussing the abduction as if he were lecturing a college class, and even now, Frantisek was looking directly at Garner with a huge smile on his face, his facial expression speaking as much as his mouth.

He continued. "On a mission like this, one cannot expect results without some, as you say in English, fireworks."

Garner understood precisely what he meant.

"Let us now adjourn to the artillery room," Frantisek suggested.

Garner was as much amused as he was curious while he followed the three men to the basement where Frantisek shoved a tall cabinet to the side and opened a door hidden behind it.

"Watch out for bats," he quipped, as he flipped on a light switch. The room was claustrophobic and contained nothing more than a workbench and a few chairs. Nothing in the room indicated this was any sort of artillery cache until Frantisek scooted the bench away from the wall.

In a concrete hideaway near the floor was a metal container. Frantisek lifted the container to the bench and opened it. "The fireworks," he said.

Garner had never seen such explosives, but the numbers on the dial of each indicated they were charges with timers.

"You need not worry about these," Frantisek told Garner. "Jan is our explosives expert." He laid out six on the bench and picked out another device similar to the rest, but Garner knew it must be something special.

Frantisek produced another box from the confines of the brick wall and opened the lid. "And this is for you."

It was a revolver in a long shoulder holster. When Garner lifted it out, he saw the silencer screwed on to the end of the barrel. Garner held the handgun out at arm's length and balanced it up and down.

"It fits you well, eh, Mr. Garner?"

Garner could not contain his astonishment with Frantisek Plauder. The man handled the explosives and revolver as if they were kids' toys, and he seemed to have a constant grin on his face. He wondered if Frantisek was like this all the time.

His expression suddenly changed, and his voice changed once again to a serious tone. "I do not want anyone killed," he said to the three. "Unless it is unavoidable."

His face was stone cold now. "From the time we enter the main gate, we will be in and out with the defector in exactly eight minutes. If we get the peasant out, I doubt we will read about it in the newspapers, however, if we kill any of the Russians along the way, there will be reprisals, and I do not want any reprisals. Is that clear?"

Jan and Emil nodded. Garner was witnessing a true agent at work, and if there was any danger written on the man's face, he couldn't perceive it.

"How do you know it will take precisely eight minutes to get Sedovskij out?" Garner dared to ask.

Frantisek's face sagged as if offended with the question. "Why eight minutes? Because I have mentally walked through the process a hundred times in my mind. It will require eight minutes."

"There are troop trucks at the compound," said Garner.

"Yes, but a transport cannot outrun us. Staff cars, maybe, but Jan will take care of them."

"What about the telephone?" Garner asked. "What's to stop them from phoning ahead and creating a road blockade?"

"Jan will take care of that."

Frantisek went on. "There are at least two platoons of soldiers inside the compound. If everything is done according to my plan, they will not know what has happened until it is too late. Once we leave the military compound, you will be airborne in less than thirty minutes. That is, you, Miss Feldman and our muzhik. You should cross the border at approximately one-ten in the morning. We have people ready to hamper communications along your escape route."

Garner could not believe the precision behind the man's words. "What if the weather doesn't hold?"

"If the weather is bad, it will be equally bad for the enemy. I am told your piloting skills can handle bad weather." He stuck out his lower lip as he eyed Garner. "You can handle it, can't you?"

"I can handle it."

Frantisek was silent, a curious look on his face, and after a few more seconds, he said, "I appreciate your questions, Mr. Garner. However, there is one question you have not asked, and that is, where is Manfried Toller?" He leaned against the workbench and folded his arms across each other. "Where do you think he is?"

Delray K. Dvoracek

It was a question Garner had pondered off and on all day. "I don't know, but I would guess at the moment he is looking for me."

"Yes, without a doubt," Frantisek agreed. "However, he does not know Miss Feldman, and he did not leave the palace until well over two hours after you and Miss Feldman left today. I suspect he is one frustrated man at the moment. Let us hope he remains that way."

"Don't underestimate him," Garner cautioned. "He's very clever and just as devious."

"Yes," answered Frantisek. "So I am told." He abruptly produced a map of the military compound and spread it on the bench.

Before he spoke, they heard the phone ring from upstairs. It rang a second time and then was silent. Garner's eyes met those of the three men. Suddenly the phone rang once more, but only once.

Emil offered an explanation. "Miss Feldman. She has arrived safely at the farmhouse."

Frantisek focused on the map again. "Timing is the most important factor and I cannot emphasize that enough." He looked at his watch. "We will review everything until our timing is down to the second, and then we shall have a toast to our success. In exactly five hours and twenty minutes, we will enter the military compound.

"From the beginning," he said as he began to run through the routine again, detailing each step of the way.

It never occurred to Garner not to go along with the abduction. These men, about whom he knew very little, had families, and they were risking not only their own lives, but those of their loved ones if they were caught.

Garner, on the other hand, had no immediate family, at least no one that would miss him should he suddenly drop off the corner of the earth. His motive was money and an opportunity to avoid a lengthy prison stay. He wondered what motive these men possessed.

And what was Trudi's motive? These people seemed to be blindly carrying out a dangerous assignment simply because they were instructed to do so. The term *patriotism* crossed his mind, a word he had rarely thought about. He began to respect the confidence and courage that each of these individuals possessed. This was indeed a rare group of people.

198

The Prague Double

"And now we have come to where we require your expertise, Mr. Garner," Frantisek was saying. He placed his finger on the rough map of the Russian compound. "This is very critical, very critical indeed..."

CHAPTER TWENTY SIX

As they rounded a curve, the lights of the town square in Zbraslav came into view. They were some twenty kilometers south of Prague and in the vicinity of the farmhouse where Trudi and the escape aircraft were waiting. Garner had been silent for the past half-hour and had managed to control his fear for most of the day, but now, seeing the lights of the tiny village brought the knot back into his stomach.

He reached inside the tunic of the Russian military uniform and touched the butt of the revolver with the silencer. He hoped he would not have to use it.

Emil was driving and was dressed in the uniform of a Russian *mladshij serzhant,* a senior sergeant. The brown uniform fit him perfectly. He had cropped his hair closely about the temples and darkened his eyebrows, making him appear five years younger. He was going to remain in Czechoslovakia with Frantisek and Jan, thus it was necessary for the trio to disguise their facial features to some extent.

Garner had learned a great deal about the three men in the past few days. They were natives to Czechoslovakia and had lived in Prague for the better part of their lives. After the war, Hitler and the Nazi regime were out, but then came the Russians. The one thing these three had in common was their extreme hatred for the *Russoks* and everything they stood for. These men had been veterans of the small revolutionary movement, which struck Czechoslovakia in the fall of 1968, just six years ago. The Communists had easily quashed the revolution, and Alexander Dubcek and his reform policies quickly disappeared. Ever since, the three had become bitter enemies of the Soviet State.

They were not actual agents for the CIA, but they might as well have been. They understood the real meaning of freedom and they hated Communism with a vehemence that would not go away. Anything and everything they could do to thwart the Kremlin Rule under Brezhnev was justifiable, and they would die for such a cause if need be.

Garner had never worked toward a goal like that.

Emil turned the vehicle off the highway and drove along a side road for a while, then pulled off behind some trees and shut off the lights.

Garner sat uneasy, the darkness crowding him. Clouds had formed, and only occasionally was the moon shining through. If the clouds did not thicken, he would be able to fly visually without any problems, but if the sky became overcast...

A set of lights flashed on the road and a second vehicle pulled up behind them.

Jan and Frantisek emerged from their vehicle and crawled into the back seat of the official looking limousine. Frantisek was still dressed in his long black coat and wearing his homburg. The only thing different about him was the fake black mustache on his lip.

Emil was dressed like Jan in a sergeant's uniform. He had darkened his mustache and eyebrows and cropped his hair about the temples.

Emil started up the vehicle, and within moments he was back on the road and circled the city of Zbraslav. Less than ten minutes later, he pulled off the road again, drove up an incline and stopped.

"Come," said Frantisek to Garner. Garner followed him up an embankment to a clump of trees. Across the road below and no more than a quarter of a mile away lay the military compound. Surprisingly, it was not very well lit.

Frantisek shoved a set of binoculars up to his eyes and scanned the grounds, then handed the binoculars to Garner. Garner looked on while Frantisek digressed.

"There are two guards at the main gate. Do you see them?"

"Yes."

"The barracks in which the defector is housed is straight across, and to the left are five staff cars."

"I see them."

Delray K. Dvoracek

Garner scanned the compound. "Frantisek, I see three guards patrolling. One in front of the motor pool, and two near the barracks. There are probably more on the outer perimeters."

"Of course."

Garner grimaced. "It looks impossible."

"Ah," remarked Frantisek. "If it *looks* impossible, then we are in luck. If it *is* impossible, we have no luck. But tonight we have luck." He turned to Garner, his face dark in the night. "How do you feel?"

"Nervous, a little sick to my stomach."

"Then you are all right. I feel the same way."

Somehow, Garner did not believe him.

A car could be heard coming down the highway that skirted the compound. Garner looked up from the glasses as a black limousine loomed into view. It slowed and turned into the main gate and stopped at the guard gate under the light pole.

"If I may be permitted," asked Frantisek. He looked through the glasses. "The plate number is correct."

Garner watched the vehicle enter the compound. By the time the gate swung shut, the limo had reached the front of the barracks. When a figure emerged from the back seat, Frantisek whispered under his breath. "It is him. He's twenty minutes early. That's good, very good. At least now we know he's there for sure."

Garner gulped. It would have been a terrible blunder to enter and not find the defector housed in the barracks.

Fifteen minutes later, the four men were back on the main highway, and as they topped a hill, the compound was suddenly before them.

"Eight minutes, Emil. If we do not make it back out within that time, you have your instructions."

A fear stabbed at Garner like darts smacking a target. Frantisek had been so sure of everything, yet now, he had just said *if* they didn't make it back out. Maybe the plan was not as simple as Frantisek had made it out to be.

As they rolled up to the gate, Garner felt the sweat on his forehead. One of the guards, a Russian sergeant, approached the vehicle and bent down to look in the window, and when he noticed

Garner in the Major's uniform, he offered a salute.

"*Bumagi, pozhaluista,*" he said asking for their papers. His eyes widened when Jan stuck a pistol in his face.

"Call your friend over here," Jan said calmly in Russian.

The soldier didn't hesitate. "*Vladij, syuda!*"

Just as the corporal approached, Emil stepped from the car with his pistol drawn. The second soldier, like the first, stiffened when he saw the weapon, but neither resisted as Emil pulled the clips from their semi-automatic rifles.

"You," Emil commanded to the corporal, "back to the guardhouse." Once there, Emil clubbed him over the head. The soldier slumped to the floor without a sound. The sergeant standing next to the vehicle saw what happened and didn't dare move.

Jan warned the Russian. "Stay in that same position if you want to see the morning sun come up."

Emil triggered the gates, and as Jan drove through, Garner glanced back. The sergeant with the shouldered rifle was as stiff as a statue, and Emil was now in control of the guardhouse.

"Very good," said Frantisek. "We are on schedule."

Garner couldn't believe how calmly the men had reacted. In less than fifteen seconds, they had overtaken two guards like clockwork in plain sight under the lamp pole.

Jan pulled up in front of the barracks and stopped. "Watch for the guard," Frantisek cautioned him. "He is fifty yards beyond the parking area.

"Come, Tovarish Major," he said to Garner as he opened the car door. "It is time for our grand performance, and we want to be in and out before the fireworks start."

Frantisek walked on ahead of Garner to the barracks swinging a briefcase as if he were one of the returning dignitaries of the conference.

The two reached the entrance door to the outer office, but when Frantisek tried the handle, it would not open. He could clearly see the Russian officer inside looking back at him. The officer seemed puzzled with their appearance, and when he reached for the telephone, Garner stiffened.

"Be patient," Frantisek told him. "He is calling the guard post to confirm our arrival. Emil will take care of it."

They saw the Russian officer nod his head, and then the door buzzed. Frantisek stomped right past the officer to the second inner door. "Why did you keep us waiting outside?" he barked in Russian at the soldier. "What do you take us for, burglars?"

The sentence struck Garner funny, but he kept a straight face. Frantisek rattled the next door that led to the interior, but it, too, was locked. "Open it, lieutenant, before I piss my pants."

Garner couldn't believe the audacity Frantisek Plauder exuded. The officer seemed embarrassed but on the defensive as he ran his finger down a list. "Excuse me, sir, but I don't find..."

"Professor Gerhard Kersten, Berlin," snapped Frantisek.

"Yes sir, one moment." He scanned the list again and then reached for the phone. Garner made his move and shoved the silencer into his belly before he could pick it up. The young officer's face drained white as he stared at the weapon.

Garner lifted the soldier's pistol from his belt and calmly said, "Open the door."

The young officer licked his lips, his eyes nervously on the barrel pressing into his side.

Frantisek commanded now, "Open it!"

"*N-ne mogu.*" The officer was scared but still trying to be a hero.

Frantisek's cold stare hit Garner.

Garner delivered a threatening tone. "Open the goddamn door or I'll open up your gut!" The soldier still didn't respond. Either he was still trying to be a hero or else he was so scared that he couldn't respond.

Garner jammed the gun barrel into the Russian officer's pocket. The man jerked when the barrel reached his groin. "When this goes off, it won't kill you, but your balls are going to come out through your boots, and you'll never screw another Lolita again. You understand?"

"*P-ponimayu,*" he stuttered. The fear still gripped his face and sweat had beaded up on his forehead. He carefully moved his foot on the carpet, and when the door buzzed, he grunted and jerked back as if the gun had gone off in his pocket.

Frantisek ducked inside, and when he reached the top of the stairs, a door opened on the opposite side of the corridor. Garner had a clear view of him through the glasswork. Frantisek was pumping his arm up and down engaged in conversation with a man in civilian clothes.

Garner felt the seconds slipping away. On and on Frantisek went, jabbering with the man until finally he disappeared down a hallway. The man Frantisek had been talking to came down the few steps, opened the door and stuck his head into the room.

"Is everything in order here?" he asked.

The officer was quick to respond. "*Da. Vsyo v poryadke.*" The soldier had a slight waver in his voice, but evidently it went by unnoticed. The man at the door nodded and headed back up the stairs.

Garner glanced at his watch. Four and one half minutes had passed already.

The officer mustered up the courage to speak. "It is impossible to escape. The post is surrounded. You will never..."

"Get out of here?" finished Garner. "If we don't get out of here, neither do you. Understand?" Garner was calm when he spoke, so calm that he surprised himself.

But after another minute passed and Frantisek still had not returned, Garner's own anxiety was growing.

Finally, Frantisek and the defector were coming down the steps, but a Russian officer was with them, and he was wearing a pistol at his side.

"I can assure you," Frantisek was saying as the three entered the room, "everything is order. You may ask the lieutenant at the desk." Frantisek was playing his role well, but an unmistakable fear was riding Sedovskij's face, and the officer with them sensed it.

Frantisek had barely made a step toward the desk when the first explosion outside shook the building. Fire rained in the air as a car less than twenty yards away rolled over in a ball of flames. The officer next to Frantisek grabbed for his pistol, but Garner fired a shot point blank and spun the man backward to the floor, his arm a bloody mess.

Delray K. Dvoracek

"Go!" shouted Frantisek.

Garner shoved the young lieutenant just as another blast blew out the window behind him and sent shards of glass crackling across the room.

Now, men came running down the stairs from inside the barracks.

"Go!" shouted Frantisek again to Garner as he snapped the cap on a device and tossed it to the floor. Yellow smoke spewed out of the bomb and engulfed the room as the two ran out.

A third blast sent another staff car hopping into the air nearby, and right afterwards another thunderous roar rocked a building a couple hundred feet away and all lights went out in the compound. The front of the motor pool was on fire now, and men were scurrying in all directions.

Gunfire erupted from somewhere across the post just as Jan pulled up in the vehicle. The three clambered inside, and as they raced toward the front gate, bullets pinged off the metal of the car. The white flashes of two more blasts lit up the compound like lightning. A barrage of gunfire from somewhere shattered the rear window, sending glass flying inside the car.

"Ram the gate!" hollered Frantisek. The gates flew to the side as Jan charged through. He screeched to a halt, and as soon as Emil climbed in, the car raced off. When Garner looked back, the sergeant at the guardhouse was running toward the compound just as a final blast lit up the sky.

Any fear Garner possessed was now overridden with excitement. They were still in sight of the compound just as a troop truck pull onto the highway. Frantisek did not seem concerned. "It is no matter," he said calmly. "They will not be able to keep up with us."

Jan pressed the accelerator to the floor, and within a few minutes, they reached the main square of Zbraslav. Jan passed through town and turned off, and five minutes later, they reached the second vehicle.

"You know the way," said Frantisek to Garner as he, Jan and Emil scrambled from the car. "Good Luck!"

Garner and Sedovskij got in the front seat with Garner behind the wheel. He jammed it into gear and whirled the vehicle around. At the first intersection, he swung off and saw the other vehicle racing off in a different direction.

A heavy relief swept over Garner, yet, a nervous energy tingled within him as he stared ahead into the ray of the headlights. It had seemed impossible, but now he understood why Farrington had never explained originally what the real Prague assignment was. He had been deceived all along the way, but at the moment, it all seemed worth it.

"How far must we go?" Sedovskij asked.

Garner was happy to see him a little calmer now. "Ten kilometers."

"And then?"

"Our escape is by aircraft. A couple hours from now, we'll be in West Germany." Garner glanced up at the sky and grinned. The weather seemed to be holding.

Sedovskij sighed a heavy breath. "I can't believe you people managed to get into the compound and out again with so few people. It was so heavily guarded."

"Frankly, I can't believe it either."

Sedovskij eased himself back into the seat, seemingly relaxed.

Out of nowhere, a set of headlights blared in the rearview mirror. Garner stiffened. They did not appear to be lights from a troop truck, since the beam was too steady.

Sedovskij also noticed the lights, and when he turned around, Garner saw the fear in his eyes. "Is it following us?"

"I don't know." Garner was driving seventy kilometers per hour and increased his speed to ninety, but the vehicle was still gaining.

Garner's mind was working ahead. At an intersection two or three kilometers away, he would swing off onto a dead-end road. The way would become winding and hilly with a lot of trees, and once he crossed the bridge, he would be less than a kilometer from the farm. If the car following him also turned at the next intersection, for sure it would be tailing him.

He kept his speed steady and was heading down hill now through a line of trees. The vehicle behind was still gaining, and when Garner swung left, the car closed to within a block.

Garner's nerves crawled. No one else knew he would be traveling this stretch of road at this time of night. The lights, only yards behind, were blinding in the rearview. He heard a ripping sound on metal.

"They're shooting at us!" Sedovskij yelled. He buried himself into the seat as Garner jammed the accelerator to the floor. The speedometer raced upward, but the vehicle behind was still maintaining its pace. Garner heard more loud cracks of gunfire as he fought the wheel. Three small but sharp rising hills were up ahead, and after the third, a sharp curve to the right would take them across the bridge. His mind pounded. If he could hold hitting his break lights after the third rise, then perhaps...

He shoved the accelerator down even more. The car almost left the ground on the first hill. He fought the wheel to hold it on the narrow road, and when the second rise was upon him, again his car leaped over, his wheels leaving the ground. Sedovskij bounced and hit the ceiling and was blathering now, his hands braced against the dash, his feet stiff against the floor.

Sedovskij was frantic. "They'll kill me! It's all for nothing! I've failed!"

Garner's stomach jumped into his mouth as the car reeled over the third rise. He resisted hitting the brake pedal to avoid letting the trailing car see his taillights flash. The car pounded downward tearing up the gravel, and as soon as the curve loomed ahead in the lights, he hit the brakes forcing the car into a skid. Sedovskij slammed against the windshield and flopped back when Garner wheeled the vehicle around the curve. The vehicle behind flew over the rise, but he was not as quick to react. The car slid sideways and plunged into the ditch into some trees. The beam of headlights showed high at an angle when the car came to rest.

Garner smiled nervously and pressed the accelerator, but seconds later, he cursed when he looked in the rearview. The headlights behind him were back up on the gravel.

Garner's mind raced again. A slight curve preceded the bridge. From there, the farm was only a minute away.

Garner's eyes hung on the rearview. He had gained the precious few seconds that he would now need. "I'll slow at the bridge," he told Sedovskij. "When I jump out, you take the wheel!"

"What? I don't understand?"

"Take the goddamn wheel and drive ahead!" The anger in his voice left the man speechless.

As the bridge loomed in the headlights, Garner braked sharply.

"Now!" he hollered as he opened the door and jumped from the vehicle. He hit hard against the gravel and felt his body twist and pound as he tumbled down the ditch. He got to his knees and pulled the silencer from inside his tunic.

Sedovskij drove on ahead, sparks flying as he scraped the side of the bridge. The second vehicle was coming, and as it broke around the curve, Garner leveled the silencer and fired at the windshield until the weapon was empty. He pulled the Russian automatic pistol from his holster, and as the vehicle raced by, he aimed for the driver's door. The muzzle of the weapon flashed orange as the bullets exploded in the night and ripped into the side of the vehicle. When the automatic quit firing, he shoved in the spare clip, but by now the car had slid sideways across the road. The front fender caught the bridge railing and flipped it end over end. The car plummeted over the bridge rail and impacted on the opposite side of the creek. Seconds later, an explosion rocked the darkness, and flaming metal chunks whirled fifty feet into the air, displaying an array of sparks like some gigantic rocket.

Garner ran to the bridge railing and peered down at the flaming wreck. The rear of the car was ablaze, and the trees and riverbank around it were as brilliant as day.

Intense heat from the vehicle kept him at a distance, but he was close enough to see the two figures in the front seat.

Behind the wheel was Max, Toller's body guard. His face was twisted grotesquely upward, lying flat and motionless against the wheel, and his eyes were wide open as if he was staring back at Garner.

In the flickering light, Garner saw the blond hair of the second man. He could only see the back of his head, but there was no doubt

Delray K. Dvoracek

in his mind, it was Toller.

Ironically, in the bank where the front of the vehicle had hit, an imprint of the grill and bumper was visible in the clay, just like the imprint Vulcek's vehicle had left in the ravine near Darmstadt.

Ahead on the road, Sedovskij had stopped the car, and by the time Garner reached him, his face was still torn. "Who were they?"

"Nobody you knew," said Garner.

A dim light burned inside the farmhouse as the two left the car and hurried up the walkway. Once inside, Garner called out Trudi's name but heard no response. In the living room he found her lying on the sofa, her back to him.

"Trudi? he said as he crossed to her. When he rolled her over, he gasped. Her cheek was heavily bruised, and a clot of dried blood hung from her lip. Garner sensed the danger too late. He had just reached for his revolver when he heard the voice from behind him.

"Let it drop, Frank."

The words were cold, but Garner recognized the voice. He turned slowly to see Manfried Toller holding a gun on him. His thoughts flashed back to the bridge. He should have known. Toller always had two bodyguards with him.

"Lift it out slowly," Toller repeated.

Garner pulled the automatic from its place and let it drop to the floor.

"You too," said Toller pointing the gun at Sedovskij.

Sedovskiy was stunned. "I don't have a weapon!" Toller carefully searched him, then approached Garner and shoved the automatic against his chest. With his free hand he frisked Garner's tunic. Satisfied, he backed away.

Garner sat on the couch and helped Trudi to a sitting position. She was trembling, in shock for all he knew.

"How did you know to follow her here?" Garner asked

"That took a little doing," said Toller. "I guessed that the Academy of Sciences was what drew the defector here, and last night, Max luckily spotted you and Miss Feldman when you left the palace reception. He was unable to follow you, but this morning when your pretty accomplice showed up without you, I put two and two together. When she left the conference, Max simply followed her here."

He laughed. "I knew you wouldn't leave without her, but what I didn't know was that you would bring an extra person along. I must give your people credit. They're very efficient.

"I'm surprised you haven't run in to Max and Helmut yet. They were going to arrange a reception for you once you left the military compound."

"Unfortunately they met with an accident back at the bridge."

Toller shrugged. "Oh, well," he said quite casually as if Garner's words meant nothing. "No matter. Bodyguards are easy to come by."

He looked at Sedovskij, pointing his gun at him. "And I'm guessing this is the defector. The KGB will be happy to get him back."

Sedovskij, sweating and with quivering lips, did not respond.

"What do you want? Money?" asked Garner. "I've got connections."

Toller gave a snide laugh. "You insult me. This isn't business, this is pleasure. A man must have some pleasure in his life, don't you think? But then you wouldn't know that's how I work. Frank would have known, but you wouldn't."

Toller's words startled Garner.

"You were very clever, Mr. Garner. Once your girlfriend began to talk she became more and more obliging."

His eyes were on Sedovskij, who sat stoically in his chair not understanding the situation. Toller addressed the Russian. "Oh, didn't you know Mr. Garner was impersonating Frank Vulcek?"

Garner was watchful, hoping for a moment to catch Toller off guard, but he was very much on guard, very much in control. It probably didn't make any difference if he killed all three of them. The KGB would prefer Sedovskij back dead rather than not at all.

Garner stalled for time. "How did you know I wasn't Vulcek?"

"Your girlfriend didn't tell me, if that's what you're thinking. She just supplied your real name. You had me going for a while. It was Dieter who first convinced me you were Vulcek, and that night when I first saw you in the parking lot of the Golden Horse, I, too, was convinced. Wearing Frank's ring was a nice touch, and I did believe perhaps you survived the accident. Your face certainly had me fooled.

"But, after what I did to Frank and Helga, Frank wouldn't have played cat and mouse. He would have killed me at the first opportunity. Yet, you didn't, which surprised me."

"You had an opportunity to kill me, too," responded Garner. "Why didn't you?"

"I thought maybe I could make the same deal with you that I had with Frank. I didn't even know a defector was involved at the time. My contact in East Berlin indicated something strange was going on in Prague. I knew about the conference at the Academy, and when Frank had a name to sell and was headed this way, I just pieced it together."

"You struck a deal with Frank Vulcek on a hunch?"

"It's no longer a hunch." He eyed Sedovskij. "You two just confirmed it. When I asked if he was the defector, neither of you denied it."

Garner swore at himself, but it didn't seem to make any difference now.

Toller was in a confessing mood. "Frank shouldn't have been fooling around with Helga."

"You killed Vulcek just because he was seeing Helga?"

"Sort of. He was using her to get to me. One night I saw her going through my files and followed her to Frank. You can guess the rest."

"And you got rid of Dieter because he knew you killed Vulcek."

Toller nodded. "Dieter suspected it. He desperately needed money, and I didn't know what he was working with you, but with him out of the way, you had to deal with me."

"How are you going to explain Dieter's death to your friends in Berlin?"

"No need to. When I turn the defector over to the Russians, East Berlin will once again have nothing but praise for me. They'll forget about Dieter."

Sedovskij cringed.

Slowly, Trudi came around, and when she saw Toller, her eyes were a living fear.

She turned to Garner. "I'm sorry, he made me tell."

Toller sneered. "It didn't take much. She's weak like all women."

A rumbling noise from outside shook the quiet of the moment as a set of headlights flashed across the front window.

"What's this all about?" Toller asked as he caught a glimpse out the window.

Garner knew, and it made no difference now. "A troop truck from the compound. The Russians followed us."

"How convenient," said Toller. "All three of you may well have earned a stay of execution. A temporary one, that is. It will give me no greater pleasure than to turn you all over to the Russians."

"No! no!" Sedovskij said as he jumped up from his chair. "You can't turn me in! Make any demands! Anything at all!"

Toller made a face. "Mr. Defector, what could you possibly give me once you are in the hands of the Americans?"

Sedovskij was sweating, shaking profusely as he slumped back in his chair.

The sound of the truck abruptly ceased, and then a loud voice boomed out in Russian. "Come out one by one with your hands on your heads. No harm will come to you."

Toller understood the Russian. "I believe we should oblige them, don't you agree?"

He did not wait for a response. "My vyidyom!" he hollered in Russian. *We're coming out.* As he slowly opened the door, Garner prayed a machine gun burst would rip the man in two, but once again he heard the Russian voice commanding them to come out with their hands up.

"You first," Toller motioned to Garner.

It was useless, Garner decided. He was about to help Trudi up when suddenly Sedovskij screamed out at the top of his lungs, "Otkryvai ogon!" With the Russian command to *open fire*, a barrage of gun shots tore through Toller's body, flinging him back into the room.

Delray K. Dvoracek

Garner's mind charged. "Get down!" he commanded to Sedovskij and Trudi as he picked up his automatic. He fired three shots through the front window, shattering the glass.

Gunfire erupted again from outside as bullets tore through the side of the house pounding their patterns into the walls. Hanging plaques shattered, a painting ripped from its mounting. The flurry of shots was incessant, and as bullets pinged all around, the lights suddenly went out.

"Get Sedovskij to the plane!" Garner told Trudi.

As the two hugged the floor and made their way to the back door, Garner fired the remaining shots from the automatic through the front window, and again, a barrage of gunfire ripped into the house. When the firing subsided, a voice hollered for them to come out.

Garner crawled to Toller's body and grabbed his automatic. He fired blindly through the open door until the clip was empty, and when the soldiers outside returned fire, he scrambled through the kitchen. The gunfire was still blasting away as he slipped out the back and ran through the trees. By the time he reached the clearing, the gunshots had ceased. He knew it would be only moments before the Russian troops stormed the home, and soon afterward, they would be searching the area.

He kept running, his lungs heaving as he raced across the field toward the bunker. Now he could see the shadowed outline of the plane. Sedovskij and Trudi had cleared away the netting and were pulling the craft out into the open.

"Get in!" he shouted as he neared. Exhausted and out of breath, he clambered inside. Trudi was next to him, Sedovskij was huddled behind the seats.

In moments, the prop turned over, and after a few seconds, it was spinning wildly. He shoved the throttle to the wall and pulled back on the wheel taking the weight off the nose. The aircraft held in place as the engine labored, then slowly, the craft inched forward.

It seemed to take forever for the plane to pick up speed, but eventually the speedometer climbed, and when the nose wheel lifted, the craft surged.

"They're shooting!" Trudi shouted.

Garner saw the figures of two men a couple hundred yards ahead and off to his right. Orange flames spewed out of their rifles when they fired, their shots barely audible above the roar of the engine. Garner could barely see the swath of trees ahead that had been cut away. He would have to maneuver the aircraft through the opening, but now the two soldiers realized it and started running in that direction.

Garner cursed, but kept the engine full throttle. The soldiers reached the passageway and again raised their rifles to fire, but Garner was bearing down on them.

The narrow passageway was closer now.

"*Slava Bogu!*" exclaimed Sedovskiy from the back. "You'll never make it through!"

"Lean forward, lean forward!" Garner exclaimed.

Trudi and Sedovskij pressed their bodies forward as Garner triggered the flaps down a few degrees.

The craft lifted off the ground and was now heading directly at the two men in the opening. Garner saw more orange flashes from their weapons, and then both jumped to the side as the aircraft passed within feet of them.

He heard shots now, coming from behind as the plane lifted some more. Sedovskij was still babbling when a wing tip thumped against the edge of a tree, and moments later, the aircraft broke free above an open meadow.

Garner veered left out of the line of gunfire from the soldiers behind, but the aircraft was still only a few feet off the ground and he was not gaining much altitude. He needed more air speed. As he raised the flaps again, the aircraft dropped and bounced on the gear.

Sedovskiy cried out again.

The engine was full throttle and laboring from the extra weight inside. Ahead, a line of trees was rapidly approaching.

"Oh, god," he heard Trudi mumble.

The airspeed indicator was passing eighty knots and Garner could wait no longer. He dropped the flaps a few degrees and pulled back on the wheel. A shudder shook the aircraft as the propeller and gear clipped the tree tops. Barely skimming the trees, he let his airspeed climb and gently raised the flaps.

They were climbing steadily now, and Garner felt the relief as the balled up muscles in his shoulders fell back in place. He was thankful Sedovskij didn't weigh two hundred pounds, for if he had, they never would have made it.

The altimeter indicated they were gaining only a hundred feet per minute, which meant under the best circumstances, the aircraft would have a tough time reaching 8000 feet, the prescribed altitude on the flight plan.

He had no idea what sort of ground defenses lay on the border, but he guessed a high altitude would protect them against any potential ground fire.

No one anticipated a troop truck would follow him to the farm, and now that the Soviets knew the escape route was by air, it was very probable that an aircraft could be sent out to intercept them. He had no more than an hour and a half of flying time at best and no radios that he could monitor.

He could climb and hope that a Soviet fighter wouldn't find them, or stay close to the ground and risk small arms fire when he approached the border.

He checked his fuel gauges and noticed the left tank was lower than the right. Against the faint moon, a white stream was visible trailing off of the wing. Garner knew right away that one of the bullets had hit a fuel tank. Now, Trudi and Sedovskij saw the trail of fuel.

Garner grabbed the flight map. "Looks like we go to plan B."

CHAPTER TWENTY SEVEN

Garner leveled the aircraft at 700 meters. Climbing would waste more fuel, and now, to conserve what fuel he had, he switched to the left tank only. It appeared that the tank had been hit near the top of the wing, so to conserve even more fuel, he banked the aircraft to the right, peddled the left rudder in to keep the plane steady and pulled back on the wheel. Although they were flying a fairly straight course, the aircraft was banked to the right, as if they were in a slight right turn. To save even more fuel, Garner leaned out the carburetor.

For twenty-five minutes, they flew at this strange attitude, and when the engine began to choke, Garner switched to the right tank and leveled the aircraft. They had at most three gallons of fuel left.

A cloud bank formed ahead, giving him no choice but to fly underneath it. Occasionally, the moon rays penetrated the clouds leaving a faint reflection of the Vltava River as his only reference. He had to rely on the lights of the cities below for navigation, and as he looked down, he believed he was passing the city of Pisek. If he was on course, the first major set of lights ahead would be Czeske-Budejovice where he was supposed to bank the aircraft to the southwest on a new course. But with the cloud cover and absence of any larger city lights, the view ahead was now very dark.

He checked his watch knowing that he was supposed to cross the border as close to 1:30 as possible. He reasoned that someone on the ground may have knocked out the communications system at that time, allowing them safe passage into West Germany. He no longer considered an intercept aircraft as a threat since they were below radar detection.

He had slowed his speed to conserve more fuel, and in the process lost a precious fifteen minutes. It was 1:30 now, and the needle on the right tank showed near empty.

Sedovskij had been monitoring the fuel gauge. "Will we make it?"

Delray K. Dvoracek

Garner's silence indicated the worst. He stared blindly ahead and downward, looking for any landmark, any reference, but the landscape was too obscure. All he could do was maintain a compass heading, which he believed was the shortest route to the border. He was supposed to land on a grass strip north of Passau, but now that was out of the question. He would have to bring the aircraft down in a field once they crossed the border, but he had absolutely no idea where the border was.

The motor choked, and with the propeller now wind milling, the aircraft began to lose altitude.

Sedovskij panicked. "We'll never make it! I've failed!"

Garner trimmed the aircraft for best glide. At 700 meters, roughly two thousand feet, he could glide no more than a half mile. He had to set the aircraft down immediately.

"Watch for trees!" he hollered at the two, as he kept his eyes on his speed and angle of descent. Trees were the worst obstacle.

"I see a light!" Trudi said.

It could be nothing more than a lamppost or a light from a building, but no matter what it was, Garner banked slightly and headed toward it. He lowered the flaps to slow his speed and give him more lift.

"It's a border post!" Trudi said as they passed over no more than a hundred feet off the ground.

Garner cursed the fact the aircraft did not have a landing light, but he forgot everything when he saw the fence line coming up at them. The left wing caught the rippling barbwire on top, and metal on metal screeched in the night. The plane slammed hard into the ground and folded the gear. Dust flew from the churning prop as the craft skidded along the ground, and then sparks swirled like a spinning wheel as the propeller wound itself into the wire fence.

Garner heard shouts in the night as he scrambled from the cockpit and pulled Trudi out. Sedovskij followed and fell to the ground shaking.

"What side of the border are we on?" he asked.

Garner had no idea.

A set of headlights flashed as a vehicle sped in their direction, and at the same time, figures on the other side of the fence were running towards them, flashlights bouncing in the night.

As the jeep jerked to a halt, two men in military uniforms quickly crawled out.

"Kill them! Sedovskij hollered as he ran away from the aircraft. "They're Czech guards! Kill them!"

The two men were nothing more than black silhouettes against the headlights and did not appear to have any weapons drawn. It made no difference if they did, since Garner did not have a loaded weapon.

On the far side of the fence, more running figures were advancing, and now their flashlights were beaming on him. They were shouting, but Garner could not understand what they were saying.

As the two from the vehicle neared, Garner stiffened. He could easily see Sedovskij running away, his clothing flashing in the beam of the headlights.

"*Sind wir in Deutschland*?" Garner asked.

"*Nay. Oestereich.*" came the reply.

Garner put an arm around Trudi. "Looks like we're home."

He shouted in Russian at Sedovskij, who was still running in the night. "*Tovarish*! We're in Austria! Come back!"

One of the border guards heard the Russian language and scrutinized Garner's uniform more closely. "Are you Russians? Are you escaping to the West?"

Garner grinned. "One of us is. How far are we from Passau?"

"Twenty-five kilometers that way," the soldier said as he pointed off. "But, I'm afraid we must first take you to the Austrian authorities."

Garner was still holding Trudi tightly. He had never heard such welcome words.

Delray K. Dvoracek

EPILOGUE
August 9th, 6 days later

Through a two-way mirror, Arthur Farrington and two other men were observing Anatol Sedovskij seated at a table with two agents in the next room. For the past three days, ever since Sedovskij had arrived at the CIA complex in Langley, he had been grilled with hundreds of questions by several different agents.

Some of those conducting the debriefing were military men and some were scientists, however, the two now questioning him were counter intelligence agents connected with the Prague assignment.

Anatol Sedovskij appeared to have a photographic memory. He had not brought any documents with him, but on a map, he was able to mark dozens of tunnel systems and silos that had been drilled into the earth in the Soviet countryside. These underground operations housed the firepower of the one nation that could initiate a successful attack on the United States or retaliate from any attack on their soil with reasonable success.

Sedovskij proved to be an expert on multiple warheads, and from what Arthur now knew, Soviet intercontinental ballistic missiles could be retrofitted to carry out chemical warfare as a deterrent to war. Initial analysis indicated the firepower of the Soviet Union was far more superior than the United States had ever suspected.

So far, everyone who had interrogated Sedovskij was impressed with the knowledge he possessed. The man was a walking encyclopedia on military might, and Arthur was more than pleased with the results.

He knew the Russians would discount the defection in their newspapers, and in the past six days, not one mention of Sedovskiy's defection had been reported in the media. An insignificant article appeared in a Czech newspaper stating that a minor fire had broken out at the military compound near Zbraslav, but that it had been easily contained. Everyone connected with the defection enjoyed a huge laugh over that.

President Nixon was informed of the results of the Prague assignment, but because he was so deeply involved in the Watergate scandal, the CIA had not yet received an official response from the White House. And that didn't seem likely for several more days since the scandal had come to a head, and Nixon had just announced his resignation from the presidency.

Arthur returned to his office and had no sooner sat at his desk when the intercom buzzed. "They're here," his secretary informed him.

When Phillip Garner and Trudi Feldman entered, the grin on Arthur's face was solid as if it had been glued in place. Sit down, sit down," he offered.

"We're not staying long," said Garner.

"I know," Arthur said excitedly as he swiveled his big frame around to face them. "I've been informed you've finished up with your debriefing, and I know why you're here." Arthur shoved an envelope across his desk. "Your check, Mr. Garner."

Phillip placed the envelope in an inside pocket without even opening it.

Arthur saw the flat face before him and took in a deep breath. "I see they've removed the scar from your throat." The scars around Garner's eyes were still visible, but they were beginning to fade, just like the makeup artist had assured Garner they would.

"Miss Feldman," he said to Trudi. "You've been granted a month's leave."

"Yes," she said simply.

Arthur crawled out of his chair and paced a bit. "I'd like to say one more time, it was an impossible assignment, and I very much appreciated your cooperation."

The displeasure on Garner's face said it all. "You didn't leave me much choice, did you? You lied to me from day one."

Arthur sat again, the grin on his face now gone. He had definitely blackmailed the man. He had lied from the very beginning, and though he wasn't proud of it, he did believe it was necessary. The results justified the means.

Arthur looked down twisting his fingers together "Your background has been cleared." That was Arthur's biggest lie. The CIA and FBI never had anything concrete on him, but Arthur wasn't about to spill that information. "Any and all records of your South American activities have been wiped away. You are free to come and go as you please."

There was a long silence.

"Do you have any immediate plans?" Arthur asked. The answer he got was what he expected.

"Nothing you'd be interested in," Garner said as he stood up. He took Trudi by the arm and headed for the door.

"I'll see you back here in a month, will I not, Miss Feldman?"

"We'll see," she said.

When the door slammed shut, Arthur sat with a blank look on his face. His intercom buzzed again. "Arthur, Mr. Kendrid would like to see you in the conference room."

Arthur left his office and walked down the corridor to where Kendrid and a few others were seated around a table, among them, William Colby, the director of the CIA.

Mr. Kendrid sat at the head of the table, his big frame filling his chair, and spoke as he motioned for Arthur to take a seat. "I assume you've read the preliminary reports on Sedovskiy's debriefing?"

"Yes, sir, I have."

"We are very pleased with the results of the Prague assignment, Arthur. You were very fortunate to have found this Prague double, something we never anticipated would work out."

"Thank you, Mr. Kendrid."

"I assume Mr. Garner has received his compensation?"

"He has. However, he's not very happy. He knows we used him all along."

Mr. Colby had just filled his pipe and lit up. In a rather soft-spoken voice he said, "Well, that's sort of the nature of our business, is it not?"

The other men chuckled along with Arthur at the comment.

"We have something to show you, Arthur," said Mr. Kendrid. He waved an arm, and when the lights dimmed, a slide projector snapped on from behind them, and a slide slid into place on a screen.

Arthur focused his attention to the man depicted on the slide as Mr. Kendrid began his narration. "If you look closely, you will recognize this man as Manfried Toller, the lawyer from Frankfurt. This photo was taken eight weeks ago in East Berlin. An interesting man. We had no idea Frank Vulcek was dealing with him, however, we did know Frank had a lead on a group of freelancers working for the KGB. Your man, Mr. Garner, discovered Manfried Toller for us. Very good, very good indeed. Further investigation of this Toller fellow has led us into some interesting circles."

"Yes, sir," answered Arthur. He wasn't sure where the information was leading him.

A second slide appeared on the screen as Mr. Kendrid went on. "You will recognize Toller again. The man he's with is an East Berlin agent named Rozmanov, who runs a camera store as a front for the KGB."

Another slide fell into place.

"This is Rozmanov in Moscow a few days later making contact with Soliy Kolokolchik, a high-ranking KGB agent attached to Kremlin security."

The slide switched to a street scene on which four men were depicted entering a limousine. "Moscow," said Mr. Kendrid. "Zoom in, please," he asked the projectionist.

As the faces came clear, one of the men was Kolokolchik, the agent from the Kremlin security. The man next to him caused Arthur to gasp.

"Good God!" exclaimed Arthur. "Anatol Sedovskij!"

"Yes," said Kendrid. "Sedovskij is an agent for the KGB. He's a mole."

"Are you certain?" Arthur could not take his eyes from the slide.

Mr. Kendrid went on. "His real name is Dmitri Treblisk. The KGB has been planning his defection for over three years. Frank Vulcek was the only person who knew him by his face, but since the KGB gave Treblisk a new identity, we were unable to trace him. That is, not until your Prague double picked out his photo. Mr. Garner was our only means of enticing the mole back into the defection, and quite candidly, no one here thought it could be pulled off."

"What do you mean, *enticing him back* into the defection?" asked Arthur.

"Well," said Mr. Kendrid matter-of-factly. "Frank Vulcek and a few of us here were the only ones from the onset who knew Sedovskij was a plant."

Arthur's jaw dropped. Now it made sense why Vulcek had been so secretive about everything. Arthur wasn't supposed to know that Sedovskij was a mole! How many times had he held back information from his operatives because they weren't supposed to be privy to certain facts, and now he was a victim of the same deception.

Kendrid went on. "The defector hasn't supplied us with much information we didn't already know. Oh, a few trivial things, but nothing of any real significance."

Arthur was still shaken. "Then why did you go to the trouble to break him out of a military compound when you knew he was a plant?"

Mr. Kendrid chuckled. "We had to make it look good. We couldn't just whisk him off in broad daylight. Nobody would have believed that. With all the trouble we went to in order to free the defector from the compound, the Russians are sure to believe we don't suspect anything."

Mr. Kendrid leaned in closer. "This has become a two-way deal, Arthur. We now very discreetly supply Treblisk with all the misinformation we want to send back to the Kremlin, and he becomes our direct pipeline."

Arthur sat back in his chair, his face hanging. "You knew about this all along and never told me?" He looked at the faces around the table. "You all used me."

"Well," said the director once again in his soft voice. "That's the sort of business we're in, isn't it?" He puffed on his pipe and shrugged. "Don't feel bad, Arthur. The Russians took great pains to get the defector into the Prague conference. From what we know now, very few people inside the Kremlin knew the defection was to take place. Even the defector's personal bodyguards didn't know."

"What?" asked Arthur.

Mr. Kendrid smiled. "I think the Russians were so sure we could get him out that they let us set the course. I can imagine Treblisk was sweating it when he learned we were going to break him out of a military post, and I imagine the Soviet leadership can hardly believe we would go to such extreme measures."

Mr. Kendrid waved his hand, and the lights came back on. "Thank you, Arthur. You did an excellent job. And by the way, as of this moment, the five of us in this room are the only ones who know the defector is a double agent."

Arthur's mouth dropped some more. "You mean the men interrogating the defector don't even know?"

William Colby simply looked across at Arthur and shrugged as he blew out a puff of smoke.

"I know," Arthur said almost under his breath. "The nature of our business."

As the men got up to leave, Arthur smiled politely. The result of the assignment was, after all, a great achievement, but he felt cheated. His own coworkers had lied to him from the very beginning.

When he returned to his office, he crossed the carpet to a window and looked out, his gaze wandering aimlessly at the buildings in the distance. His eyes drifted downward to the street below where he caught a glimpse of Phillip Garner and Trudi Feldman as they stepped into a taxi. He watched the yellow cab until it dipped under a viaduct and disappeared from view.

Arthur took in a deep breath and sighed. He knew he would never see either one of them again.

Delray K. Dvoracek

Novels written as Delray K. Dvoracek

The Baltic Sea Incident

The Lady from Prague

Letters from Lydia

The Mirror Man

The Guys from Fargo

The Prague Double

Short story collections written as Kent Kamron
Charlie's Gold and Other Frontier Tales
A Time for Justice and Other Frontier Tales.
The Dime Novel Man and Other Frontier Tales
Shootout at Skinner's Saloon and Other Frontier Tales

Delray K. Dvoracek is a former college teacher of German and Russian. During his Air Force enlistment as a Russian linguist, he spent a year in Turkey and three years flying reconnaissance missions in a C-130 aircraft.